Also by Louise Allen

The Earl's Practical Marriage
A Lady in Need of an Heir
Convenient Christmas Brides
'The Viscount's Yuletide Betrothal'
Snowbound Surrender
'Snowed in with the Rake'
Contracted as His Countess
The Duke's Counterfeit Wife
The Earl's Mysterious Lady

Liberated Ladies miniseries

Least Likely to Marry a Duke
The Earl's Marriage Bargain
A Marquis in Want of a Wife
The Earl's Reluctant Proposal
A Proposal to Risk Their Friendship

Discover more at millsandboon.co.uk.

HIS CONVENIENT DUCHESS

Louise Allen

MILLS & BOON

First published in Great Britain 2022
by Mills & Boon, an imprint of HarperCollins*Publishers* Ltd,
1 London Bridge Street, London, SE1 9GF

www.harpercollins.co.uk

HarperCollins*Publishers*
1st Floor, Watermarque Building,
Ringsend Road, Dublin 4, Ireland

His Convenient Duchess © 2022 Melanie Hilton

ISBN: 978-0-263-30190-8

09/22

MIX
Paper from
responsible sources
FSC® C007454

This book is produced from independently certified FSC™ paper
to ensure responsible forest management.
For more information visit www.harpercollins.co.uk/green.

Printed and Bound in Spain using 100% Renewable Electricity
at CPI Black Print, Barcelona

Chapter One

‿‿‿‿◦◦◦‿‿‿‿

Chalton Castle, Wiltshire—3rd June, 1817

> *The Princess Rosalinda sat in her turret
> and gazed across the assure (azzure?) rip-
> ples of the river towards the far bank. She
> was yearning to be free from her wicked
> uncle (stepfather??) the King. When would
> her gallant knight (prince??) come to res-
> cue her from durrence vile?*

Lady Katherine Trafford sucked the end of
her much-chewed pencil and frowned down
at the notebook spread open on a board across
her knees. 'How do you spell durance? And do
you think I should put something about Rosalinda's long flaxen tresses at this point, or keep
that until later, when gallant Sir Marmaduke
first sees her?'

'One r. And it's an a, not an e. And one z in azure.' Her elder sister Lady Chloe looked over her shoulder as she passed, the starched apron over her neat sprig muslin dress weighed down by hens' eggs, still warm from the nest. 'Rosalinda and Marmaduke? Are you certain about that, Kat?'

'I am basing my heroine on Rose, but that isn't a romantic enough name,' Kat explained earnestly. 'And Marmaduke has glamour. Or not? What do you think, Rose?'

Lady Rose Trafford, perched ten feet up the wreck of the spiral staircase of a small turret, now in such ruin that only half of its outer wall remained, looked down at her younger half-sisters. 'What do I think about what?'

'Marmaduke as a name for the hero.'

'He sounds like the kitchen cat, to be frank,' she said. 'Although Oswald would be worse. Is this your new romance, Kat?'

'It is and I am going to make our fortunes with it,' Kat stated confidently. 'It is called *The Knight and The Imprisoned Princess*, although I may make him a prince. What are you doing up there, Rose? It is a very good place, because if a knightly hero comes galloping across the meadows to our rescue you could see him from up there and wave a spangled scarf to attract his attention.'

'That would be difficult, as I do not possess a spangled scarf,' Rose said. 'I'm afraid I would make a very unsatisfactory heroine, Kat because what I am doing is contemplating setting fish traps in the moat.' She studied the turgid green water, stirred by the wake of a small flotilla of ducks. 'We do not have time to sit dangling rods in it in the hope that something will bite, but a few traps might catch something. Probably only a very muddy-tasting carp.'

She gathered up her divided skirt, revealing boots and breeches beneath, and picked her way down carefully from her favourite, but precarious, perch. 'Time for breakfast and I am sorry to disappoint you, Kat, but the only men in sight are Billy Austin taking his plough horses down to the forge and that lad from the village, the one with the sniff. He's leading a goat on a string which must be the one I bought from Widow Lambton last market day. The one thing we are *not* going to see riding up to our drawbridge is a gallant knight, let alone a prince.'

Northminster Castle, Wiltshire, seat of the
Duke of Northminster—the same day

'Where is my castle?' the Fifth Duke of
Northminster demanded. He stabbed a long
tanned finger at the rows of folders spread out
on the library table, each neatly labelled with
the name of one of his many newly inherited
properties. The Burmese ruby set in the ring
on his left hand flashed in the sunlight like a
baleful eye. 'I do not see it among these.'

'Er…here, Your Grace?' Mr Barclay, his
land agent, ventured, making a vague gesture
towards the arrow slit high in the library wall.

'Not this one, Barclay. And while we're on
the subject, what confounded idiot put a library
in a round tower? No, don't answer that. I suppose it has been in here since fifteen seventy.
I mean Chalton Castle.'

Marcus was still sizing Barclay up, as he
was all his newly acquired staff and servants.
The man looked like a nervous mole, but at
least he stood his ground under pressure. Presumably he'd had enough practice with the last
two Dukes.

'Oh, that was sold last year, Your Grace.'

'Sold?' Marcus looked up, eyes narrowed,

and Mr Barclay swallowed visibly. 'Entailed property may not be sold or otherwise alienated.' He might know more about ships' lading and the import duties on silk than he did about the inheritance of land, but he was very clear on that point.

'You are quite correct, of course, Your Grace. But Chalton was not included in the entail for some reason and the Fourth Duke and his father sold all the non-entailed property.'

'When?'

'Over the last seven years, Your Grace. As you know matters became a trifle… That is to say, there was the need to secure ready money for…er…various reasons.'

His cousins' debts, in other words. Father and son appeared to have been alike in reckless extravagance. 'Do stop calling me "Your Grace" every second sentence, Barclay,' Marcus said, more moderately. 'It makes me feel like an archbishop.' It wasn't the poor devil of an agent who was at fault here: he would have had to follow orders or lose his position and there was nothing illegal about selling non-entailed property.

Marcus frowned down at the spread of folders. 'Why were the properties that were sold not entailed?'

'All of them except Chalton Castle were recent purchases, made at the end of the last century by the Second Duke, Your Gr…er…sir. They were small farms or parcels of land, for the most part. I assume the intention was to add them at some point. Chalton was acquired in the fifteenth century when it was already in a very poor state, I understand, and the farmland was never significant. For some reason it appears never to have been included in the entail.'

'It came with Isabelle de Chalton in 1491,' Marcus said. 'Only the gatehouse towers were in any state of repair even then and they were turned into a house by the farmer who leased the land. He built a dwelling of sorts in the space between the towers where the entry had been. The last time I saw the place the curtain walls around the bailey were tumbling down, but the moat was still there.'

Marcus blinked and the image of sunshine on water, of the deep shade cast by ancient ramparts, swam back into his mind. For a moment he felt again the thrill of learning to fish, to use a bow and arrow; the magic of weaving fantasies of knights and battles. The balm of pure serenity and healing, uncomplicated, happiness.

'You knew it well, sir?'

'Yes, very well. Buy it back, Barclay,' Marcus said. 'The castle and all the rest of the land that was sold. Offer five per cent over what was paid, that should do it.' The peace that followed Waterloo had triggered an agricultural decline and farmers would be glad to sell at a profit.

'I am sure I can secure the agricultural lands, but I doubt very much we will be able to buy back the castle, sir,' the agent said doubtfully. 'The lady who purchased it seemed to have very definite plans in mind.'

'A *woman* bought Chalton? A farmer's widow or some such, I assume.'

'No, sir. A single lady. Quite a young one, in fact: the Lady Rose Trafford. A home for her and her sisters, she said. It seemed very strange to me, her being the daughter of the late Earl Wighton. I could understand a spinster in middle age investing in land, but this…'

'I will speak to her myself.' It was, indeed a mystery. Young, unmarried, female aristocrats did not go purchasing rundown castles with some scrubby farmland attached. Marcus took an old copy of the *Peerage* from the shelf and paged through it until he found Lady Rose, born 1792, daughter of the Second Earl. No sign of sisters, but then, this edition was ancient. His late cousins were not men who could ever have been described as bookish and the library was in a shocking state of neglect.

He did some rapid mental arithmetic. Lady Rose was aged twenty-five. Ridiculous that she should be buying land for herself at all, let alone a tiny tumbledown castle and a few acres.

Clearly this was some spoiled chit either sulking after a family row or with delusions of playing at being Marie Antoinette on her fantasy farm. Her brother must be out of his mind to allow it.

The two castles were a mere eight miles apart across country. Not so very far to ride in order to travel back in time more than fifteen years, Marcus thought as he put the nervy chestnut at the first gate.

He had inherited his second cousin's stables as well as everything else, and William's choice of horseflesh did nothing to change the poor impression he had of the man. William Cranford had been the Earl of Milbrook and twenty-two when Marcus had last set eyes on

the man, and as arrogantly pleased with himself then as only the over-indulged heir to a
dukedom could be.

For anyone who read the newspapers it
would have been impossible to miss William's
transit through society, marked as it was by
scandals with married women, two flamboyant duels, tales of wild extravagance and a series of sporting idiocies marked by huge bets
and, in the end, lethal danger.

The previous year his cousin, sixteen months
a duke, had challenged his cronies to a mid-
night steeplechase. The riders had all been
drunk and William's horse had the reputation
of being unmanageable by anyone but him. If
this particular animal was anything to go by,
Marcus thought grimly as his mount did its
best to deposit him in a ditch, his cousin preferred flamboyant looks to well-bred manners.
Which just about summed up the man himself,
in his opinion.

Halfway around the steeplechase course the
Duke's horse had baulked at a bank and ditch,
William had gone over its head and landed on
his own. He was lying face down in the mud,
his neck broken, when they found him.

The death of an unmarried duke without

brothers had sent many people to consult their *Peerages*, intent on discovering who the lucky inheritor of a lofty title, neglected lands and an empty bank box might be.

The First Duke, raised from an earl by George I for reasons the family was always somewhat evasive about, had sired four sons. The eldest had two sons, but Lord Arthur, William's only uncle, had died unmarried, several years before his elder brother, the Third Duke. This meant that the inheritance would have gone to the male descendants of the second son, Lord Francis, but he had fathered only daughters. The third son, Colonel Lord Ludovic Cranford, suffered a somewhat intimate wound in the course of the battle of Culloden that crushed the Forty-Five Jacobite Rebellion, and his hopes of paternity vanished along with the dreams of Bonnie Prince Charlie.

As a result, when the College of Heralds consulted the records to determine the new holder of the title, they had to move to the descendants of the fourth son, Lord Maurice Cranford, Marcus's grandfather. Given that younger sons, let alone the sons of fourth sons, were expected to get on with supporting themselves, it was not surprising to the Heralds to discover that Mr Gregory Cranford, Marcus's father, who enjoyed a quiet but undistinguished career in the London offices of the East India Company, had married the daughter of an obscure country clergyman. On his death in the year 1798, his small savings had left his widow reliant on a return to her father's home, along with her daughter.

His son Marcus, the Heralds found, had spent five years as a ward of his father's cousin, the Third Duke, and had then, at the age of fifteen, been sent as a junior clerk, or 'griffin', to the East India Company, to take a riskier path than his father amid the perils of the subcontinent.

'*That* Marcus Cranford,' Rouge Dragon Pursuivant remarked when one of the secretaries deposited the paperwork on his desk. 'Well, well, well. This *will* be interesting.'

The letter requesting that he present himself at the College of Heralds had landed on the desk of Mr Marcus Cranford, head of the flourishing London And Orient Trading Company, one hectic Monday morning. Marcus tossed it aside to concentrate on business and he did not discover until dinner time that, providing he could produce satisfactory proofs of his identity, he was now the Fifth Duke of Northminster.

His partners visibly braced themselves for an explosion when he told them the news, but it did not come. Marcus was not pleased, but he was resigned: there was no way to disinherit himself and he hated to see anything done badly. He was now a duke, so he had better learn to be a good one. He could hardly be any worse than the previous two, as he pointed out to Mr Richard Farthing and Mr Arnold Gregg, his associates. They would have to take on more responsibility and, with it, a greater share in the profits of the company, so they were, he suspected, considerably happier about the situation than he was.

'I thought you'd have hundreds of servants to look after the estates and so forth,' Arnold had observed as they opened a bottle of brandy to toast their newly negotiated working agreement. 'Surely all you need to do is stroll through St James's looking superior, spend a great deal of money with your tailor and enjoy all the delights of London society.'

'That was my cousins' approach and the results are what you might expect if you combine inadequate supervision of great estates with a desire to extract as much profit as possible without reinvesting,' Marcus observed. He had taken a first look at the books and was still reeling at the incompetence and greed. Unlike his father he had flourished in the Company and learned to profit from an unsuspected talent for business.

Now, as he held his mount to a steady canter across meadowland, he wondered at his decision to gather up the dispersed properties. It hardly made good economic sense and he was surprised by his own instinct to win back every square foot of lost territory. Perhaps he was more of an aristocrat than he had believed.

Or perhaps he was simply a sentimental fool, because there was Chalton, just coming into view above the water meadows, and his vision blurred for a moment.

As castles went, it was not impressive, he thought, as he reined in to recover his equilibrium and to see whether it bore any resemblance to the sun-dappled Eden of his memories.

It had always been tiny, commanding a shallow valley where the stream had been diverted to the left to form a moat, to the right to feed the village watermill. Originally a curtain wall had surrounded the bailey: a courtyard filled with stabling, lodgings and the kitchen. At one end had stood the long-vanished wooden great hall of the de Chalton lords.

Once, an imposing pair of towers had flanked a defensive gate. The towers still stood, but only as the flanks of the little farmhouse that had been built where the portcullis and entrance arch had been by that first Tudor tenant farmer. That man had made a permanent bridge across the moat to a jagged gap in the walls as his farmyard entrance and that was defended by nothing more threatening than a five-barred gate.

As he held the chestnut to a walk and drew nearer Marcus saw that the gate was closed. Not only that, but apparently guarded by a small figure in skirts. She perched on top, feet dangling. This could not be Lady Rose, he saw at once. The girl was ten, or perhaps twelve, years old and she sat swinging her legs to reveal sturdy boots and much-darned stockings beneath skirts that, Marcus suspected, had been cut down from some older sister's discarded gown.

She glowered at him fiercely from beneath a

mass of brown curls until he reached the edge of the moat. 'Halt! Who goes there?' she demanded.

She made an unlikely sentry but, mellowed by memories, he was prepared to play along with the game. 'Marcus Cranford, Duke of Northminster.' He had a vague feeling that if he repeated that often enough, he would come to believe it.

The child's eyes widened when she heard his title, but she still demanded, 'Friend or foe?' Despite appearances, her voice was educated. Surely this urchin was not one of the Trafford sisters?

Marcus was tempted to say, 'Foe', just to see what the reaction would be. Possibly she would produce a longbow from behind those skirts.

'Friend. I have business to discuss with Lady Rose Trafford.'

'Pass then, friend.' She jumped down and pulled open the gate for him to ride in. 'My sister's over there.' She pointed at a crumbling turret. 'Rose! Here's a duke to see you! Not a knight at all.'

The shrill shout sent the chestnut plunging and curvetting over the bridge and Marcus arrived in the bailey feeling more like a trick rider from Astley's Amphitheatre than a dignified visitor.

'Good morning,' said a clear, amused voice.

He found himself facing a young woman improbably perched on the exposed steps of the inside of the turret. She was blonde, hatless and appeared to be using a flat part of the ruined wall as a desk because, as he urged the horse forward, she closed a ledger and put down a stub of pencil. Her elevated position brought her face on a level with his and vivid blue eyes regarded him critically.

Marcus brought the chestnut under control and found he was being assessed with faint scorn.

'Do not blame me,' he said, responding to the look. 'I didn't buy the confounded animal.' The derision was replaced with a twitch of the lips and he doffed his hat. 'Marcus Cranford. Am I addressing Lady Rose Trafford?'

'You are,' she conceded. 'Are you the brother of the man from whom I bought the castle?'

'His cousin. Once removed.' Marcus discovered an instinctive desire to distance himself as far as possible from the late, unlamented, William.

He became aware of people moving around

him. The child from the gate came and stood close by, staring up at him as though committing his appearance to memory. Another brown-haired girl, rather older than the child, and wrapped in a vast and spotless white pinafore, walked down from the other end of the bailey, and an unprepossessing youth leading a very handsome nanny goat followed her, his mouth hanging open.

Lady Rose made no move to stand up or to invite him into the little house. All three onlookers, girl, youth and goat, stared fixedly at him and, to add to his discomfort, a solid middle-aged woman with her sleeves rolled up over strong arms and wearing a blood-streaked apron, appeared in the farmhouse doorway. The broad knife in her hand glinted in the morning sun and she held it with the ease of long familiarity.

'Forgive me arriving without writing first,' Marcus said, reflecting that he'd had warmer welcomes in some of the wilder parts of the Spice Islands. 'But I have a business proposition, Lady Rose. Perhaps your agent or man of law—or your bailiff, perhaps—are available to talk for me to speak to?'

'I have no bailiff. My lawyer is in London.

You had best state your business to me, Your Grace.'

She was treating him like an equal and Marcus found he appreciated that. But negotiations over property were not a woman's province.

'I wish to buy this castle and its land,' he explained. 'If you give me your lawyer's direction, I will write to him.'

'Then he would have to write to me and I would write back to him saying *no*, and then he would write to you—and we would be no further forward and a great deal of time and paper would be wasted.'

'You have not yet heard my proposition, Lady Rose.'

'I do not need to. The castle is not for sale under any circumstances.'

Marcus had politely refrained from staring at her, but now he looked directly into her face. Her thick plait of pale gold hair fell over the shoulder of a man's frieze coat. Cool blue eyes studied him from under brows just a little darker than her hair and her wide mouth was unsmiling. He was reminded of the Swedish sailors he met sometimes on voyages—a frank gaze the colour of the sea, handsome, strong features and an uncompromising attitude.

But this was in no way an unfeminine creature, he thought. Her regard was assessing him as a man, just as his was considering her as a woman.

Attractive, he thought. *A very unconventional beauty. A stubborn, wilful handful and a challenge to make a man's blood run hot. However, the feeling does not appear to be mutual.*

He was unaccustomed to being looked at by women with quite that degree of *hauteur.* Or perhaps it was simply uninterest. It would have been false modesty to pretend that he did not know he was generally considered to be a handsome man and he could not recall any other occasion when he had been eyed as though he had just emerged from under a stone.

'Not for sale even at twice what you paid for it?' Marcus asked, goaded into a reckless offer just to provoke some reaction.

'Not even then.' She stood up in a swirl of fabric and he realised with shock that she was wearing a divided skirt. He caught a glimpse of tight breeches over shapely thighs and long, scuffed, boots before the dun-coloured serge settled into decency again.

Marcus managed not to let his jaw drop—if this confounded female wanted to scandalise him then she had certainly succeeded, but he was damned if he was going to oblige her by showing it.

'Lady Rose.' He resumed his hat and inclined his head. 'I was perhaps too abrupt. I will leave you to consider my offer at your leisure and hope to hear from you in due course.'

'I doubt it,' she said, standing like a Valkyrie on her precarious rocky outcrop.

Outrageous, but magnificent. Under him the chestnut shifted uneasily at some unconscious pressure of his hands.

'This castle is my dowry, Your Grace. It is far too precious to barter for mere money.'

'Madam. Good day.' Marcus got the chestnut to turn and to walk sedately out of the bailey and across the bridge. Possibly the animal was as stunned as he was.

Her *dowry*? Was Lady Rose Trafford actually *proposing* to him?

Chapter Two

'Rose?' Chloe, for once shocked out of her usual ladylike poise, stared wide-eyed at her half-sister. 'Whatever did you mean, your dowry?'

Rose picked her way cautiously down the stairs to the grass. Her knees felt unaccountably shaky. Wearing her divided skirt and breeches was all very well in her own farmyard, but to confront a duke in them—any man, come to that—was downright shocking. She felt ready to sink, because it was her own fault. If she had just stayed sitting down he would never have noticed her garments. But no, she had become flustered and anxious and had overreacted to hide it and now he'd had an eyeful of her legs.

'You know it is,' she said. 'It is all our dowries—it is the only asset we have. That is why

I bought it. Land always has some value and it keeps us in most of our food while we live here. As for what I said to the Duke—arrogant man—I was merely, er, simplifying to make a point. I had no intention of explaining our circumstance to him.'

Not that this tumbled castle, or the smallholding that went with it, had much value in truth, and it was a mystery why the Duke had offered her twice what she had paid. Those cold, hooded eyes set under uncompromising brows had given nothing away, even though they had managed to send disturbing shivers down her spine. That was a very large, imposing male creature that she had sneered at and then frustrated, and he wasn't pleased.

Chalton Castle might not be much, but they were settled here now. They were self-sufficient in eggs and milk and grazing for their donkey and cow and were growing most of their vegetables. The roof was sound, there was no rent to pay. If she couldn't think of any better scheme, then, when Chloe reached marriageable age, she would try to shame their brother Charles into paying for a Season for her and providing some kind of dowry. If it wasn't sufficient, then she would sell Chalton to fund Chloe's come-out.

Charles, now Earl Wighton, was, like Chloe and Kat, the child of their father's second marriage. He was the longed-for son and heir and the apple of their father's eye. A rotten apple spoiled by indulgence, in Rose's opinion.

Charles had found himself Earl at the age of nineteen two years before, when their father had died within days of his second wife during an outbreak of influenza. He was also encumbered, as he saw it, with three sisters whose expenses fell on him.

Rose, in his freely expressed opinion, was on the shelf at twenty-three. She had attracted seven proposals during the course of three Seasons and had refused them all. Charles considered her excuses—that the hopeful suitors were either too old, too dissolute, too dull, or, in one case, all three combined—were foolish whims. The chit, he had declared, was a born spinster. Chloe was several years from needing a come-out and Kat a mere child. As his father had done, he decided that he could continue to ignore them all until some distant point in the future.

And when that time arrived, Rose thought,

there was a fair chance that Charles would have run through a sizeable fortune on his own pleasures and fancies and would have none to spare for his sisters. It was clear that, if the girls were to have a chance in life, then it was up to her to provide it.

What would happen to her then was something she tried hard not to think about. Her sisters had to come first. From the day they were born she had loved them and been loved fiercely in return. Together they had made a family within the cold shell her father's neglect had created.

'Well, you certainly shocked the Duke,' Chloe said. Of the three of them she was clearly the one destined to make a suitable match, provided she could be put in the way of respectable gentlemen in a few years. She was already pretty, with a charmingly serious demeanour and ladylike manners which had survived unscathed, despite the daily toil among the chickens and vegetables. 'His jaw almost dropped open when you stood up, did you see? He caught it just in time and then he managed to glare down his nose at you. He is very good looking in a fierce sort of way,' she added thoughtfully.

'He would be just right for the hero Marmaduke in my book,' Kat observed. 'He's big and strong and he looks as though he could fight off villains and dragons and so forth, like a real hero has to do. But I can't have Marmaduke the Duke, it sounds silly. I will have to change his name.'

'This one is called Marcus,' Rose said, wishing they would stop pointing out the Duke's physical features. They were quite obvious enough for her to notice all by herself. Yes, he did look big and strong and capable of most things.

She was honest enough to admit to herself that she agreed with Chloe. He was handsome and she had felt a small, and very secret, frisson, just looking at him. Not many attractive men came into her life these days and frissons were in very short supply.

But he was stubborn too, she added mentally as a necessary corrective to thoughts about long legs in tight breeches and the strength of those thighs as he had controlled that horse. He was used to getting his own way, judging by the set of that chin, and he wasn't going to give up, although why a man who must possess half of Wiltshire, and goodness knew what else besides, wanted with her little castle, she could not imagine.

'Marcus. Duke Marcus the Bold? Marcus the Magnificent?' Kat was muttering. 'Duke Marcus Maximumus?'

'That is a ridiculous name,' Chloe observed with sisterly candour. 'Do you mean Maximus?'

'I like it. It has splendour,' Kat retorted. 'And it fits: there is a lot of him.'

Rose left them bickering and walked across to where Dorothy, their cook and general household dragon, was still planted in the doorway, knife in hand.

'Who was that, then?' Dorothy demanded. 'Didn't like the look of him. Too sure of himself.'

'The Duke of Northminster. He wants to buy the castle from me. I told him it was not for sale.'

'Hmm. Didn't look like any duke I've ever seen. Not that I've ever seen any, come to think on it. But where did he get that colour, I'd like to know? Gentlemen aren't that brown. Been on board a ship, if I'm not mistaken. Whatever he is, he won't take no for an answer, you wait and see. Rabbit pie for dinner suit you? There's the remains of the ham and some cheese for midday.' Taking consent for granted, she stomped back inside.

The sisters had arrived at the castle with Jack Baines and two ladies' maids. Jack, an undergardener sacked by Charles for carelessly leaving a rake on the front lawn where the new Earl could trip over it and fall flat on his face— and dignity—took to small-scale farming like a duck to water. The two maids had fled in horror after a week.

Dorothy Hedges had turned up the next day, said that she'd heard the maids talking as they waited for the stagecoach and announced that three young ladies couldn't live by themselves. 'It isn't fitting.' She'd produced a vast white apron from one of the baskets she carried and tied it on.

'Vicar'll give me a good character,' she informed Rose as she swept into the kitchen. 'I was working up at the Grange for years, but old Mrs Giddings died last week. I'm a respectable widow, I am,' she'd added when Rose, rendered speechless for once, had just stared at her. 'What were you paying those two useless bits of town frippet? I'll take the same as the two of them together—you'll get three times the value out of me, I'll tell you that now—and my board.'

Rose had found sufficient voice to agree to a month's trial and Dorothy had been with them ever since. Rose felt she had managed to secure the services of a cook, a housekeeper and a ferocious guard dog, all in one sturdy package, and was deeply thankful for the chance that had brought Dorothy to their door.

Now she went and took the deeds from the little iron chest that served as her strongbox and studied them all over again, worried that she had overlooked something. But no, it was as she remembered: she had bought the freehold outright from the late Duke. His successor had no claim on either castle or land, but she had an uneasy feeling that Dorothy was right—this man was not going to accept a refusal and she had a lowering feeling that he was not going to be easy to stand up to.

Which was absurd, she told herself. He was a nobleman, not some criminal uttering threats of violence and harassment. All she had to do was keep saying *no* and sooner or later he would give up, or make her an offer so ridiculously vast that she could accept it. The trouble was that, even at a distance, she had felt the force of his personality, of his will, and she had felt a curious weakening of her own.

It was because he was so physically powerful, she told herself as she locked up the chest. Not what she would call classically handsome, but intensely masculine: big, hard and competently relaxed as he'd sat on that ill-mannered chestnut. Straight nose, level brows, cold grey eyes made chillier by the tanned skin Dorothy had noted. When he'd doffed his hat it revealed a ruthless crop controlling thick black hair that, Rose suspected, would curl given half a chance.

And what was a duke—or any gentleman, come to that—doing with tanned skin? It was not what one would expect, although she had never met a duke and had dealt only with the agent of this man's cousin. But the late Duke, from what she had picked up from local gossip, had been a fop, a spendthrift and a town beau. His successor might have any number of bad habits—she felt another of those unwelcome little shivers at the intriguing thought of what those might be—but an idle man about town he was not.

Nor was he the gallant hero that Kat fondly imagined was going to ride to their rescue. The

Fifth Duke looked as though any interaction he might have with virtuous maidens in distress would be to toss them over his saddle bow and make off with them. And presumably after that their virtue would no longer trouble them. Rose smiled wryly at herself. Yes, that was a titillating fantasy. In real life she was sure she would do her very best to maim any man who tried it with her, even if he was an annoyingly, inexplicably, attractive duke.

'No luck, sir?' Aubrey Farthing, Marcus's new secretary, stood up when he walked into the study and tossed his riding crop and hat on to the nearest chair.

'It is that obvious, is it?' Marcus began to strip off his gloves.

'You do not exactly have the air of someone who has concluded a satisfactory transaction, no, sir.' Aubrey was the younger brother of one of Marcus's business partners and had been working for him as a clerk when he had received the news of his inheritance. Marcus knew Aubrey to be hard-working, good with figures and honest and he liked his quiet sense of humour. He could also be relied upon to do what the new Duke wanted and not what convention dictated. He had already proved blandly indifferent to the disapproving stares that Heathcote, the butler, directed at him every time he failed to say, 'Your Grace.'

'Lady Rose Trafford refused my offer of twice what she paid,' Marcus said as he went to stare at the map of the holdings that hung on one wall.

'Mr Barclay reports a good response from the farmers who bought the other unentailed properties.' Aubrey put down his pen and consulted a list. 'He is confident of securing all of them. No doubt Lady Rose wishes to consult her man of law: one cannot expect a young lady to understand such matters and to know how generous an offer it is.'

'You haven't met this young lady, who isn't quite as young as you clearly think: twenty-five, according to the *Peerage*. And I suspect hoyden might be a more accurate description than lady. I found her perched on some crumbling masonry, supervising a farmyard and wearing breeches to do so.'

'Breeches?' The usually phlegmatic secretary looked startled.

'Breeches. Under a divided skirt.' Marcus resolutely ignored the warm glow the memory caused. Just because Lady Rose did not behave like a gentlewoman, that was no excuse for ungentlemanly thoughts. 'She turned my offer down flat, supported by a sturdy henchwoman armed with a large knife, a small girl apparently under the impression that she was a sentry at the gates of a medieval fortress, a prim little body with an apron larger than she was and a youth with a goat and a number of chickens.'

Aubrey made a sound suspiciously like a swallowed laugh. 'Ah… Er… Lady Rose would appear to be an original, sir.'

'An original what, I wonder?' Marcus said darkly. 'Her parting shot was to remark that the place was her dowry. For one moment I thought I was being proposed to.'

'Perhaps you were, sir. It does seem rather drastic to marry for the sake of a ruinous castle and a few acres of land, but she is the daughter of an earl, after all.'

Marcus snorted. 'I suppose I'll have to do something about the succession at some point. The College of Heralds turned collectively pale when I asked about the next in line, because it appears that I am the only male Cranford left standing, unless one goes right back to my great-great-grandfather and then looks at the descendants of his brother. But I draw the line at marrying a breeches-clad chicken farmer who exhibits a strong dislike of me, even if she does come with her own goat.'

That proved too much for his secretary, who developed a fit of coughing and left hurriedly to reappear a few minutes later, muttering apologies about a crumb in the throat. 'How do you intend to proceed in the matter, sir?'

'A friendly approach did not work.' Marcus sat down at his own desk and drew a sheet of paper towards him. 'I shall see what some formality will achieve.'

'How much are you prepared to pay, sir?' Aubrey, used to working in a commercial environment, asked.

'Whatever it takes.'

'Of course. It has been in the family since the fifteenth century, after all,' Aubrey said, tactfully nodding his understanding of such unwise extravagance. 'One can quite see why you are concerned to have it back.'

Then one is quite wrong, Marcus thought as he dipped his pen in the ink. *I don't give a hang about ancestral lands as such, but I do object to some self-indulgent spendthrift cutting up a perfectly good estate and I object violently to him disposing of Chalton Castle.* My *castle.*

He held the pen poised over the paper for a moment, then began to write.

'We have some post!' Waving a letter, Kat bounced into the kitchen, where breakfast was being set out.

'We?' Rose put down the teapot abruptly. Letters these days were unlikely to bring good news.

'Well, it is addressed to you, I suppose.' Kat studied the letter in her hand. 'It's lovely thick paper. May I have it when you have finished with it if they haven't written on both sides? Only—'

'Kat, give me the letter.' Rose held out her hand, her apprehension growing at the sight of the large red seal.

It was not from Charles, anyway. She didn't recognise the crest which seemed to be some kind of coiled serpent. Or a dragon, perhaps.

'Open it!' Kat was bouncing up and down on her chair now.

The single thick sheet was smooth as Rose spread it flat on the table, the emphatic black handwriting seeming incongruous as it lay be-

tween the marmalade pot and the bread board.
She read it.

Madam,
I propose to do myself the honour of call-
ing upon you tomorrow, the 5th June, at
two o'clock, to discuss further the ques-
tion of the sale of Chalton Castle and it
appurtenances.

If this date and time is inconvenient to
you and your legal advisor, I would re-
quest that you suggest the earliest suit-
able appointment as I wish to conclude
this matter with the least delay possible.

I note your refusal of my initial offer
and I am prepared to consider whatever
reasonable price you may suggest. Should
you require assistance in securing a more
congenial replacement home for your-
self and your sisters, or help in moving
to such an address, then I am more than
willing to place the matter in the hands
of my secretary and land agent, who will
assist you to their utmost.

I remain, your obedient servant,
Northminster

'Obedient servant! That man has never been anyone's servant, let alone an obedient one.'

'Who is it from, Rose?' Chloe asked with a reproving look at Kat, who was half out of her chair in an attempt to read the letter.

'The Duke, of course. He is going to do himself the honour, if you please, of calling upon me tomorrow afternoon. Presumably, an informal approach not having worked, he now intends to overawe me with formality.' She passed the letter to Chloe and dug marmalade out of the jar with a vicious twist.

'You could ask him for three times what you paid,' Chloe suggested, frowning at the page. 'And demand assistance with finding a new house and removals, as he suggests. It would be a substantial return on your investment, after all.'

'Oh, no,' Kat wailed. 'We could never find another castle. This one is *perfect*. I don't want to leave.'

Rose tried to think. 'It is too soon,' she said at last. 'We have to keep saving until shortly before you can make your come-out, Chloe. Then will be the time to move to a respectable lodging in London. If we move now we will have to find money for all our food and we will need more staff, too—a better house will mean keeping up appearances locally and maintaining the property, or the investment will lose value.'

'In a year or so, surely Charles will realise the importance of funding my come-out,' Chloe said. 'I know he was horrible before and complained about a pack of girls costing him money and blaming you for not finding a husband when you had your own debut, but he will be settled as the Earl by then and he will be older and more…more sensible. More responsible.' She grimaced, as if recognising how unlikely that was.

'And pigs might fly,' Rose retorted. 'I cannot imagine Charles becoming anything but more spoiled, more selfish and, I fear, less solvent. He is going to go on spending on his own pleasures until the money runs out and then beyond that. It will be two years before you can do your Season, because inflicting that on a girl of seventeen is just cruel.'

'Did you hate it so much?' Chloe asked.

'All three Seasons, yes.' Rose concentrated on spreading the conserve evenly across the toast, right up to the edges, then cut it into four neat triangles. 'But the first one was the worst.

The terrifying Patronesses at Almack's, the young men who all thought they were God's own gift, the adder-tongued matrons all on the look-out for the slightest slip.' She shuddered.

'It sounds horrid, but I cannot imagine why you did not "take",' Chloe said. 'Gentlemen must be blind and foolish.'

'I received seven proposals,' Rose said calmly. 'And I did not wish to marry any of the gentlemen concerned.'

'Seven? Goodness. Is that why Charles was so cross and says such nasty things about you wasting money? I cannot see what business it is of his—Papa was alive then.'

Rose sank her teeth into another piece of toast. Seven proposals, but not the one she had wanted, dreamt of, yearned for. Seven men had wanted her for their wife, although none had ever showed a greater emotion than mild liking and admiration for her blood lines. And how could she marry any of them when she loved another?

Captain Christopher Andrewes. She let herself think his name, an indulgence she rarely permitted herself. She had misread his intentions, his feelings—everything about their relationship. She had thought theirs would be a great romance; he thought she was a friend and the perfect way to get closer to the woman he loved, Rose's best friend.

Clearly, she did not understand men's emotions. She had realised that after the first bitter realisation of how wrong she had been and how close to humiliation she had come by letting Christopher see how she felt. She had to accept that she could not trust her own judgement when it came to their feelings, but it did not mean she could not understand their ambitions, their motives and their weaknesses.

She took a reviving mouthful of tea. 'If we move from here now, it will not just be the new house that must be kept up to scratch. No one pays any attention to us here, but in a respectable neighbourhood we must dress the part, socialise, entertain and so forth, or rumours will spread about us and we cannot afford that. When the time comes we must emerge as though we have been in seclusion on one of Charles's estates.'

'So what will you tell the Duke?' Kat said. She had been following the conversation like a spectator at a game of shuttlecock, her head turning from one sister to the other.

'I will refuse, whatever he offers me.'

'You could always marry him,' Chloe said demurely. 'He is doubtless in need of a wife. I looked him up in the Vicar's copy of the *Peerage* yesterday when I delivered the eggs. He was just plain Mr Cranford in that. And single. It was last year's edition, so I shouldn't think he's had time to get married in the interval.'

'Marrying him is the last thing I—'

'Oh, *no*,' Kat interrupted. 'Rose cannot marry a mere duke. She is a maiden imprisoned in this castle until a prince comes to rescue her. I have decided that a knight is nowhere near high-ranking enough. And when I thought about it some more for my book, I realised that dukes never rescue maidens in any of the legends. They are usually the villains.'

'If there is any rescuing to be done, I am the one who will be doing it,' Rose said grimly. 'Although if Northminster falls in the moat, he can save himself.'

Chapter Three

Marcus gave considerable thought to his approach to Lady Rose. Clearly, she had felt confident—defiant even—on her own ground, enjoying shocking him. His arrival on that damned horse hadn't helped. The feeling of confidence would put her in a position of strength in negotiations, so the first thing must be to undermine it.

She was a lady born and bred, therefore reminding her of that, while refusing to acknowledge her frightful clothes or her pose of unfemininity, would unsettle her. It had to be bravado, surely? Undoubtedly she would appear at their meeting in an equally unconventional guise, hoping to unsettle *him*.

He therefore dressed with care, gratifying his new valet enormously. His late cousin's personal servant had made little secret of his feelings at being asked to demean himself by dressing an upstart merchant. The man had been dismissed within days.

Bettany, the new man, had ventured a few disapproving sighs, a cautious *tut*, over most of Marcus's sartorial choices and had not unbent when it was pointed out to him that a life running a trading company, much of it spent at sea, was more comfortably and efficiently lived in clothes fit for the purpose.

'But you are not at sea now, Your Grace,' the man had murmured, setting out evening knee breeches and a swallowtail coat.

Marcus had felt like retorting that 'all at sea' was exactly how he felt, but he tolerated Bettany because the man clearly felt that dressing a duke with a good figure far outweighed whatever Marcus's past life might have been.

Now he eased a ruby stickpin into the elegant folds of his neckcloth, selected a watch chain with two fobs and submitted to having a clothes brush whisked over his coat.

The carriage awaiting him at the door had been polished to within an inch of its life and the pair drawing it were perhaps the best behaved of any of the animals in his cousin's

stables. He doubted the inhabitants of Baron's
Chalton would have seen anything so smart
in their lives.

At the castle the carriage drew up at the site
of the original drawbridge, now a narrow stone
structure leading to a heavily studded front
door. Tudor, he supposed. In all the time he
had spent at Chalton as a boy it had never occurred to him to analyse the castle's structure.
Now he could see plainly how the sixteenth-
century half-timbered house filled in the gap
between the two gatehouse towers. It made a
nonsense of the architecture, but it added a certain fairy-tale quality of unreality to the little
fortress as it sat in the sunshine, its reflection
shimmering in its moat.

'Sir?'

Marcus controlled the jerk of surprise. How
long had he sat there, forgetting that Aubrey
was beside him and the groom waited patiently
at the carriage door? Today he needed his wits
about him and all his concentration—day-
dreaming was foolish. He nodded to the man
to open the door and climbed down, followed
by Aubrey clutching a portfolio.

'The condition of the place appears better

than I had expected,' he remarked, by way of explaining his abstraction. Not that a duke needed to explain himself to his staff. He had to get out of the habit of discussing everything as he had with his partners—debating decisions, arguing over tactics and strategy.

'Yes, sir. It looks as though it reached a certain point of decay and has been held there for years.' Aubrey gave a small snort of amusement. 'Quite picturesque, in fact. Just think how many landowners would pay a fortune to have this constructed as a romantic folly in their parks.'

The groom was already crossing the bridge to rap at the knocker, a large ring of twisted iron. The door opened to reveal the cook, not armed with any offensive implements this time. Her sturdy form was clad in a vast, and very clean, white apron, her hair topped with an equally snowy mob cap.

She stood aside as Marcus entered, his secretary at his heels. 'Lady Rose is expecting you, Your Grace,' she said with a stiff bob. 'If you would care to come through to the drawing room.' She walked ahead down a short passageway created by erecting a wooden wall on one side of the curve of the tower.

Drawing room? When Marcus had lived there the ground floor consisted of the central kitchen, a warren of storerooms in the left-hand tower and a living room of sorts in the right-hand one.

The woman opened a door and announced, 'His Grace the Duke of Northminster and his man.'

Marcus heard another snort from Aubrey, although whether that was offence or amusement he couldn't tell because he was too busy taking in the room in front of him. It was clean, for a start. Instead of bare gritty flagstones there were rugs on the floor. In the place of a drapery of cobwebs there were bright blue curtains at the windows and the arrow slits had been closed by pieces of glass set over them.

Old oak furniture gleamed with polish, there were flowers on virtually every flat surface and on the wide hearth and, facing him, side by side on a sofa, sat three perfect young ladies.

They stood as Marcus entered and each dropped a curtsy, albeit a rather wobbly one from the child at the end.

'Good afternoon, Your Grace,' they chorused.

It took him a moment to recognise the tallest

of the trio. Her smooth blonde hair was swept up into a simple chignon, her gown was one of elegant simplicity in a shade of periwinkle that brought depth to her eyes and she wore pearl drops in her ears and touches of fine old lace at neck and cuffs. She smiled at him serenely and he read unholy amusement at his surprise in those wide blue eyes.

'Lady Rose.'

The neat figure next to her was easier to recognise, her pin-neat appearance unchanged except for the removal of her pinafore. 'Lady Chloe.'

Which meant that the child at the end, brown ringlets loose on her shoulders, her simple dress just right for a schoolroom miss, must be the miniature terror who had challenged him so fiercely at the gate. 'Lady... Kat?'

'Katherine,' she supplied with a grin.

'Lady Katherine. Ladies, may I present my secretary, Mr Aubrey Farthing?'

More curtsies. 'Will you not sit down, gentlemen? May we offer you tea?'

He almost refused, but it was his intention that afternoon to keep the upper hand, to remind her constantly that this was an unsuitable place for three daughters of an earl to be liv-

ing, let alone farming. 'Thank you. That would
be delightful.'

Lady Katherine went out, presumably to
order the tea, and Marcus sat back, crossed
his legs clad in biscuit-coloured pantaloons and
relaxed. He enjoyed negotiating, bargaining,
getting the better of his opponents, whether it
was over the price of tea, silk or stowage on
one of his vessels.

Aubrey, as instructed, launched into polite
comments about the weather and the beauty of
the countryside. Lady Chloe remained silent,
her eyes on her clasped hands. Lady Rose up-
held her end of the conversation as though she
had never seen a goat, let alone perched on
a crumbling wall in breeches while chickens
pecked in the dust below.

Marcus took the opportunity to assess the
room. It was, on second glance, certainly neat
and clean and arranged with taste, but everything was old, some of it worn. There were
darns at the edges of the rugs, the elegantly
placed drapes on the sofas probably hid dam-
age and he suspected that the ladies' gowns had
been remade at home at least once, if not twice.

The mystery of what three daughters of the
aristocracy were doing living in genteel pov-

erty on what was effectively a labourer's small-holding deepened.

The cook returned, carrying a loaded tea tray, with Lady Kat behind her balancing a plate of cakes in each hand. There was the usual genteel fuss associated with pouring the tea, placing convenient side tables, offering cake, then more polite nothings were exchanged while they all sipped, nibbled and, in Aubrey's case, inhaled, several small cakes.

Finally, when further cups had been refused, Lady Rose turned to her youngest sister. 'I am sure Dorothy would be glad of your assistance, Kat.'

To Marcus's surprise the girl got up, bobbed a curtsy to him and went out carrying the tea tray. Lady Chloe rose, too, picked up a sewing basket and retreated to a far corner of the room.

So, battle is about to commence and you have cleared the field, my lady!

This whole scene was carefully orchestrated, Marcus realised. Lady Rose had recognised the formality of his letter for what it was, a veiled threat about his status and influence, and had answered it by reminding him that she, too, was an aristocrat and not to be intimidated by his rank.

'You wished to make me an offer, Your Grace.' She nodded graciously, as though giving a tradesman permission to show off his wares.

Marcus smiled, enjoying her resistance. This was almost like the challenges of a flirtation. 'I did. It might save time if you were to name your price, Lady Rose.'

'This place is not for sale. Not at any price. I had hoped I had made that clear at our previous…encounter.' She sat, hands gracefully folded in her lap, and smiled too. A sweet, ladylike and very false smile.

'I—'

'Why does a duke require more than one castle?'

It had not been a deliberate interruption and not a planned one, either. Lady Rose was curious and that curiosity had overridden what he was certain was a carefully planned series of statements.

'This one is tumbling down and Northminster is, so they tell me, magnificent,' she went on. 'So why so anxious to secure Chalton Castle? Your predecessors clearly considered it of very small account if it was not even included in the entail.'

'An oversight which requires correction. We have held it since 1491,' Marcus said, casually. Beside him Aubrey, trained in the hard school of business negotiations, was perfectly still.

'And you dislike having anything escape from you,' she observed with a nod as though settling a question to her own satisfaction. 'You must be a devil on the hunting field, Your Grace. I pity the fox.'

'I do not hunt.'

'No?'

'I do not have the time to waste.'

'Of course, you were recently in trade. I had forgotten.'

She had done no such thing. Marcus thought it a certainty that Lady Rose had gathered every scrap of intelligence about him that she could. She was dropping that insult—and anyone with pretensions to the *ton* would regard it as just that—with the care of an artilleryman lining up a shot. Yet, oddly, he did not think she personally thought it was anything to be ashamed of. There was watchfulness and hostility in those lovely blue eyes, but not scorn.

Those eyes. Marcus was uncomfortably aware of a feeling that had no place in negotiations, nor in a lady's drawing room, come to that. He re-crossed his legs, switched his gaze to her mouth, decided that was an even worse idea and told those parts of his brain that were functioning to concentrate on the reason he was here.

'Lady Rose, let us come to the point. I am sure this place is romantic and charming in the summer sunshine, but winter will bring rain and mud. A very great deal of mud. The late queen of France found playing at milkmaids at Versailles an amusing diversion, but I can assure you that she was not mucking out pigsties during a November gale.'

'Playing? You think I am aping Marie Antoinette and *playing*?' Lady Rose leaned forward, then held out her hands to him. 'We have been here through all the seasons and are quite familiar with mud. Look. Touch. Then tell me that I am playing.'

Startled, Marcus sat forward and did as she asked. Her hands lay on his own outstretched palms. Her fingers were long and slender, but were dwarfed by his. The touch was warm, steady, barely perceptible. He looked closer. Her fingernails were clean, but cut close, except for two that had been torn, exposing the quick. A red scuff across the knuckles of her right hand looked sore and there was a healing cut on the left wrist.

She turned her hands so they lay palm up. Faintly he could feel the blood pulsing under the fine skin. With his thumb he stroked across the swell at the base of her fingers, felt the hardening of the skin that betrayed callouses. There was a blister on her right index finger.

'Why?' he demanded, his grip closing so he held both hands imprisoned in his. Now her pulse was thudding against his. 'What the devil is the daughter of an earl, the sister of an earl, doing working like a farm hand?'

'Because I choose to. And kindly do not use such language in front of my sister.'

Marcus had forgotten Lady Chloe, stitching in her corner. Forgotten his own secretary sitting silently right beside him.

'I apologise, ladies,' he said and released the hands that had lain passive in his. But that stillness had been the result of will, he knew—the stammer of her pulse had betrayed her.

Fear, anger or something else? Marcus met Lady Rose's steady gaze and saw the betraying darkness as her pupils widened. Arousal?

Then he told himself not to be a coxcomb. Just because he was finding this strange battle stimulating, there was no reason to suppose she felt anything for him except dislike or distrust. Probably both, he thought wryly.

'Lady Rose, I am offering you an escape from this drudgery, enough money to purchase a home of elegant comfort for yourself and your sisters and assistance in finding it. I fail to understand why you should refuse me.'

'Your lack of comprehension is hardly surprising, Your Grace,' she said coolly. Whatever emotion he had stirred was well under control now. 'You know nothing about me. You have come suddenly into wealth and position in a world that, I imagine, is unfamiliar to you. You cannot comprehend what might cause me to shun that world and I feel no compulsion to explain myself to you.'

She stood and he and Aubrey had no option but to rise to their feet.

'Rest assured, Your Grace, that if pigsties and autumn mud wear me down, you will have first refusal on Chalton Castle. I should warn you, however, that those pigs will be airborne before such a thing should happen in the foreseeable future.'

The stifled giggle from the corner was the last straw. He had rehearsed any number of arguments to persuade her. Now those vanished in a wave of exasperation, a good part of it at himself.

Marcus bowed. 'When you find yourself driven to sell, Lady Rose, you may still find me open to consider the matter. However, I would not count upon it. Good day to you, Lady Chloe.'

Lady Chloe saw him out and closed the front door behind them so gently that it was as effective as a slam.

'I cannot believe it,' Aubrey said when they were seated in the carriage once more. 'It is unaccountable. Lady Rose must have taken leave of her senses. I have never seen such eccentricity.'

'I mishandled that,' Marcus said, scrubbing his hand across his face. A faint drift of scent—rose petals?—rose from his skin. It must have been her soap. 'And I committed a cardinal error in any negotiation.'

'Sir?'

'I did not investigate the other party in depth. Lady Rose is not indulging a whim, nor is she playing games. Something very strong is chaining her to Chalton and I will not shift her from that castle until I understand what is keeping her there.'

He stared out of the window as the carriage rumbled across the uneven cobbles of Baron's Chalton village. There was the forge, but the burly young man shoeing a plough horse outside could not be the smith he remembered. This was his son, perhaps. And there was the bakery ahead. Marcus dropped the window down and breathed in the once-familiar scent of hot bread and spiced buns. There were still small boys playing in the puddles around the pump on the green, still a flock of geese menacing a dog—direct descendants, perhaps, of the flock that had once chased him across the grass and treed him in the great oak that hung its branches over the ancient stocks and whipping post.

He tugged up the window strap, shutting out the past.

'Sir, may I ask a question? A personal one.'

'Of course.' Marcus smiled faintly. 'I do not undertake to answer it.'

That was one reason he had taken Farthing on as his secretary—the young man's enquiring mind.

'Why do you want Chalton Castle so badly, sir?'

'It used to be my home.'

'Oh. Er…you must have delightful memories of it. I quite understand why you would not wish to lose it now.' Tact, and perhaps a knack for reading faces, stopped Aubrey from making any further comment.

Understand? I doubt if you do, Marcus thought. With all the things he had to deal with, all his new responsibilities piled on top of his old ones, this driving need to recover Chalton might seem an indulgence. But it was not. It felt as necessary as air to breathe. As necessary as an anchor to a ship.

'I must be careful how I go about investigating Lady Rose,' he said, changing the subject abruptly. 'To make any open enquiries about a young lady risks her reputation. My London acquaintances are all men, which means I have no way of discreetly gathering gossip about a lady. This will take some thought, because I am reluctant to employ an agent about the matter. If it were the Season I would go up myself and I imagine a duke, even a newly minted one, would soon find himself drowning in invitations, but now society will be dispersed for the summer.'

'My aunt Aurelia married a baronet,' Aubrey offered. 'And when he died she married a viscount and *their* daughter, my cousin Georgiana, has just finished her first Season. She's lively, intelligent and popular—and she is also very discreet. I could ask her what she knows about the whole family.'

'You are certain of her discretion?'

'Absolutely, and besides, I would not give her any idea why I am asking.'

'Try that, then. There is more to this than three wilful young women playing at farming.' And make-believe farmers did not have blisters on their fingers or callouses disfiguring their hands.

Georgiana's answer came by return from her father's country house, where the family were entertaining a large party of guests.

'"*Mama is hoping to marry me off to some chinless Algernon or Henry with a large fortune and excellent prospects,*"' Aubrey read out loud over breakfast. '"*But not Lord Wighton, you may be sure! I heard Papa telling Mama that I was not to be allowed to dance with him at Almack's because he is a gazetted fortune hunter and not to be trusted.*" Three exclamation points,' Aubrey added.

'"*Whatever do you want to know about him for, Aubrey?*"' he continued. '"*The Duke isn't*

*intending to marry one of his sisters, is he?
His half-sister is quite on the shelf—Mama
says she was wilful and opinionated and threw
away her chances—and the younger ones, his
full sisters, are far too young, I think. As for
the Earl himself, Gordon says—"* that's her
brother, sir *"—that he is a scapegrace and a
sneaksby and he wouldn't play cards with him
under any circumstances. Gordon also says
that the Earl will be under the hatches soon
and he's in deep with the gullgropers. Then
he became quite flustered and said he had no
business using cant terms to me and wouldn't
tell me what it meant. But I asked James, the
third footman, and he says they are usurers
who lend money to gamblers at great rates of
interest and if they aren't paid back then they
resort to violence. And James said that he'd
heard that Wighton is also in the clutches of a
real Captain Sharp, who is leading him to the
devil. That, he tells me, is a cheat who lures
young men into huge debt and then screws
money out of them. It sounds horrible. You
don't play cards, do you, Aubrey? I hope not.
I am quite resolved now not to play, not even
for chicken stakes."'*

Aubrey skimmed through to the end. 'That is all to the purpose, sir.'

'Your cousin sounds a delightful young lady and a good reporter.' Marcus cut into his steak and chewed thoughtfully for a while. 'I can quite see why Lady Rose does not want to live with her half-brother and especially why she would not want two young girls in that household. But it does not explain why they are not comfortably established in some pleasant villa in Hampstead or Margate. There is more yet to discover, but I fail to see how to get at it.'

His instinct was to offer help, but that would certainly be refused. Those chilly blue eyes had held no plea for assistance, no weakness. Marcus admired her spirit even as he deplored her stubbornness. He had got off on the wrong foot with Lady Rose and it was clear that now she thoroughly disliked him. It was unfortunate, he thought wryly, that he was disposed to feel quite differently about her, exasperating female that she was.

Chapter Four

'That is an entire week passed with no word from the Duke,' Rose said, stretching her back and leaning on the spade. Potatoes apparently had to be 'earthed up', although why you had to bury healthy foliage under soil she was not certain. Still, that was what Thomas Mawe's *Every Man His Own Gardener* said and, as the introduction stated that it was designed to 'convey a practical knowledge of gardening to gentlemen', she had adopted it as her guide.

'That is good, isn't it?' Chloe said absently. She was perched on one of the rhubarb-blanching pots, studying the book in her hand. 'It says here that we should be working on our melons and cucumbers in frames, but we haven't got any of those, so that's all right. Oh, and sowing lettuce.'

'I bought the seed yesterday. And, yes, it is excellent news that the Duke seems to have given up on us.'

Although it was rather unsettling—all that intensity and then...nothing. Those chilly grey eyes melting into disturbing heat as they focused on her, the touch of his hands, big and cool, with rider's callouses. The man was a menace, of course, making her anxious about their security, tempting her with money when common sense told her she was doing the right thing. But he was strangely attractive. Or perhaps it was not so very strange—he was good to look at, intelligent and powerful.

And he thoroughly disapproved of her. He was irritated by her obstinacy, shocked by her working clothes and exasperated that she was refusing something he wanted. Dukes were presumably not used to encountering opposition, even ones who had only recently inherited. And, apparently, he had been a very successful trader and, she guessed, one did not achieve that without astuteness and a certain ruthless turn of mind.

'That's that done.' Rose stuck the spade in the soil and peeled off her gloves. 'I thought I would take a walk up the stream. It should be cooler there and I want to look out for watercress. There is some growing down below the mill leet, but that's not our water, so I don't like to pick it. Will you come with me?'

Chloe shook her head. 'I am going to sit under the shade of the oak tree and let down the hems on Kat's dresses. The light is better outside than in and if they aren't done soon she will be showing her knees.'

'Bless you, that will be a help.' Rose found a basket and a knife, just in case she found some cress, and left through the yard entrance, crossed over the moat and then walked northwards until she met the little River Chal where it split into two. One arm went off to the east to form the mill stream, with a pond south of the castle, and the other fed the moat which overflowed back into the millstream.

The land that went with the castle was shaped like a teardrop and the castle within its moat sat in the middle of the fat end, surrounded by a few acres of land. The stream ran up through the narrowing valley that formed the top of the teardrop.

To call the Chal a river was giving it more status than it deserved, Rose thought as she picked her way along the bank. It was perhaps two feet deep as it chuckled along over its bed of pebbles, the clear water revealing strands of waving weed. Watercress needed fairly shallow, clean, running water, she knew. Was this shallow enough? Perhaps she needed to go further upstream into an area she had so far not explored. If it didn't contain useful land, then she hadn't been interested when they first arrived.

On the right bank a small copse stretched away up the hillside. That would provide wood for the fire and perhaps for fencing. There might be blackberries in the autumn and mushrooms and hazelnuts. On the other bank there was rough grazing. If they could afford to fence it, perhaps the pigs might turn it into something more useful by turning the soil.

Deep in thought about pigs and fences, she almost overlooked the tufts of greenery poking above the water on the far side. Was that cress? She was going to have to get in to pick it and see. Rose sat down and pulled off her sturdy leather shoes and the thin wool stockings she wore with her breeches, then discarded the long-skirted waistcoat she put over the boy's shirt she had found on a market stall. This was her garb for rough work and the waistcoat's skirts came almost to her knees, providing a nod to decency by disguising her breeches. Now she glanced around cautiously, having no wish to scandalise any of the villagers who might be about. They thought her eccentric enough as it was.

No, she was quite alone. Rolling up her shirt sleeves, Rose waded in with a little shiver at the cold. But the water was refreshing and she picked her way carefully over to the plants. Yes, that was cress. The knife she wore at her belt cut through the stems easily and she picked a bunch. The peppery freshness of cress would be good with cheese or ham and all the old herbals said it was invigorating for the blood.

Best to leave the rest and see if she could find some more patches, because she had no idea how fast it would regrow. Pleased with her find, she climbed back up the bank and walked barefoot over the grass with her basket, leaving her waistcoat and shoes to pick up on her return journey.

After a few minutes she saw a bend in the stream ahead and heard the splashing of falling water as it fell over a tumble of rocks across the riverbed. They formed a natural weir, or perhaps it was ancient and man-made. Whether artificial or natural, there would be a deeper pool upstream, so perhaps the ancient inhabitants of the castle had created a fish pond here.

A kingfisher flashed past downstream, a streak of azure from the pages of an illuminated manuscript and, enchanted, Rose stopped, hoping it would return. Then, over the gurgle and splash of the steam came a single *plop*. An otter? She craned to see around the bend and glimpsed something that had not been there before, a thin, diagonal dark line against the water. At the end a red float bobbed on the surface.

A fishing line? Someone was stealing her fish!

Not stopping to recollect that the largest fish she had seen so far was a stickleback, and quite forgetting how she was dressed, Rose marched along the path, around the corner and found her poacher.

The man was relaxed, sitting on the bank, bare feet in the water, his back propped against the stump of a tree. He glanced up as she pushed past a bush and into the open, then hissed, 'Shh!'

'Don't you *shh* me! You are poaching, this

is my stream…' Her voice trailed away as she recognised him.

The Duke must have realised who she was at the same moment. His eyes widened, then he looked away and lifted a finger to his lips. 'It is, but harangue me quietly or you'll disturb the fish.'

The very care he was taking not to stare at her made Rose aware of just how she was dressed. Or hardly dressed. She froze, but he made no move to either glance her way again, or to get to his feet and do anything…anything untoward. Tentatively Rose slid one foot behind her. If she could just ease away into the bushes, then run down to where she had left the rest of her clothes she could get covered up and pretend this had never happened.

No, I can't, she thought, looking down at her legs, bare to the knee, at her breeches, at her simple shirt, open at the neck. *This is going to be branded on my memory. It certainly will be on his.*

'This is definitely your stream, but are you positive that you purchased the riparian rights?' the Duke asked, still unmoving, his gaze steady on the rod and line.

His tone was conversational and, recalling

that swift glance when she had surprised him, his expression had been neither lecherous nor disapproving. His coat was hanging on a bush, his boots and stockings lying beneath. There was no sign of his neckcloth and he had rolled up the sleeves of his shirt. A curl of dark hair was visible at the open neck and his forearms were dark with springing black hairs, too. He was, for a gentleman, positively undressed.

She should turn tail at once, but some stubborn instinct told her to stay. Cautiously Rose pulled her shirt free of the breeches' waistband. It was a typical countryman's shirt, full and long, and as she let go of the hem it fell as far as her knees.

Feeling slightly better now the worst of her clothing was covered, she put up her chin and prepared to do battle. The Duke was on her land and she was not going to be routed. Besides, he had seen her shocking garments now and running away was not going to make him forget them.

Rose was not at all certain what riparian rights were, let alone whether she had paid good money for them, but she was not going to admit either. 'Naturally I own the rights,' she stated, hoping she sounded confident.

'So, the fish are yours. Well, if I catch any-thing, I will give it to you. Is that fair?' This time he did glance at her and she had a nasty suspicion that the twist of his lips was more amusement at her appearance in the flapping shirt than general friendliness.

'I—I suppose so.' Given that she had no idea how to fish, so was certainly not going to catch anything herself until she worked it out and purchased whatever gear was needed, it seemed foolish to turn down the chance of free food to put on the table for supper. 'But you *are* trespassing,' she persisted.

The Duke had turned his attention back to his float and she relaxed a little. 'This is an an-cient way that all the villagers have used for centuries,' he remarked. 'They may not gather your timber, hunt in your wood or fish in your stream, but it is the quickest way north from the village. You aren't intending to block it off and set mantraps, are you?'

'Certainly not,' Rose said stiffly.

'So, we have established that I am not tres-passing and you have given me permission to fish. Come and sit down next to me and I will see if I can't catch you something to go in that basket along with your watercress. Tread quietly, or you will scare every fish in the river away.' His tone was neutral, his expression unreadable, but certainly amiable. Where was the formal, harsh-faced man of their first meeting, or of that encounter over the tea cups?

She should, of course, turn around and leave, not stay here bandying words with him. And what on earth was he doing, fishing in this little stream? Surely he had perfectly good rivers of his own, stocked with fat trout.

Curiosity got the better of her. 'Why are you here?' she asked as she sat down on the bank, a foot away from him, her legs curled under her to hide their bareness. She shifted so she could spring to her feet at the slightest sign he would take advantage of her closeness. 'And do not say, *fishing.*'

'I am indulging an attack of nostalgia,' the Duke said, surprising her. 'I dreamt about this place last night and came to see whether it was still as I remembered it.' He was looking at the bobbing float, but Rose wondered what he was seeing in his mind's eye.

'How can you be nostalgic for Chalton? I thought you inherited everything from a cousin.'

'I did. But I lived here once as a child, for

four years. It worked its magic on me as I suspect it is doing on your youngest sister.'

'Whatever brought you here?' Rose asked bluntly. It had been inhabited by tenant farmers for ever, as far as she knew. Distracted, she sat up straighter and put her feet into the water. The sudden coolness was welcome, because it had become unaccountably warmer, despite the shade.

The Duke shrugged broad shoulders. 'It is not important.'

That was a clear snub. Rose bit her lip and wondered what to say next. Something tickled her foot and she looked down to find inquisitive sticklebacks nibbling at her toes. They had found the Duke's feet, too. Rather nice feet, she thought, admiring long bones and sharply defined tendons. Ridiculous to find a man's feet attractive.

'Your Grace,' she said. Whether it was the bare feet or the quiet beauty of the place or whether his mood had changed, softened, since their last encounter, she was not sure, but the dislike she had felt for him was fading. Perhaps it had never been him at fault, but only her bruised feelings about the general selfishness of men and the power they wielded.

'Call me Marcus,' he said abruptly. 'I have to become accustomed to being a duke, I suppose, but someone called me *Your Grace* the other day and I turned around expecting to find the Archbishop of Canterbury behind me. Ridiculous.'

'You will soon get used to it,' Rose said, the softening she had begun to feel about him vanishing. Did he really expect her to feel sympathy because he had been elevated to the highest rank in the country below the royal family? Surely he wasn't pretending he did not want the title, the land, the power? 'Are you saying that you do not want to be a duke?' She made no attempt to hide her disbelief.

'Not particularly,' he said, not reacting to the sarcasm in her tone. 'No, that's not true. Not at all, to be honest. It's a confounded nuisance. But there isn't much to be done about it: the Heralds almost fainted away when I asked whether I could get out of it.' He turned, gave Rose a quick, rueful, smile and went back to contemplating the stream.

'Er… Why don't you want it?' The charm of the smile took her aback. He seemed a different man. 'You have power, status, wealth now—some people would kill for that.' Would he snub her again?

'I don't give a da—a toss about the status. I have yet to discover a use for the power and as for the wealth, there is precious little of that. This inheritance is going to cost me money because I refuse to just abandon estates and tenants and hundreds of employees and neglect land the family has nurtured for centuries, just because two wastrels did their best to suck it dry.'

He took a breath that was audible and went on more moderately, 'At least my cousin broke his neck on the hunting field before he could complete his father's work of spending every penny in their coffers. The last Duke's grandfather, my grandfather's eldest brother, was a high spender too, but most of that money at least went on the house and the estate rather than into the pockets of loose women, racecourse touts and card sharps.'

His cousins sounded like her brother. Rose fell to thinking about that and began to feel some sympathy again. 'Officers in the Navy have to pass examinations before they can be promoted, unlike the Army, where preferment can be purchased,' she said. 'Perhaps aristocrats ought to undergo an examination before they inherit their title.'

The Duke—*Marcus*—gave a snort of amusement. 'That is an excellent suggestion. Papers on agriculture, land law, investment and land drainage, perhaps?'

So he had a sense of humour. 'Mmm,' she said, relaxing still further. He was showing no sign of wanting to pounce on her—not that she was presenting a very tempting sight, she was sure, but men were men, after all. Nor was he almost flirting, which was what some of their exchanges over the tea cups had felt like.

They fell silent again, but it was companionable now. Rose found herself wondering how she had come to be so comfortable in the presence of her adversary. Only he wasn't that, she realised, struggling to do him justice. The Duke—Marcus—had simply asked for what he wanted. Quite assertively and directly, it was true, and he hadn't been above trying a few tricks, like alternating a casual approach with something formal and legalistic, but there had been no aggression, no threats, no deception.

The man was a trader, of course, and that was what he had been doing—attempting to make a trade. And offering her a very fair price into the bargain, one that anyone else would have been delighted with.

And now she came to think of it, there were any number of underhand ways a duke could force her out of the castle if he wanted it that much. She had not been exaggerating when she had spoken of the power Marcus Cranford now held. A word in the ear of local tradesmen and she would have found people unwilling to do business with her. A hint or two to his tenants whose land abutted hers and no doubt fences would be broken, cattle would stray on to her property.

Or he could have started some very nasty rumours about her in society, here and in London, she realised. It would not take much to ruin Chloe's chances of an eligible match, as she was only too well aware. Who would believe that the three sisters of a profligate and foolish young earl were living in a tumbledown castle in the depths of the country simply to raise chickens and grow vegetables?

Marcus did not even seem hostile or disapproving of her personally now. He certainly entertained no lecherous thoughts—his reaction, or lack of it, to her revealing costume proved that.

'Eventually, in a few years' time, I will need to sell the castle,' Rose said abruptly, surprising herself. 'You may have first refusal then, but I warn you, I shall want every penny I can squeeze from it.'

The line jerked, scattering droplets of water as the float came clear of the surface. It was possible to startle an imperturbable duke after all, it seemed.

'Your word on it?' Marcus asked, his eyes dark and intent on her face.

'My word, if you trust the honour of a woman.'

'I trust yours,' he said slowly. 'I do not understand you, not in the slightest, but I trust you.' He held out his hand. 'Shall we shake on it?'

The clasp of his fingers was cool, slightly damp with river water. Rose returned the slight pressure and nodded. 'The castle will be yours.'

'Thank you. You had no need to tell me.' Marcus released her hand promptly. 'But I am glad you did. Or perhaps you thought I would plague you and pester, use some of that ducal power you spoke of.'

'You could have done all of that, but you did

not, I realised just now. That is why I said what I did—oh, look! Your float.'

The fishing rod had slipped from Marcus's fingers to the bank when they clasped hands and he had to grab for it before it slid into the water.

'What is it?'

'A dace or chub, I expect.' He reeled in his line and, after a few moments, had a fat brown fish with reddish fins flapping in his hand. 'Chub. This will go nicely with your watercress.' Shall we see if I can catch you some more? You can find some patches of cress further up above the pool if you do not have enough already. Walk quietly, though.'

Half an hour later Rose came back to the pool, with her basket half filled with cress, to find four fish on the bank beside Marcus. He looked up as she approached, although how he heard her barefooted tread on the grass she could not imagine.

'You must have sharp ears.'

'It pays to have in some of the places I have found myself. Mind where you walk—that patch there is mostly thistles.' He looked away again.

'These are my gardening clothes. I took off everything else when I waded in after the watercress,' she explained, answering the question he had not asked. 'I had been earthing-up potatoes earlier.'

'Very creditable, I am sure. Er...why?'

'I have no idea, but my gardening book says I must, so I do.' Rose sat down, her feet drawn up and her chin resting on her knees. 'Do you know anything about gardening? I could ask Jack Baines, who came with us when we moved here. He used to be an undergardener, but he didn't enjoy it much and he's far happier looking after the pigs and the cattle. Besides, I want to learn for myself.'

'I know not a thing,' Marcus said cheerfully as he laid the fish in her basket and drew the damp greenery over them. 'I can tell a rose from a radish, but I spent six years in the East India Company's employ and that, then the life of a trader, does not give much opportunity for planting potatoes.'

She wanted to ask about his previous life, about the East, but something in Marcus's manner warned her off. This was a man who gave personal information reluctantly and in small doses, she guessed. 'Thank you for the fish.'

'They are your fish,' Marcus pointed out. He stood up and held out his hand to help her to rise.

'Yes, but you caught them, I never could have done.' He released her hand the moment she was steady, she noticed. It was slightly galling that he did not even attempt to flirt a little, although, of course, she was grateful for that, she told herself. It would have made her feel very uncomfortable, here in this secluded spot, if he had shown awareness of her as a woman.

'Take this.' He handed her the rod, then tucked the hook safely into the line. 'All you need as bait for coarse fish are worms.'

'But… I cannot take your rod,' she protested.

'I have more. There is an entire case of the things in the gunroom at Northminster.' He lifted his coat from the bush where it was hanging and picked up his boots. 'Good day, Lady Rose.'

'Good day, Marcus,' she murmured, standing there with rod in one hand and basket in the other and certain there was more she should be saying. Marcus turned away to follow the path upstream and she called after him, 'And it is just Rose. Call me Rose.'

Marcus half turned and raised one hand. 'Good day to you, Rose. Goodbye.'

That sounded very final, she thought as she picked her way back down the path in the opposite direction. Of course, there was no reason for him to come to Chalton again, not for a busy man with massive responsibilities and now with her promise that the castle would be his in a few years. He could hardly be expected to have an attack of nostalgia for his childhood very often.

She should be glad, of course, because she had more than enough to worry about without thinking of ways to fend off tall, dark, handsome dukes. The foolishness of that thought made her smile to herself—Marcus had shown no signs of wanting to do anything that required fending off.

Rose reached the spot where she had left her clothes and propped the rod and line against a tree while she sat to pull on stockings and shoes, then stood to shrug on the waistcoat. When she picked the rod up again she saw scratched letters at one end and tilted it to read them.

Marcus Cranford Chalton Castle 1798

How old had he been? She did some mental arithmetic as she made her way back downhill, faster now that she had sturdy shoes between her feet and lurking thistles. She guessed he was about thirty now, although when he was relaxed he looked a little younger. Those lines at the corners of his eyes must be from squinting against fierce sunlight and there was no silver at his temples. So…if he was thirty now, then he had scratched his name on that rod when he was nine or ten.

What on earth had a young boy of good family been doing living here? Perhaps he had been orphaned, or his parents were unable to have him with them for some reason. But his cousins had a vast home at Northminster Castle that could accommodate any number of related children without the need to lodge them with a tenant in a tumbledown smallholding, she thought, puzzled. Perhaps he had been a very naughty small boy.

Rose was still brooding when she put the basket of fish and cress on the kitchen table. Dorothy pounced on them with a grunt of satisfaction, but Chloe and Kat both fixed her with quizzical stares.

'When did you learn to fish, Rose?' Kat demanded.

'You didn't have a fishing rod when you left,' Chloe added. 'We don't own one.'

'I met the Duke and he was fishing in the stream and gave me the rod.' Quite why she felt reticent about revealing that, Rose could not think.

'He was poaching?' Chloe sounded incredulous.

'Hardly that, as he gave me his catch. I believe he was enjoying a little nostalgic relaxation. Apparently he lived here in the castle for a few years as a child.'

'So that is why he wants it,' Chloe said. Then her expression darkened. 'Unless it was all a trick to get your sympathy.'

'How could it be? He had no reason to suppose I would come across him all the way up there. It was the merest chance. You sound very hostile to him, Chloe.'

'I don't know why you trust him.' Her usually demure sister was frowning now.

'He spoke about the things he wanted to do to his estates and he clearly has a strong sense of duty and responsibility. And then I thought about all the nasty tricks he could have used to force us out and realised that he has been quite open and honest with us. So, I told him I would be selling in a few years and that I would give him first refusal when I did and he seemed quite content with that. I cannot imagine we will see him again.'

'Oh,' Kat said, pouting. 'I had such hopes of him. I have been reading about our British princes in the newspapers recently—the old copies Mr Benton at the inn gave us—and they seem to be very unromantic and not at all what I had hoped for. They are fat and... deca...decadent, whatever that is. Unless some foreign princes come to England now the wars are over, I think a duke is the best hope for you, Rose. And there aren't very many of them, are there? Not unmarried ones.'

'I do not want a prince, foreign or not, and I certainly do *not* want a duke.' A mental picture of long limbs, of bare, wet feet, of strong forearms revealed by rolled-up shirtsleeves filled her mind and she could feel her colour rising.

Yes, you do and the sooner you stop thinking about him in that disgraceful manner the better, my girl.

'You are a damsel in distress and you live in a castle,' Kat said stubbornly. 'All the best fairy stories begin like that.'

'This is not a tale,' Rose said, beginning to feel that the arrival of a fairy godmother willing to turn her two sisters into something resembling sweet, obedient and decidedly un-curious young ladies would be very welcome. 'I am not in distress. The Duke has gone and that is the end of it.'

Chapter Five

Marcus sprawled full length along one of the cushioned benches on the back terrace of Northminster Castle. There should have been a satisfying and beautifully composed view of lawns sloping down to the remains of the moat, now part of the ornamental water garden. Instead there was an unkempt hay meadow and an expanse of muddy water.

Mercifully this distressing aspect was partially blocked by another bench, this one occupied by the firmly upright figure of his secretary. Aubrey was, Marcus was sorry to see, clutching a bulging folder of papers.

'I thought we had finished with business before luncheon.'

'London and Orient Trading Company business, yes. Everything seems to be going very smoothly, I thought, sir.'

Marcus grunted. Yes, it was gratifying to discover there were no problems, disasters or shipwrecks, that several lucrative deals had been struck and that the cash flow was exceedingly healthy. It was also disconcerting to discover that all this was happening without his presence.

His mouth twisted into a wry grimace of self-mockery. He had chosen his partners well, he had set the business up so that it ran smoothly and it was arrogant to imagine it needed his hand on the wheel day in, day out. The truth was, he knew the work of the company inside out, but learning to be a duke was something else altogether and he would have snatched at an excuse to rush back to London to deal with a shipping crisis, a fall in the price of tea or an unexpected opportunity to buy fine carved teak.

And now he no longer had the excuse of collecting back all the land that had been sold because, with the exception of Chalton, the purchases were agreed with farmers all too happy to take a quick and solid profit. He couldn't even indulge himself with nostalgic visits to 'his' castle. Lady Rose had offered him first refusal on a sale in a few years' time and he had frittered away yesterday afternoon with rod and line—and her company—at his favourite childhood fishing pool. Time to put memories and dreams aside and deal with duty.

'So what are you clutching there?'

'Correspondence about the market at Chalton Magna, sir. Apparently the grant of a weekly market and an annual fair was made to your ancestor in the reign of King Edward the Fourth and most of this correspondence consists of representations from the burgesses of the town and farmers in the surrounding area, which your cousins chose to, er, ignore. There is a need for repairs to be made to the market hall and for the better management of the market. Apparently there are endless disputes about stalls and pitches, the livestock pens have spread out into places that cause a nuisance and no one takes responsibility for clearing up afterwards and—'

'Do you know, Aubrey, when I was told I was a duke I thought it would be a burdensome round of Court appearances, endless debates in the House of Lords and problems with agriculture and tenants. Never, in my worst forebodings, did I imagine that I would have to concern myself with sweeping up rotten cabbage leaves, penning pigs or soothing borough officials.'

'No, sir. I'm sorry, sir.'

'I suppose I had better go and look for myself. When is market day? Monday?'

'Tuesday, sir. Tomorrow.'

'Your Grace.' Heathcote, the butler, somehow managed to radiate disapproval both of Marcus's posture and Aubrey's informal address to his employer without any change in his expressionless face.

'Yes?'

'Are you at home, Your Grace? Viscount Langford, Lady Langford and Miss Langford have called.'

'Show them into the drawing room, Heathcote, and order up refreshments.' He watched the butler's rigid back as the man went back indoors. 'I swear if we installed Heathcote in the kitchens we could produce iced desserts at a greater volume than Gunter's,' Marcus remarked as he stood up and gave a tug to his neckcloth. 'You look thoroughly respectable. Do I?'

'If I may…' Aubrey twitched at Marcus's

coat tails and picked something off his sleeve. 'Lichen, I presume, sir.'

Marcus was still grinning when he walked into the drawing room and beheld the prettiest girl he had ever seen.

Big brown eyes smiled shyly back at him They were set in a heart-shaped face with a mouth that could be described as *rosebud*. The pink lips curved shyly beneath a tip-tilted nose and around this enchanting countenance were glossy chestnut ringlets escaping from a pert, high-crowned bonnet.

Marcus dragged his gaze away, found he was now staring at a petite, but curvaceous, body and hastily switched his attention to the couple standing beside this vision.

'Langford, Lady Langford. A pleasure.' He advanced, shook hands and managed a decorous smile when the Viscount introduced him to his daughter.

'Our daughter Delphine, Your Grace.'

Delphine curtsied and blushed. The effect was perfect, like the inside of a seashell, Marcus noted. A glance at Aubrey had him hoping that he did not appear quite so poleaxed himself.

'Mr Farthing, my secretary.'

As was proper, Marcus focused on Lord and Lady Langford when they were seated, leaving Miss Langford to Aubrey.

'So kind of you to call. I had understood you were away from home.'

'We were. Visiting my mother-in-law, Lady Armitage, in Somerset, you know. She has not been in the best of health, but we have installed her in Bath with her companion and are confident that the waters will be beneficial.'

'I do hope so.' Marcus maintained his share of the social chit-chat, then when all the obvious topics had been exhausted, remarked, 'I imagine you will be more familiar with Northminster than I am myself, being such close neighbours. Your lands march with mine to the east, I believe.'

'They do.' Lord Langford looked a trifle uncomfortable. 'Your late cousin, and his father, did not entertain widely—not their neighbours, that is. We have rarely… They preferred a more sophisticated set.'

His wife's rapid glance at their daughter did not escape Marcus. It seemed his relatives' reputations had been as dubious in the country as they were in town. On the other hand, he could see very clearly why the Langfords had hastened to pay their respects as soon as they came home to find him in residence. Marcus knew he was one of the most eligible catches on the Marriage Mart, despite the taint of trade, and Miss Langford was a very enticing young lady indeed. Their hopes must be high.

And I must be equally wary, he thought. It would be all too easy to raise expectations by familiarity with close neighbours and although the young lady had parts of him very interested indeed, his brain had no difficulty dominating the internal struggle.

Too young, too sweet, too conventional.

'You will remain at Northminster for the summer, Your Grace?' Lady Langford enquired.

'That is my intention. It has probably not escaped your notice that the estate is in need of some attention.'

'All your properties must be,' Lord Langford interjected. 'The Fourth Duke was not much interested in his lands, I believe.'

'Quite. I have an excellent man touring the rest of my estates and sending me back reports, but Northminster must be my main focus for now.'

'But you will open up Northminster House

in London for the Season?' Lady Langford, a prudent mama, was clearly determined to pin down his movements.

'Certainly.' Yes, he must do that and search for a bride and take his seat in the Lords.

'Oh, the Season! Drawing rooms, balls—I am so looking forward to it,' Miss Langford said.

'It will be your first Season, Miss Langford?'

'Yes. I will be presented at Court, you know. I am terrified of that!'

'So will I be,' Marcus said, smiling at her naive enthusiasm. Goodness, but the child was young. He realised he was comparing her to Rose, who, of course, was several years older and would have had at least one Season herself. 'I must make my bow to the Regent myself and I expect my knees will be knocking.'

She beamed at him and he turned his attention back to her parents. Yes, he needed to be very cautious here.

When Marcus returned from walking the Langfords to their carriage he found Aubrey gazing into space.

'You look like a landed carp. Pull yourself together,' he told his secretary.

'Isn't she the most divine creature? Those eyes, that sweet face...'

'Miss Langford is very pretty, very fresh—and very, very young,' Marcus said repressively.

'She will be the success of the Season.' Aubrey sighed.

'You may dangle after her to your heart's content—I won't stand in your way, but don't get your hopes up or expect me to protect you from her infuriated father if he finds you making up to her. They have ambitions for that little miss.'

Aubrey snapped out of his rose-coloured daydream with a rueful grin. 'Oh, I know I don't stand a chance. Besides, her parents know exactly whom they want for her.'

'So do I. And they are going to be disappointed: cradle-snatching holds no appeal for me whatsoever. Now, I assume markets start early and, if we are to satisfy the good citizens of Chalton Magna that I am taking an intelligent interest in their problems, I suppose we had best be there by eight.' He glanced up as the butler came in to check on the footman removing the tea tray. 'Breakfast for six-thirty tomorrow, Heathcote. And, Aubrey: dress for mud.'

He had been right, there was considerable mud, Marcus observed as he strode down the High Street towards the market hall the next morning. There would be even more by the day's end. And worse than mud, given the cattle, pigs and sheep being herded into pens off to one side.

The street itself was lined with stalls and, at the end, more were grouped in the shelter of the market hall, raised on wooden pillars above the pavement.

'The hall looks shabby,' he remarked to Aubrey.

'The roof leaks, apparently.'

'Let's talk to the stallholders as we go, see what they think requires remedying.'

'You'll be swamped with demands, sir,' Aubrey said gloomily, but he produced notebook and pencil and followed.

'Oh, Your Grace!'

Marcus turned around from a tempting array of cheeses and found Miss Langford approaching, a maid at her heels. 'Miss Langford.' He doffed his hat and looked about. 'Are your parents with you this morning?'

'Mama is in the milliner's shop and Papa is talking to someone about cattle, so I thought I would explore on my own and then I saw you.' She dimpled at him and then, her attention diverted from looking where she was going, gave a squeak as her foot slipped.

'Take my arm, it is treacherous underfoot.' Marcus stepped forward and she tucked her hand under his elbow. 'May I escort you somewhere?'

'Oh, no. I only wanted to look around. I mustn't divert you from your own business.' She remained firmly attached to his arm.

'Apparently I have some responsibility for the market, so I was going to form an impression before I speak to the burgesses. Shall we view the stalls on this side?'

They progressed slowly along. With a lady on his arm Marcus could hardly stop for discussions with the stallholders. They passed vegetable displays, some agricultural hardware and a table of dead rabbits. That made Miss Langford squeak again. Marcus made a mental note that his future wife would not squeak.

'Oh, what a pretty goat!'

Marcus looked at the next stall where a handsome nanny goat with a glossy chestnut coat and a white blaze down her face was standing next to a board with the chalked notice, 'Fresh goat's milk here'. He stared at the goat and it stared right back at him through its strange, vertically slit pupils. It looked very familiar.

'Mama says that goat's milk is exceedingly good for the complexion,' Miss Langford observed brightly.

'I am sure you do not need it then,' he said, as he was no doubt expected to do. 'But shall we go and look?'

A girl stood up from the stool beside the sign as they approached. Yes, he had recognised the goat and the girl was Lady Katherine, dressed in a mob cap and voluminous smock and looking the perfect farmer's daughter. She came up to them, took Marcus's arm and tugged.

He bent down obediently and she whispered in his ear, 'You don't know me.'

Marcus straightened. 'Yes, that does sound a most reasonable price.' He turned to Miss Langford, who was staring in bemusement at their antics. 'Shy,' he murmured. 'Tell me,

Miss, is it true that goat's milk is good for the complexion?'

'I don't know.' The child studied his face. 'You don't need it.'

Miss Langford giggled. Marcus added giggles to his mental black list as she freed her arm and went to pet the goat.

Marcus surveyed the stall set out alongside the tethered animal. Cream cheeses, bunches of cress with water still sparkling on the leaves, a basket of brown eggs and another of salad greens. And behind the blue-and-white-checked cloth was Lady Rose wearing a straw bonnet, her simple blue gown covered by a large white apron.

'Good morning.' A glance showed Miss Langford was happily engaged with the goat which was tolerating having its ears scratched. 'Where is La—I mean, Miss Chloe?'

'At the castle. I do not want to risk her being seen like this,' Rose said quietly. 'Is there anything we have that you might be interested in, sir?' she added more loudly.

Yes, you, a treacherous voice in his head said. Rose looked fresh and intelligent and interested. And interesting. Miss Langford might be five times prettier and several years younger, but she could not hold a candle to Lady Rose, he realised with a faint sense of shock.

'Some of the cream cheese and two bunches of cress, please. How much is that?'

'Nine pence, sir.'

'Thank you. I will collect them on my way back if you could put them aside.'

Marcus found the coins and dropped them into her outstretched palm. There was a new blister at the base of her fingers, which angered him. What the blazes was her brother thinking about, allowing her to live like this?

'I discover I have a responsibility for the market and that all is not as it should be. As a stallholder, can you make any suggestions for improving matters?'

'I'll think about it, sir, and tell you when you return.' Rose was regarding Miss Langford and the goat with slightly raised brows. 'Perhaps you should tell your lady that she risks having her gloves eaten.'

He almost retorted that Miss Langford was not *his lady*, but bit back the defensive answer. 'Yes, I should see if we cannot find her mama. She is rather young to be wandering about a crowded market by herself.'

That made the brows rise higher and Rose looked at him, amusement in her eyes. 'Ah, yes. Do take care, sir, the place is strewn with dangers. The sooner you can restore her to her mama, the safer you will be.'

Marcus moved on, detaching Miss Langford from the goat in passing. He had thought for a moment that Lady Rose had been exhibiting some jealousy of him squiring a younger, prettier, lady. Now he was certain she was laughing at him for being manoeuvred into offering his escort.

'There is your mother,' he said with some relief, sighting Lady Langford on the steps of a shop.

She beamed at him when he returned her daughter to her. 'So kind of you, Your Grace. Her maid is a most reliable girl, but a gentleman's escort is always to be preferred in a crowd.'

'My pleasure, ma'am. If you will excuse me? I have some business at the market hall.'

Marcus strode off, perhaps rather too abruptly, feeling as though he had escaped by the skin of his teeth. If one hopeful matron was enough to rattle his nerves, then he had the sinking realisation that the London Season would leave him feeling like a hunted stag. Some men might enjoy the sense of power that being so sought after would bring, but he could gain no pleasure from something that had nothing to do with him personally, only his title.

Yes, he needed a wife, but he wanted something more than simply pretty looks and respectable breeding.

'What has amused you, sir?' Aubrey, still clutching his notebook, had caught up to him.

'I was thinking that I have negotiated with a Chinese war lord, held my own with any number of exceedingly sophisticated Indian merchants and faced down Malay pirates and yet I am rattled by a prime example of the English matron on the hunt. I had not thought myself a coward before.'

Aubrey gave a snort of laughter. 'I doubt you are, sir. No more than any other eligible gentleman when sighted by a pack of hopeful mamas, that is.'

'After that encounter I feel able to deal with any number of mayors and burgesses. Shall we get that over with?'

An hour later Rose saw Marcus emerge into the sunshine from the shadows of the market hall, shake hands with the mayor and stroll towards her stall. His secretary, Mr Farthing, was at his side, notebook in hand. There was no sign of Miss Langford. It was none of her business to speculate, of course, but he had seemed most attentive to what must be the prettiest girl for miles around. She was a viscount's daughter, so an acceptable match, if not brilliant. But the girl was so young, as young as she had been herself when she had been thrust on to the Marriage Mart. She felt her mood darken. It was pity for Miss Langford, of course. The girl needed another year or so, and a nice young man nearer her own age, but it was too much to hope her parents might think that.

'A dozen eggs, if you please,' someone said impatiently. It was one of the numerous housewives who were bustling around the market with their lists of provisions.

Rose started. 'I do beg your pardon. I was wool-gathering. A dozen, you say? They are fresh this morning.'

She was placing the eggs carefully in a rush basket held out by the woman, but out of the corner of her eye she could see the two gentlemen draw closer.

The younger man's clear voice reached her

easily. 'I am not at all convinced that it is your responsibility to deal with all of this, sir.'

She paused to try to catch the reply, ears straining. It was disconcerting to meet Marcus again so soon after their encounter on the river bank. She had hoped that his absence would stop the daydreams she kept falling into when she should have been concentrating on the housekeeping accounts, or working out how much she could afford for nails and wire so that Jack Baines could mend the gap in the lower pasture fence.

'I shall think about it.' The Duke's deeper voice was quieter. 'My cousins appear to have neglected their duty to the neighbourhood and I should remedy that. We will see what La… What some of the stallholders have to say on the matter.'

That showed a respect for the less attractive responsibilities of his new position that she had not expected the new Duke to possess. It was certainly a mark in his favour that he had troubled himself to be jostled in a muddy market at this hour of the day.

They reached her as she was counting out the change for the eggs. She gave them an automatic, polite smile, then exchanged a cheerful farewell with her customer before she turned to him.

She had been unwisely happy to see Marcus earlier, Rose thought. Now she felt positively depressed and she feared it was because of Miss Langford, which was humiliating, as well as quite pointless. Her smile was false, she knew, but she managed to keep her tone cheerful.

'Your Grace. Good day, Mr Farthing. Miss Langford is safely returned to her parents?'

Bother. Why did I say that? He will think I am taking an interest in his affairs.

'She is.' Clearly, Marcus did not want to discuss Miss Langford.

Surely he doesn't think I am...jealous?

It was bad enough that she felt like that, but the idea that her feelings might be visible was appalling.

Marcus looked at her for a long moment, a crease settling between his brows. Rose had the uneasy feeling he was trying to read her thoughts, but when he spoke all he said was, 'Have you any suggestions for me about the market?'

'I have, but I will write them down and send them to you,' she said crisply, attempting to sound like the mature, organised woman that she was. At least, when she was not mooning like a schoolgirl over a handsome man… 'But they are too disorganised to keep poor Mr Farthing standing here while I dictate them.' They were certainly chaotic—and fragmentary, because she had been thinking about Marcus and Miss Langford, she realised.

'You must not put yourself to the trouble and expense of posting your notes. I can ride over to Chalton in a day or so and collect them.'

'As you wish. You will find us at home whenever you call. Market day is the pinnacle of our wild social whirl.' Her smile still felt as though it had been pasted on. Why had she lost all her poise? She ought to be quite capable of putting on a bland expression of polite interest—she had learned that the hard way during her London Seasons, where revealing one's true feelings was thought positively gauche.

She had been so at ease with Marcus beside the stream, yet now she felt stiff and awkward. He was looking at her with that furrow between his brows as though he was frowning over a puzzle. Or perhaps wondering what on earth he was doing wasting his time talking to her when Miss Langford was in town.

The secretary stepped to one side to use an upturned barrel as a table for some last-minute notes and they found themselves alone for a moment, the stall a still island in the river as the bustle of the market swept past on either side. Rose reached to rearrange the remaining eggs in their basket.

'I wish you would allow me to help,' Marcus said abruptly.

'With what?' She turned to him, still holding an egg.

'With whatever it is that is weighing on your shoulders.'

Her fingers tightened and she felt an ominous crack. Rose put the egg hastily back in the basket. 'Nothing is weighing on me, except why one of the piglets is not thriving as the others are. And the fact that we cannot afford cucumber frames.'

Marcus made an abrupt gesture with his hand as though dismissing her attempt to deflect the question. 'Is it something to do with Earl Wighton?'

'What do you know of my half-brother?' she demanded before she could stop herself, then realised how defensive she must have sounded.

'I have never met the man,' Marcus said.

'But I cannot think much of a brother who allows his sisters to scratch their living as the three of you are doing.'

'Charles has nothing to do with us.' And she could only hope and pray he did not think to take an interest now.

'That is exactly my point. Rose—' He reached out, as if to catch her hands in his to make her listen to him and respond, then stopped himself abruptly. The gesture shook her, not because he reached out, but because he was clearly so caught up in what he was saying that he forgot that they were in public like this.

'Rose, I can tell something is wrong. You spoke to me before of the power that a duke must have—will you not let me exercise it in your cause?'

'There is no *cause*.' But she knew her gaze shifted under his and instinctively attacked to fight off his concern. 'You are simply trying to find some reason to account for my apparent eccentricity. You want the world to be tidy and according to how you expect it to be and I offend your sense of order. The problem is with you, Marcus.'

They stood staring at each other, his face a picture of exasperated frustration, hers, no doubt, set in unflattering defiance. Then something tugged at her apron and she looked down to see Kat at her side.

'Rose. I've got some bacon, like you said. Mrs Herring exchanged it for half a pint of milk, half a dozen of the eggs and some watercress.' She clutched a bulging greasy package to her smock and looked up at their faces. 'What's wrong?'

'Nothing is wrong, Kat. The Duke and I were discussing the things that might be improved here at the market, that is all. Well done—that was excellent bargaining for the bacon.' She found her bright smile again and met Marcus's eyes squarely. 'Good day, Your Grace. Here is your cream cheese and cress. I will set down my thoughts for you in a day or so.'

Faced with a clear dismissal, there was nothing a gentleman could do except take the brown paper parcel, doff his hat and walk away with what dignity he could muster. Mr Farthing, the secretary, was having an equally uncomfortable time of it, Rose noticed. The goat had twitched his handkerchief from his pocket and was contentedly chewing it.

Chapter Six

Two days later Rose sat at the kitchen table and attempted to write a coherent report from the mass of jottings she had made about the market. She would have to post it, of course. After she had so firmly rebuffed Marcus, he was hardly likely to come and fetch it in person.

The worst of the disorder and disputes would be solved by the appointment of a good man as some kind of bailiff or beadle for the market—a retired sergeant, perhaps, someone with authority. There was once, I hear, a regular pattern set out for positioning the stalls, but this has fallen into disuse and is now the main cause of argument between the vendors. It seems to me that if—

'Rose! The post boy is coming.' Kat ran in, hopped from one foot to the other and then dashed out again.

Rose frowned. It did not seem likely that a letter would bring good news. Who would be writing to them? It was probably bills. She racked her brains, worrying that an account had been overlooked. No, no one had any cause to be dunning them. Great-Aunt Sylvia, delivering another lecture on Behaviour Unfitting For a Lady, possibly? Or, of course, one of her friends from her days in London. She should have thought of that.

Really, it was futile to sit here speculating. Rose blotted her report, put the lid on the inkwell and went outside.

The lad was leaning down from his horse and holding out a letter to Chloe. He was attempting, unsuccessfully, to flirt with her by holding it just out of her reach and suggesting that he might be tempted to give it over in exchange for a kiss.

When he saw Rose advancing towards him he straightened up, touched his hat and dropped the letter into Chloe's hands before cantering off.

'You routed him with one glance,' Kat crowed. 'Who is it for, Chloe?'

Chloe, her cheeks still pink from her encounter with the post boy, finally looked at the letter. 'It's for Rose. Oh, and it is Charles's handwriting. What can be wrong?'

It doesn't occur to any of us that it might be good news, or simply brotherly concern for our welfare, Rose thought grimly. 'Let me see.'

Yes, that was Charles's sprawling hand. She slit the seal and opened the page out, then moved into the shade to read it better.

At first she thought she must be seeing things, or that his awful script was making it hard to decipher and she was reading it wrongly. She stared at the letter, the paper beginning to shake in her hand, then she bit her lip and made herself go through it again, word by word.

'Rose? Rose, what's wrong?'

There was an odd buzzing in her ears and Kat's anxious question seemed to be coming from a long way away. She stared at the letter again. She was ill, that was why she felt so strange and this must be a fever dream.

'Rose?' That was Chloe.

Oh, heavens. Chloe…

The last thing she was conscious of was the blackness filling her vision, pressing in until her sisters' anxious faces were all that were left. And then, nothing…

There were voices, female and anxious, and a man's, reassuringly calm and familiar, and something firm was supporting her head and shoulders.

'She has fainted, give her space and air. Which is the coolest room? The sitting room? Very well, run and take the cushions off the sofa, Kat.'

She was the person he was talking about, Rose realised. She must have swooned.

But I never faint. She felt reluctant to open her eyes, because whatever was out there was too difficult to deal with and panic was lurking at the fringes of her consciousness. *Chloe.*

'Chloe.'

'I'm here, Rose. What is wrong? Was it the letter?' Her sister's voice sounded thin and frightened. She must deal with this, somehow.

'Don't read…'

'Quiet. Stop trying to talk. Steady now, Rose, I am going to lift you.'

There was a jerk, then the sensation of rising, and she realised she was in the man's arms and being carried and the familiarity she felt was because this was Marcus. The fingers of her right hand tightened on fabric and he muttered, 'Don't strangle me, woman, that's my neckcloth.'

She let go, but left her hand where it was, because the warmth of skin under the folds of muslin was comforting. She could feel the beat of his heart, steady and safe.

'That's it, Kat. Put a cushion at the end for her head. Now, down you go, Rose. Hold tight.'

And there was the lumpy sofa under her and the scent of the lavender that Chloe had sewn into the cushions. Marcus withdrew his arms and she gave a sound of protest and opened her eyes.

'Oh, Rose, thank goodness. Shall I send for the doctor?' Chloe asked.

'No,' she said, wishing she did not sound so feeble. 'Just fainted…'

Marcus put the back of his hand to her forehead. 'There is no fever. Don't fuss her, Chloe. If she doesn't improve soon, I will send for someone. Now, Kat, where's that cook of yours?'

'Dorothy's gone down to the mill. Should I fetch her?'

'She'll be back soon enough. I expect your sister would like a drink of water. Can you fetch her one? And smelling salts, perhaps, Chloe?'

Marcus waited a moment until the door closed behind them, then looked down at her. 'That has sent them both off for a moment. Now tell me what is wrong, quickly, before they come back.'

'I can't. There is nothing you can do. We must leave at once.' The fog in her brain was clearing a little. 'I must sell you the castle.' Rose struggled to sit up and Marcus put his arm around her shoulders and wedged another cushion behind her back. 'If I leave the deeds with a solicitor, and sign things, we can just take the money and go, can't we? I wouldn't have to wait for everything to be sorted out legally first?'

He slid his arm free and sat back on his heels, frowning at her a little, then stood up as the door opened. 'Thank you, Kat. I'll take that, Chloe. Your sister is coming to herself and sitting up, but she needs to be quiet, so just wait in the kitchen, will you?'

There was the sound of a protest and then Marcus's voice again, firmer now. 'No, Lady Chloe. Thank you, but it will not help to have you burn feathers under her nose.'

The door closed again and he came back, crouching down beside her. 'They doubtless have their ears glued to the panels, so we will speak quietly. Tell me what is wrong. If you need money, you may have it, but I am not going to let you run off to vanish into the depths of England in a panic.'

'I am not panicking,' she said indignantly. 'Or… Yes, I suppose I am. My head is spinning and I feel sick and I suppose that is panic. How lowering—I had always supposed I was far too level-headed for that.'

'You say that you need money and that you need to hide. So, who was that letter from?'

'What letter?' Even as she said it, she knew it was not going to help.

'Do you believe me to be so very foolish? I find you in a faint, clutching a letter. Your sister appears to think it caused you to collapse. You admit to being in a panic, to needing money and say you intend to run away. I think even one of your chickens could put that together and arrive at the fact that the letter contained something very alarming.'

'Yes, but it has nothing to do with you.' When his brows drew together in the familiar frown she added hastily, 'I mean, it is nothing you should concern yourself with.'

'From which I deduce that the men in your life, before I entered it, have been singularly uncaring or ineffectual. Perhaps both. You should expect me to be concerned.'

'Yes, but—'

Before Marcus entered my life...

He got to his feet and took an impatient few strides away from her, was brought up short by the table and turned back. 'If you say *Yes, but*...once more, I am going to read it myself.'

'It isn't your problem,' she said faintly as Marcus stooped and picked up the crumpled sheet from beside the sofa where she had let it fall.

'What kind of man leaves three young women in distress and does nothing to help them?' he demanded.

Rose swallowed. 'Thank you.' It came out as a whisper, but he heard her.

Marcus dragged over a chair and sat down. 'Now, tell me.'

'I don't know where to begin.' The panic was ebbing, but she still felt frightened and sick. And angry now. That helped. 'I suppose, at the beginning. My mother died shortly after I was born. I was her only child. My father married again, very quickly. I believe, from what I heard him say, that he was desperate to have a son and heir.

'Louisa, my stepmother, gave him that son within a year of the marriage. Then a second son died as an infant and she lost another baby before it was born. When Chloe came I was eight, old enough to understand some of the things I overheard. I knew he wanted another son because, although he doted on Charles, he was in fear of losing him: he wanted the spare as well as the heir. He and Louisa had a terrible argument and she said her health would not stand another pregnancy. She moved to a different wing of the house.'

'But Kat is Chloe's full sister?'

'Yes. I do not know whether he persuaded Louisa or… Anyway, she had been right and her fears were justified: her health was permanently damaged by the birth and she was virtually bedridden. In a way, I suppose that staying alive was her revenge—he could not marry again, so he could not get another son. As a result Charles became the centre of my father's world. He wanted for nothing, he got away with any number of scrapes, and, as he became older, things that were worse than mere scrapes.

'I had my Seasons—three of them—and proved just how unsatisfactory I was by refusing every offer that was made to me.'

'Were they all so very dreadful, the men who offered for you?' Marcus leaned forward, elbows resting on his knees, listening intently.

'Some were older than me by ten or more years and I had seen first-hand the life of a young wife with a man intent on using her as a brood mare to give him sons. Of the younger ones who proposed, I never found one who was the slightest bit interested in me as a person, who enjoyed conversation with me, who entered into my interests or wished to share his. I turned them all down.'

There had been Christopher, of course, but, then it turned out that it would never have occurred to him to propose to me.

Rose kept her voice steady as she added, 'If I had known then what the consequences were to be, I would have accepted one of them, regardless, because my father was furious at the waste of money.

'He washed his hands of me, he said. I could stay at home, keep out of his way and make myself useful tutoring my sisters. When he died we discovered that he had made no provision for us in his will. Everything had gone to Charles, with a note that he should *"take care of his relatives and dependents according to their needs".*'

'Good God. Could that not be challenged?'

'How? I did ask a solicitor, in secret, but he said it was reasonable for our father to entrust us to an adult brother's care and that I had no evidence that Charles would not discharge that trust. It soon became clear that he had no intention of, as he put it, *wasting money* on Chloe's come-out in a few years' time. Almost as soon as our father was buried he began to fill the house with his cronies. I found one of them trying to kiss Chloe and drag her into the shrubbery.'

'What did you do?' Marcus was sitting upright now, his expression formidable.

'Kicked him hard in the...the groin. Oh, you mean, after that? I knew we had to get away— I did not think Charles would care if we were gone, because it would save him money and if we were not there it would be a case of out of sight, out of mind.'

Rose took a steadying breath and tried to condense weeks of frantic planning and worry into a coherent account.

'I had a little money saved that had been left to me by my mother. Then I saw the advertisement in the newspaper for Chalton and, after enquiries, thought we could manage the smallholding with a little help. When Chloe had her eighteenth birthday I intended to sell and take lodgings in London for the Season and hope she could find a man worthy of her, someone who might be willing to sponsor Kat in her turn, when she was old enough.'

'A brave plan. And you?' Marcus asked. 'What about you?'

'I would manage,' she said, ignoring, as always, the cold little knot of fear deep inside at the thought. 'I have had my chances.'

Marcus made a sound that she could have sworn was a growl, but when she looked at him he was staring at a point somewhere over her head and she could not read his expression at all. 'And now your brother has written to you,' he said, flattening the crumpled letter on his knee. 'I saw the signature.'

'He says…' She swallowed and tried again. She was going to be no help to anyone if she succumbed to the vapours. 'He wants Chloe back. He says he has found a husband for her.'

'She is a child. Not even out yet.'

'She is just seventeen.'

'Who is this man Wighton is proposing for her?'

'His name is Soames Marlowe. He didn't say any more.'

'*Soames Marlowe?* My God. Have you any idea who that is?'

'No. I have never heard of him before. How do you know him? I did not think you mixed in London society.'

'The owner of a large trading business might not be invited to the homes of the *haut ton,* or be accepted in their clubs, but that did not prevent me from having a perfectly good social life in London and mixing with many of the gentlemen of the *ton*. I am a wealthy man,' he said with a shrug. 'I attend the same theatres, play cards in the same houses, buy my horses at Tattersall's, patronise the tailors and boot-makers and hatters of St James's. I have met your brother. Briefly. But I know Marlowe by sight and reputation.'

'He is as bad as I fear?' Rose made herself speak calmly. She had to know the worst.

'He is in his late thirties, I would guess, although hard living makes him look older. He is what is vulgarly known as a beau trap, a plausible man about town with an air of sophistication who befriends younger, greener men and introduces them to gaming hells. He will have battened on to your brother, led him into debt, lived off his hospitality. And I have no doubt that, when Charles found himself with his pockets to let, he introduced him to some amiable types willing to help a gentleman in need of funds.'

'Moneylenders,' she said grimly.

'Yes. And there are moneylenders and moneylenders. All of them charge high rates, of course, but some are more grasping and unscrupulous than others and the gullgropers, the men who prey on gamblers who are in deep water, are the worst of the lot. If they don't get their money back they will seize it forcibly and take it out of the hides of the debtors if it is not forthcoming. May I read the letter?'

She nodded mutely. If Charles was ruined,

then he had brought it on himself. If he was beaten by these men, then she found she herself indifferent to that, too—he had killed any affection she had ever felt for him. All she cared about now was Chloe and Kat.

'Is this going to make a scandal that will affect my sisters' reputations?'

Marcus finished reading, folded the letter and tapped it against his thumbnail. 'I think that is the least of your problems. My suspicion is that Soames Marlowe is playing a long game. He wants respectability—or, rather, a place in respectable society. He has deliberately put Charles in his power, because I am certain he is acting in concert with the usurer in question, and he has promised your brother relief from his debts if he gives him Chloe. Marriage to the sister of an earl will be a big step up for Marlowe and then none of you will be free of him.'

Now she truly did feel sick. 'I was right: we must leave and hide. Sooner or later Marlowe will give up, surely?'

'Have you any idea how difficult it would be to simply vanish and then support yourselves for however long it takes for this danger to pass? Your brother is your sisters' guardian, I suppose?' Marcus scrubbed his hand over his face, thinking. 'You have no legal power, of course, being an unmarried woman, even if you are of age.'

'You won't buy the castle from me?' She sat up abruptly, swayed and Marcus went down on one knee beside the sofa and steadied her.

'I didn't say that.' He felt strong and steady and she wanted to simply lay her head on his shoulder and wish the whole world away. She realised, after a moment, that he was cradling her head with one hand and his fingers moved gently through her hair as though he was soothing a nervous horse. 'I will help you, Rose. Of course I will.'

'You have ships—could you send us somewhere? Belgium is cheap, so they say.'

'Yes, perhaps,' Marcus said, although he sounded, to her sensitive ear, as though he was thinking of something else entirely. 'Don't fret, Rose. Your brother won't expect an answer for a day or so.'

'But I cannot just sit and wait!' She pulled out of his arms and, suddenly full of energy, swung her feet down to the floor. 'What if that man comes here to look at Chloe? Or take her away? We must pack, sell the animals. There is so much to do. Oh, I am so thankful you are here, Marcus. You feel more like a brother to me than Charles ever did.'

Marcus stood up abruptly and moved away to the glazed arrow slit that overlooked the moat. 'Do nothing. Not yet. I told you I will help you; give me time to work out a plan. We must keep you all safe, of course, but it is essential there is no scandal. We must not rush into this blindly.'

'No, of course not.' The sudden burst of energy fizzled out, leaving her feeling as limp as an un-watered lettuce seedling. 'Oh, if only I were a man!'

Marcus gave a snort of laughter as he turned from the arrow slit. 'If you were, then none of this would have happened because your father would have had his heir before he married again. You would have been the one he spoiled and indulged and ruined.'

'I have more strength of character than Charles,' Rose said loftily, but she had lost his attention again. 'What must I do?'

'Nothing. Wait for me. Do not frighten your sisters. Tell them your brother wants you all to return to London because he has a suitor for Chloe—that is only the truth, because if Marlowe wants a wedding that appears normal, then you should all be there. Do not tell them anything about Marlowe's character, although they must know enough to make sure they are wary of strangers. Tell them that I am devising a plan to keep you all safe.'

'We will not have to go to London? There will be no wedding?'

'I— Give me time, Rose. I have to work out the best strategy. There are options, shall we say?'

Why was Marcus being maddeningly vague? She felt so tense and anxious that she wanted to scream, but he was right to think it through, she had to believe that.

'Thank you.' She stood up and found the ground steady under her feet. When she walked towards him and held out her hands he took them in his. 'Kat was right all along—you are the prince come to rescue the maiden in the tower.'

The twist of his lips as wry. 'Not much of a prince, but perhaps there is merit in saving three maidens in one fell swoop, as opposed to only the traditional one.'

That made her laugh a little, as she supposed it had been intended to. 'I am sorry you had to deal with such swooning and drama. I am not usually so easily flustered.'

'Easily? Anybody would be excused for feeling alarm and distress at such a situation. Now, go and tell your sisters as much as you think it prudent without alarming them. It would be as well if they did not stray from home until we have this settled. In fact, I would keep your front door locked and the key ready to turn in the back door.'

'You really think Charles would try to take Chloe?'

'I do not know. The fact he has written with his intentions suggests not, but if there is too much delay in your response, then he might decide to act. It all depends how much pressure the moneylenders and his dear friend Marlowe are putting him under.'

'Let him try,' she said grimly, relieved to find that this threat was what was needed to blow away the last tendrils of panic. 'How long will you need?'

'I will come back by nightfall tomorrow.' Marcus took her hand and for a moment she thought he would raise it to his lips, but he just gave it a squeeze and released it. 'Have courage, Rose. We will keep Chloe safe, I swear it.'

Chapter Seven

'The swine.' Aubrey added a more colourful description of Earl Wighton, then flung down his pen. 'What do you propose to do, sir? I agree, attempting to hide them in this country is fraught with dangers.'

Marcus knew he could count completely on his secretary's discretion and it was impossible to deal with this without some assistance, so he had told him everything.

'What ships have we leaving port in the next few days? I could send them into Belgium as Lady Rose suggested.' That was one obvious solution, but they would be too far away to keep an eye on, too far for him to reach them fast in a crisis. And they would be in a foreign country with no friends, not even acquaintances, only themselves to rely on. They were a strong little family and that had sustained them so far, but there were limits.

Family. Marcus was not in the habit of deceiving himself and he knew what he was feeling was envy for that closeness, for the deep, instinctive love the three sisters shared. They would fight to stay together, fight for each other. It seemed a very long time since he had been part of a family and, even though he understood his mother's decision, he still found it hard to forget the pain of what had seemed so much like rejection.

On the other hand, whatever he might feel towards the younger girls, *brotherly* was not how he felt about Rose.

Aubrey pulled a file towards him and ran one finger down the topmost list inside it. 'Two for the Continent from the London Docks and one for the east from Bristol. I could escort the ladies, sir. If you go it might be noticed…' he hesitated '…and perhaps be misconstrued.'

'As an elopement?' Marcus drawled. 'That would be novel, taking the bride's young sisters along.'

The thought that had been taking shape in his mind began to assume a clearer form. He was a duke, a fact he had been exceedingly reluctant to face up to now, and, as such, he wielded a great deal of influence, if he chose to use it. And he was a rich man and quite used to the power *that* gave him.

He was also, he suspected, a great deal more unconventional than the average aristocrat and, without doubt, considerably more intelligent than Rose's fool of a brother. But that would not be difficult.

There was a solution to this. All he had to do was to approach it as dispassionately as he would any matter of business and keep inconvenient feelings, emotions and needs out of it. He pushed aside a nagging doubt that that might be easier thought than done and applied his brain to the practicalities.

'Is the Archbishop of Canterbury in residence at Lambeth Palace?' he asked.

Aubrey dropped the file. 'The Archbishop? Er, I believe so,' he said, scrabbling around his feet to gather up the scattered papers.

'Good. Then write to the good burgesses of Chalton and tell them to appoint a beadle to control the market. I will pay—but it must be a man used to exercising authority. Give me those documents you wanted signed and marshal all the business that needs seeing to in the next week. No, make that a fortnight. It must all be dealt with this afternoon.'

'Yes, sir. What do you intend to do tomorrow then?' Aubrey asked, visibly bracing his shoulders.

'Put on my armour, find a lance from somewhere and storm the enchanted castle,' Marcus said, rather more flippantly than he felt. 'Now, let us get down to work.'

Marcus woke the next morning with a plan which seemed good to him. The only fault he could find with it was that he suspected that Rose might flatly refuse to co-operate and he had no idea if his powers of persuasion would overcome her objections. She seemed willing enough to trust him and she had shared with him the story of their predicament, but he still sensed a reserve. She was holding something back.

She had certainly never given him the slightest reason to suppose she was attracted to him and that might be a drawback to what he had in mind. He could only hope that remark about him being more of a brother to her than Charles was had simply been an expression of relief at having someone to help her. But her tale of how unwilling she had been to accept any of the proposals that had been made to her came back, very clearly.

When he rode into the castle bailey, chickens flapping away from his horse's hooves in feathery panic, he found the back door closed. But a pale oval at the window showed someone was on watch and as he dismounted the door opened and the two younger sisters emerged. Neither of them looked as though they had slept very well.

Kat marched straight up to him. 'Are you going to take us to Belgium?'

'If that is what your sister wishes,' Marcus temporised.

'Can't we go somewhere more interesting? Your ships go to China, don't they? They have dragons there—'

'Kat, do not bother the Duke with your nonsense.' He noticed as she put a protective arm around the child's shoulders that Chloe had dark smudges under her eyes.

'If you will both excuse me, I must discuss matters with Lady Rose.'

The sisters looked mutinous, which he understood. They were tired and frightened and they hardly knew him. Chloe watched him with a mixture of wariness and hope and Kat pouted, but they went back into the house as Rose came out. The door did not close completely, however, and he could see them both standing just inside, watching.

Rose gave a rueful smile when she reached him. 'I am sorry; they are very unsettled and I don't think they know who to trust or believe. I hope you had a better night than we did.'

'I have a plan in mind, if that is what you mean. Shall we sit and discuss it?' Marcus gestured to a low wall and she sat, hands folded in her lap, and waited with seeming patience. But the hem of her gown vibrated slightly with the tension in her. She was dressed conventionally now. There was no sign of the breeches, or of the countrywoman of market day. It was as though she was already putting her life at the castle behind her and bracing herself for the next chapter.

'It seems to me that hiding away until both Chloe and Katherine are of age, even if you are successful in remaining undiscovered, is not going to solve anything, other than to condemn you to living on your nerves for years.'

Rose nodded. Thank goodness for her clear-headed intelligence now she had recovered from yesterday's initial shock. At least he did not have to persuade her flight was not the answer, which was a relief, because he suspected his plan was going to meet with strong resistance. It was not as though she had shown the slightest interest...

'You reminded me the other day of the power a duke can wield,' he said. 'It is considerably more than any influence a young, impoverished, rakehell of an earl can muster. I am a wealthy man—'

'No! You are not to buy him off,' Rose said vehemently. 'I'll not have it!'

'If I had time, yes, I would buy up his debts,' Marcus said, ignoring the outburst. 'That would enable me to put pressure on him to behave decently towards the three of you. But we do not have the luxury of time and, besides, Marlowe has a strong motive for keeping Charles in his power—I doubt he would sell, or persuade the moneylenders to do so. What I need is a legitimate reason to involve myself with Chloe's welfare. I therefore propose becoming her brother-in-law.'

'Her—'

I wouldn't mind at all being married to Rose,

he thought, watching the expressions chasing each other across her face. She had intelligence, courage, determination and looks that a man could never grow weary of.

'You want to *marry* me? No, of course you do not want to.' He could see her briskly adjusting to the surprise, fitting his suggestion to something she could accept. 'You mean pretend to be married and see if that would intimidate Charles?'

'I do not mean pretend. And I do mean marriage.' Her sudden, agitated movement sent that now-familiar scent of flowers from her skin wafting to his nostrils and its effect on him lent more warmth to his tone than he had meant to use. 'A true, legal marriage. I am well aware that you have turned down numerous proposals in the past, Rose, and that you cannot have any feelings of…of affection towards me. After all, we hardly know each other. But you are a lady of breeding and character and I am certain you would make an excellent duchess.'

As proposals went, that was probably one of the least romantic ever delivered, he suspected. But there was no point in pretending this was something it was not—Rose was too astute for that.

'I do not believe that you actively dislike me and I like and admire you,' Marcus added when she simply sat and stared at him. He could not discern what she was feeling, but it did not appear to be pleasure. On the other hand, it was not revulsion either. Or outright rejection.

'No,' she said after a moment. 'No, of course I do not *dislike* you.' Her voice shook a little. 'You have been very kind to us.'

Marcus managed not to wince. *Damned with faint praise.*

'You are asking me to marry you, to have your children—'

'There is no need to think about that until later,' he said hastily, as he realised that he hadn't given children any thought at all. An heir, yes, in the abstract, but he had not given any thought to the more…personal aspects of what he was suggesting. 'I would not dream of expecting, shall we say, intimacy, until we know each other much better?'

Was that clear enough without being brutally frank? She isn't just out of the schoolroom and the way she spoke of her father's relations with his second wife showed a degree of understanding of the facts of life.

He hoped his words were reassuring, even if they were a lie: he would certainly dream of Rose in his bed, he knew that.

'Oh. Intimacy,' Rose said faintly and blushed, which had the unfortunate effect of provoking a strong desire in him to take her in his arms, kiss her until she was pink all over and demonstrate exactly what he meant by the word, just in case she was in any doubt. 'Um, thank you. That is very considerate.'

She took a deep breath and said with the air of a woman who had just scrambled back on to solid earth after almost falling over a cliff, 'But even if you married me, which is impossible, Charles would still have the power over Chloe and Kat.'

'He would have the law on his side,' Marcus agreed. 'But he would be facing a duke and duchess, closely related to the young women in question, who will launch an absolute barrage of legal challenges to his fitness to be the girls' guardian. We could drag matters out for years, if need be.

'I have the resources to protect Chloe and Kat with bodyguards and to hire the very best legal minds. And do not forget, Charles's character is well known in society. It is hardly as though you were trying to drag them away from respectable grandparents, for example.'

'No,' she said, and for the first time Marcus believed she was giving his proposal serious consideration. 'But I cannot marry you simply because of my sisters. It is too much to ask any man.'

'Why? I would have to find myself a bride sooner or later. If I had met you at Almack's and proposed the next day, the highest stickler would not object to your suitability—in fact, they are more likely to be dubious about my trade connections.' And that was nothing but the truth. 'I am not selling out of the company, I must warn you, so you will have to learn to ignore sneers about that.'

Rose waved that away. 'Nobody sneers at dukes. But I am too old. I am twenty-five. You should be marrying someone like Miss Langford.'

'She is too young. Far too young.'

'I thought men liked young brides.'

'Some do,' he admitted. 'I do not. You are just right, in my opinion.'

'She is beautiful,' Rose said, with the air of a woman snatching at straws.

'She is a pretty child. Are you fishing for

compliments, Lady Rose? I suggest you look in your glass.'

'We hardly know each other.' It was almost a cry. She stood abruptly and, for a second he thought she would walk away from him. It took an effort of will not to seize her wrist, hold her there.

'How many couples in our station in life truly know each other before they marry?' Marcus argued. 'I have seen your determination and courage. Your loyalty. You knew I would not browbeat or force you out of this castle, however much I want it. You trusted me enough to offer me first refusal when you sell. And you trusted enough to confide in me when that letter came.'

'I did, didn't I?' Rose sat as abruptly as she had jumped up. 'I shouldn't say *yes*, it is asking too much of you. Beside all the other objections, you would have all the nuisance and expense of the legal battle with Charles.'

She was wavering. He sensed it would take only one nudge. 'I enjoy a good fight. I use excellent lawyers who will deal with the nuisance for us.'

He saw her take a deep breath and smiled as reassuringly as he could. Just a nudge…

'You...' He was reminded of a deer poised on the edge of a woodland clearing, one foot raised, cautiously scenting the air before taking the first step into the open. 'You would not want to consummate the marriage immediately?'

'What I want is irrelevant,' Marcus said, ignoring the protests his body were making. 'When you are ready will be soon enough. I am perfectly content to wait.'

Rose stared at the ground at her feet. Every detail—the muddy grass, a crushed dandelion flower, the hoofprints of the goat—stood out as though they had been etched by a master draughtsman. They were real. The pain in her hands where she gripped them together so tightly, the faint cluck of the hens—those were real, too. But the man next to her offering her what she had believed was a foolish daydream, a disturbing thought in the night—he must be an hallucination. Perhaps she was still in a faint, or disordered by shock and panic.

Marcus Cranford didn't want *her*, of course. He had made it quite clear. *I am perfectly content to wait*, he had said just now without the slightest hint of desire in his voice.

But he did want a wife. She could understand that, because any man in his position would. He wanted this castle, but she could acquit him of offering her marriage in order to obtain it, because she was certain he had believed her when she'd promised to sell it to him eventually.

He was a gentleman, his instinct was to help females in distress and she suspected he liked her sisters, was even quite fond of them, however they behaved to him.

There was no reason she could imagine that this offer was made for anything but the best of motives, but it would put Marcus to a great deal of trouble and expense to protect the girls. If he had offered that sacrifice for her alone, she hoped she would have the backbone to refuse, however much the idea of being married to him tempted her. But it was not she who was in danger and how could she throw away the best chance she had of giving Chloe and Kat the life they deserved?

'Are you sure?' She made herself put the question calmly.

'Very sure. Are we agreed then?'

He might as well be finalising a contract to import tea, she thought. And it *would* be a contract, with obligations on both sides. She must do her best to be a good duchess, whatever that entailed, and she must not trouble or embarrass him with her emotions and demands. Her needs. Marcus should never have cause to regret this generous offer.

'Yes, we are agreed,' Rose said before she could talk herself out of it.

The burden of gratitude was something she would have to learn to live with, even though it felt as though she was surrendering every ounce of her independence by doing this thing. The hope of one day finding a love match was gone, too. But that, of course, had always been a foolish dream, just like the growing wish that Marcus would show some sign that he regarded her as more than the woman in possession of the castle he wanted, or a practical, rather shocking, spinster it amused him to know. Or a helpless female in need of his help.

'That was a big sigh,' he said.

'Relief,' Rose explained hastily. 'And perhaps a little dread at the thought of everything that must be done.'

She looked up, finally ready to face this man she had just agreed to marry, and found Marcus was already moving back towards the house. So much for any lingering exchanges, even some talk of feelings. *A kiss*.

'If you and your sisters could pack everything you need immediately, then they will be ready when Farthing arrives,' Marcus was saying as he walked away, presumably assuming she was following. 'He should be here in about an hour with two carriages. He is bringing a maid to attend on you, so the four of you can travel in one coach and Farthing and I will take the other. A very reliable farmhand and one of the dairymaids are also on their way to remain here until we make permanent arrangements. They will look after the smallholding for you under the direction of your cook and handyman.'

Rose stared at his retreating back, then ran to catch up. 'You were very sure I would agree!'

'I know you for a woman of sense.'

It was interesting, she thought, as she stamped across the farmyard in Marcus's wake, that it was possible to find a man attractive, disturbing and desirable and yet still want to hit him over the head with the chickens' feed bucket.

'You are going to marry the Duke?' Chloe stared at her blankly while Kat gave a whoop of excitement and bounced up and down. 'When? Where? *Why?*'

'Why, because he can keep us safe from Charles's idiocy. I do not know any more,' Rose admitted. 'But Marcus has a plan.'

He came into the kitchen as she spoke. 'I will take you all to Northminster House in Grosvenor Square. Rose and I will go to Lambeth Palace to see the Archbishop of Canterbury to obtain a special licence. Then we will marry in London with as much display as possible.'

'A palace!' Kat sat down with a thump.

'A *real* archbishop?' Chloe asked.

'London?' Rose said faintly. 'Display?'

'There must be nothing hole-and-corner or suspicious about this match, because we are establishing ourselves as the respectable alternative to your brother as your guardians,' Marcus explained. 'Under normal circumstances an ordinary licence would do, but I want to be able to marry at very short notice if we have to. So, we see the Archbishop, we establish ourselves in the town house—and I warn you now, Rose, I have no idea what state it is in— we invite everyone we know to the wedding and wait for the gossip to spread. Our guest list will not be spectacular, I fear, but the visits afterwards should make up for that.'

'But how do we explain how we met, why I have not been seen in society?'

'We tell the truth—you removed yourself and your sisters from your brother's house because you feared for your moral welfare. Everyone is quite well aware of his character. We should be as frank as possible about your anxiety for the girls because of the company he keeps. Now hurry and pack, the carriages will be here soon. It will take us at least eleven hours on the road and I intend driving straight through with short stops, if you feel up to it.'

In for a penny, in for a pound...

'Of course,' Rose said firmly. 'We three are made of stern stuff.'

Rose was regretting her bravado by the time they crossed the Thames at Maidenhead. She had lost track of time and all she knew was that they were driving more slowly now it was full dark. Marcus had brought two drivers for each carriage instead of a driver and a groom, so she had no anxiety about the danger from tired coachmen, and he had been punctilious about stopping at each change of horses in case they wanted to get down from the coach or take refreshments. But none of that stopped her thoughts whirling like the dog in its treadmill turning a kitchen spit.

Martha, the maid from Northminster Castle, had long since fallen asleep and Kat was breathing deeply, curled up on the seat with her head in Chloe's lap, but Chloe was awake and Rose saw the reflection in her eyes when they passed a light in the street. She was worried and, for some reason, she was oddly suspicious of Marcus. Perhaps, Rose thought, her faith in men had been fatally undermined by the way their father and brother had behaved.

As for herself, she believed that Marcus was a decent man, a gentleman, and that his motives in offering her marriage were honest. She was certainly able to believe that he could protect Chloe from Charles's schemes. Her brother's selfish stupidity was no match for his ruthless intelligence and focus. But had she really agreed to marry a man who had no warm feelings for her, who did not even appear to desire her? What would their life be like?

It would be difficult, she suspected, because whatever Marcus Cranford felt—or did not feel—for her, she certainly liked him a great deal more than was wise and certainly wished he would kiss her. The *intimacies* that he had delicately offered to postpone would not be unwelcome to her at all, she admitted. She would be shy at first, of course, but she wasn't completely ignorant of what went on in the marriage bed and she was not afraid of him.

Only… Only, whenever she had imagined marriage and its consummation it had been with Christopher Andrewes with whom she had been in love and who, she had believed, loved her, not with a gallant, almost-stranger who was offering her his hand and name for protection only.

Rose found her reticule, pulled out a handkerchief and blew her nose resolutely. There was nothing to worry about; it was simply that she was weary and her eyes were tired and watering a little.

'Are you all right?' Chloe asked in a whisper.

'I am tired,' Rose admitted. 'We should try to sleep.'

'No, I mean about marrying the Duke. I know you are only doing it to protect us and I hate that you are sacrificing yourself.'

'Sacrifice?' Rose managed a soft laugh. It really sounded quite convincing. 'I hardly think so—I will be the envy of every unmarried woman in London and many of the married ones as well, I wager. I will be a duchess. I will be married to a wealthy, handsome man who has shown himself to be kind and resourceful.'

'But everything will be different. I loved the castle. And we have left poor Dorothy and Baines behind.'

'We still own the castle and Dorothy has help and protection and, once all this is settled, we can find out exactly what she and Baines want to do. Now, try to sleep.'

She turned her own head against the squabs, trying to find the most comfortable position before she closed her eyes.

'Why is he doing this?' Chloe whispered, almost as though she was talking to herself.

'Because I am a perfectly eligible wife and marrying me will save him all the trouble of searching for a wife during the Season. Marcus is doing us a kindness which also suits his own plans. That is all he wants.'

That is all he wants, all he wants...

She drifted off to sleep at last, the words twining into her dreams, leaving an ache in her heart.

Chapter Eight

Dust sheets and whispering, hurrying, servants. Flickering candlelight. A huge bed piled with pillows and a cup of hot chocolate, sweet and strong and comforting: those had been Rose's overriding impressions as they arrived at the London house on Grosvenor Square.

'The girls will sleep with me tonight,' she had said when Marcus carried Kat in from the carriage, Chloe stumbling half-awake at his side. 'I do not want them waking in a strange house alone.' And certainly not in this soulless great place.

Now, easing up cautiously to peer over the top of the covers, she saw her sisters were both still slumbering beside her. What time was it?

As if in answer the gilt clock on the mantelshelf chimed nine with thin, silvery notes.

Rose slid out of bed and padded barefoot to the window to look out.

Below her was a large square, the centre filled with shrubs and small trees, the streets around it already busy with vehicles and pedestrians. The day had begun hours ago, there were no servants in sight sweeping front steps or polishing doorknockers, that had already been done and working Londoners were well into their day while their lords and masters—and mistresses—slumbered.

Rose pulled the bell rope and caught the maid, who came in to answer it as she opened the door. It was a stranger, not Martha, the Northminster Castle maid, who had travelled with them from Chalton.

'Shh! I do not want to wake my sisters.'

'Yes, my lady. I am Frost, my lady. I'll have hot water brought up for your bath. The men can use the other door into the dressing room. If you would care to step through to the sitting room I will bring you chocolate, or tea, while you wait, my lady.'

'Chocolate, please,' Rose decided. It was indulgent, but she felt she needed all the strength she could muster for whatever the day held.

What did one wear to visit an archbishop?

she wondered. Something modest and neat, she supposed. And also something that made her look her full age, because there must not be any doubt about her right to assent to the match.

By the time Rose was bathed and dressed, Chloe and Kat were awake, wide-eyed and more than a little awed by the echoing, rather dusty, splendour of the rooms. Trafford Hall, where they had grown up, was a fine house, but it had a country air about it and the younger girls had never been to the family's town house a few streets away from Grosvenor Square.

The girls dressed and even Kat was subdued enough by the atmosphere to stand still while her hair was brushed.

'Breakfast is served downstairs, my lady. Unless you wish to take it here?' The answer the maid was expecting was clearly *no* and Rose guessed that Marcus was downstairs waiting for them.

'Please show us the way, Frost,' she said composedly. Unless Marcus had second thoughts, or she lost her nerve, this maid and all the other staff would soon be answering to her and if she was to have the respect of the household then she must start by looking calm and confident.

The idea that she was about to become a duchess was still too impossible to be real, so she focused simply on being married and mistress of a household. She could manage that—at least, the second part.

Marcus was, indeed waiting for them and dismissed the footmen who were standing by the buffet. 'We will serve ourselves,' he said as the door closed. 'Then we can discuss our tactics freely.' He lifted the lids of two of the dishes as he spoke and Kat's eyes widened.

'Your household is well prepared for guests arriving unexpectedly,' Rose said, helping herself to creamy scrambled eggs and crisp bacon. 'Kat, that is quite enough—you may always return for more.'

'I sent a groom on ahead,' Marcus said, spreading butter on toast and passing her the plate.

'If they had enough warning to be this prepared, then you were very confident that Rose would say *yes*,' Chloe observed, her tone critical.

'Chloe!'

'I was confident that your sister would give very serious consideration to any plan to keep you safe, yes,' Marcus said evenly, making

Chloe colour up. 'If she had refused me, then no harm would have been done.'

Kat, who had demolished her plateful, fixed Marcus with a hopeful look. 'May I have some buttered toast and strawberry preserve now, please?' When he glanced at Rose for permission, she added, 'I'm growing and Dorothy says I have hollow legs.'

'*Kat!* Marcus, I apologise for both my sisters.' If they were going to behave like this— one of them prickly with distrust, the other behaving like a hoyden in the making, then Marcus would soon have good reason to regret his offer.

'I am sure it will do me good to be reminded of the give and take of family life. I was ten years old when I last lived in the same household as my sister.'

'Is she older or younger than you?' Kat asked,

'She was a year younger. She died while I was in India with the East India Company.'

'Oh, I am so sorry. What was her name?' Kat asked immediately.

Rose almost hushed her, but Marcus was smiling, just a little. Clearly talking about his sister, however painful, was welcome.

'Penelope. She had blue eyes like Rose and brown hair and freckles and she was very fond of her pets.'

'Lady Penelope—'

'Not *Lady*. Our father was plain Mr Cranford. He was the son of the fourth son of the First Duke, so he didn't have a title.' His smile broadened as he looked at Kat. 'I was plain Mr Cranford, too, which makes being a duke a bit of a shock.'

That effectively silenced Kat, Rose was relieved to see. 'At what time should we set out for Lambeth Palace?'

'I had thought shortly after breakfast.'

'I want to come, too, and see the palace,' Kat announced.

'It isn't a *royal* palace,' Chloe told her. 'There will not be any guards on duty or anything like that.'

'You can visit St James's Palace another day and see the guards on parade, Kat. But, yes, I think you should both come to Lambeth Palace with us,' Marcus said.

'And meet the Archbishop?' Chloe looked nervous.

'I doubt whether we would. I am sure matters such as licences are dealt with by his staff, who then take them to him to be signed and then we'll receive it after a day or so. I could go to Doctors' Commons, near St Paul's, of course, but I want to make as much stir as I can. It would not be a bad thing if you are both seen, both of you looking as young as possible,' he added with a glance at Rose.

Of course, the more people saw how unacceptable it was for Charles to be pushing forward a match between his friend—if the man who was leeching off him could be described in those terms—and Chloe, the better it would be.

'Of course. Come upstairs, Chloe, and I will redo your hair. I think perhaps the blue frock.'

'It is too short.'

'Exactly. Hair down, skirts up. We want you to look as though you are just out of the schoolroom.' She should have thought of that. In fact, it would be a good thing if she stopped feeling so glad that Marcus was looking after everything and began to think for herself again. It really was not fair to the man to expect him to consider every detail.

Unless, of course, he was the kind of man who liked meek little females who depended on him for everything. Surely not. She wouldn't like him as much as she did if he was that sort of person.

And she did like him, Rose admitted to herself. Liked him too much for comfort, if truth be known. He was decisive, considerate, effective, warm and patient with the girls—and respectful of her. Which was what she wanted of course, Rose told herself. Respect.

A gentleman whose proposal had been accepted might be forgiven for expecting at least kisses from his betrothed. But Marcus had not even made a move to embrace her, had shown not the slightest sign of regret, or of having to exercise self-control, when he spoke of allowing her time before consummating the marriage.

A lady should be delighted for such delicate consideration, but a woman who found the man in question attractive had grounds for feeling more than a little flat. Rose was coming to realise that the detachment with which she had previously viewed men since Christopher, and the satisfaction with her lot that she had convinced herself that she felt, were illusions.

Besides, she was not at all certain that Marcus's *delicate consideration* was not simply a complete lack of interest in whatever charms she possessed. Perhaps he had a mistress. Yes, of course he had, he wasn't a monk. Probably he would keep her even after he was married, because why should he suffer celibacy because of Rose's supposedly delicate sensibilities?

'Rose?' Chloe stood on the landing, looking down at her where she stood, five feet from the top of the stairs. 'Are you all right?'

'Oh. Yes. Sorry. There is just so much to think about.' She ran up to join her sister and put her mind to making Chloe look as much like a schoolgirl as possible. She, on the other hand, was no schoolgirl and she was old enough to understand just what was disturbing her so much. It could only be physical attraction and liking though, couldn't it? Not tearing jealousy at the thought of Marcus and a beautiful, sensually experienced woman.

Lambeth Palace, on the south bank of the Thames, proved tiresome to reach. 'It is easiest by boat from Millbank, just south of the Houses of Parliament,' Marcus explained. 'But that sky looks as though it is about to rain and I have no desire for us to arrive at the Palace damp and bedraggled.'

In the end they had to travel down past the

Queen's House and take the roads cut through to the new Vauxhall Bridge. Once across the river they then drove north, skirting the famous Vauxhall Gardens and past more industry than Rose had expected to find so close to Westminster. Distilleries, a mustard manufacturer and a brewery all added their own pungent aromas to the atmosphere and the sight of the Millbank Penitentiary's great octagonal walls looming on the opposite side of the river gave the prospect a sinister tone.

The ancient stone gatehouse of the Palace seemed almost incongruous in this setting. Kat was disappointed that it seemed so small, but as they passed through and into the great courtyards beyond, she fell silent. Rose could only hope she did not look as apprehensive as her little sister.

Inside all was orderly and busy, but unsettling in some way. Then Rose realised what was so strange—there were no women. Everywhere were men in sober clerical garb, some with wigs, almost all with fluttering white bands at their throats.

They were greeted politely and then, when Marcus produced his card, with considerable deference and shown to a small parlour to sit while someone was fetched to assist them.

They all looked up when the door opened and a young man peered in. 'Why, Lady Rose, it *is* you. I could hardly believe my ears when I heard the porter.' He came right into the room and revealed himself to be a slight, sandy-haired man in clerical black. 'Geoffrey Cass?' he said. 'Perhaps you do not remember me?'

'Oh, yes, Mr Cass. You must forgive me. I have been away from London society for so long that I had not realised that you had taken holy orders.'

He gave an awkward wriggle of a shrug. 'My father insisted I find an occupation. This seemed… But never mind me. Is someone looking after you, Lady Rose?'

Rose smiled and did her best to ignore her dislike of the man. He had been one of Charles's friends. Harmless enough, but a hanger-on and, she suspected, a bit of a sneak, the kind of person who would read any letters he found lying about open. Was he still a friend of Charles? No, surely not if he had mended his ways and become a clergyman.

'Yes, thank you. Marcus, I must introduce you. This is Mr Cass, whom I met when I lived in London. Mr Cass, the Duke of Northminster, my sisters Lady Chloe and Lady Katherine.'

'Your Grace.' The young cleric looked almost alarmed. 'An honour, sir. I will inform the Archbishop's secretary immediately.'

'There is no need, Mr Cass,' Marcus said, his voice cool, as though he had picked up on her dislike of the man. 'The person in charge of special licences is being informed, I believe.'

'Special—' Geoffrey Cass looked from one to the other. 'You mean—'

'Lady Rose and I are to be wed, yes,' Marcus said. 'Ah, I believe we are called,' he added as another young clergyman came into the room and requested that they come with him.

Cass was left with nothing to do but bow them out as they followed their guide.

The new young man guiding them was smoothly polite and seemed incapable of speaking above a murmur, which prevented Rose from hearing what he had to say in response to Marcus explaining their errand. It seemed they were to be moved on, presumably to the functionary who dealt with special licences.

They were led down a long corridor, oak

panelled and stone-floored, to a heavy door. Their guide knocked softly and it opened.

'His Grace Dr Manners-Sutton will see you now, Your Grace.'

The flurry of *Graces* confused her. Then, as they were ushered into a chamber that was clearly a study, even if it was the size of the average dining room, she realised whose room this must be.

A tall man with a long, pale face and a rather feminine mouth advanced towards them, hand held out. 'Northminster.'

'Your Grace.' They shook hands, which was a relief, because Rose had been wondering whether one was supposed to kiss the Archbishop's ring. Perhaps it was the Pope she was thinking about.

She curtsied and the girls followed suit and Marcus introduced them all, then they sat down while he explained the reason for their visit.

The Archbishop listened. He nodded at intervals but did not ask why a special licence was required. It seemed that it was only to be expected that a duke would ask for one without giving any reason why an ordinary licence would not do.

Marcus said nothing about Charles or why they were marrying.

Chloe nudged Rose and whispered, 'The Duke is very articulate, isn't he?'

Rose had to agree. This was what Marcus must be like when he was conducting his business: efficient, cool, in command of his facts and his argument.

'That all seems perfectly in order. Lady Rose is of age and free from parental control? Yes, quite. There is a document to be drawn up and sworn to. Doctor Smithers will take you through that, if you would care to accompany him, and then I will sign it. The three young ladies may remain with me.'

Beside her Kat gave a small squeak, but remained still. Rose said, 'Thank you, Your Grace.'

'I am pleased to see a young man with such responsibilities entering into matrimony,' the Archbishop said. 'There is doubtless a great deal for him to attend to and the support of a wife is invaluable. You are the daughter of the late Earl Wighton, I believe.'

'Yes, Your Grace.'

'Your brother is much seen about town, I

understand.' That was not said with any great warmth.

'Yes, Your Grace. Charles's social life is very…lively and, um, sophisticated, which is why I felt it best if my sisters and I lived quietly in the country.'

He seemed to approve of that. 'And where do you intend marrying?'

'That has not yet been decided, Your Grace. I am leaving all the arrangements to the Duke.' Chloe gave a faint snort, which she turned into a cough, but Dr Manners-Sutton nodded grave approval at this meekness. 'In church, I hope,' she added. That was not due to any particular piety on her part, although she was a regular attender, but the thought of a marriage in that great echoing house was unnerving, even if a special licence made it perfectly legal.

As if all this is not unnerving enough.

That clearly pleased him. 'And have your sisters been confirmed yet?'

'I have, Your Grace,' Chloe said. 'Not long ago. Katherine is only twelve, so next year, we hope.'

That was clever, Rose thought. It implied that Chloe was younger than she truly was.

'Excellent.'

At which point the door opened to admit Marcus and Dr Smithers, who was carrying a vast piece of parchment with dangling red ribbons. He was attended by a young man with some kind of spirit burner and a brass pot. 'For your signature, Your Grace.'

The document was spread out on the desk, the Archbishop signed, and then a round box was placed at the end of the ribbon, molten red wax was poured into it and a great seal pressed down. A lid was added and then the document folded by Dr Smithers and his assistant. It involved much advancing and retreating to make all the folds and they looked so much as though they were setting to partners that Rose almost found herself humming a country air to accompany them.

Kat gave a great sigh when they found themselves outside in the courtyard again, Marcus gingerly balancing the licence which, folded, measured at least a foot square and was crowned by the seal in its box.

'That was *lavish*.'

'It was? I thought you would be bored,' Rose said as they settled into their seats.

'Oh, the Archbishop and all those men in

wigs were dull, but wasn't the palace wonderfully ghostly? The stone floors, the dark panelling—you could almost hear the screams of the prisoners in the dungeons below.'

'You are thinking of the Spanish Inquisition, or the reigns of the Tudors,' Marcus said. 'This is the Church of England in the nineteenth century. No one is being tortured in dungeons.'

'Oh.' Kat wrinkled her nose. 'It would have fitted beautifully into my new novel. The hero creeps through the passages to rescue the heroine from the cell where the evil inquisitor is threatening her with awful torments...'

'You will have to set it in sixteenth-century Spain,' Chloe said. 'And I for one do not want to read about awful torments.'

'I will hint at them. Subtly,' Kat declared. Her sisters exchanged despairing glances—subtlety was not one of Kat's virtues.

'Tell me about your writing,' Marcus said. 'You are working on a Gothic novel?'

'It will make our fortunes,' Kat explained gravely to the man who, Rose guessed, possessed more wealth than her little sister's wildest dreams. 'I will tell you all about the plot so far.'

'You did ask,' Rose mouthed at Marcus.

He nodded gravely. 'Please proceed.'

The tortuous explanation of the plot lasted all the way back to Grosvenor Square. Marcus was still nodding, but he soon learned to keep silent after the first question had produced a complex digression into the relative virtues of princes or knights as gallant rescuers of distressed maidens and why a duke wouldn't do as the hero.

Rose's head was buzzing with questions, none of them relating to works of fiction. Where would they be married and when? Who would be invited? What on earth was she to wear? What happened afterwards?

'Thank you,' Marcus was saying and she realised that the carriage had come to a stop. 'That was most enlightening. Do you have sufficient paper to continue your work, Kat? If not, I will have some found for you. Ah, I see Heathcote has arrived from Northminster to strike terror into the household.'

A dark-clad individual with a pale, bony face and an air of infinite superiority was waiting just inside the front door. Anyone would be forgiven for thinking this was the Duke, but

Rose had encountered superior butlers before and gave him a cool smile when he was presented to her.

'Heathcote, there is a great deal to be done here in a short time,' Marcus said. 'I require that their ladyships' rooms are given priority, then the public rooms. Guest bedchambers can be left for now.'

Rose guessed that a great deal of the butler's frigidity was due to chagrin that the house was not in perfect condition. Time to pour a little oil on the waters.

'No doubt the late Duke insisted that resources were diverted to Northminster Castle, where he preferred to entertain,' she said. 'I am sure you and the household will be delighted to be able to bring this house back to the standard you are used to maintaining.'

There was the slightest unbending on Heathcote's part. 'Exactly so, my lady.'

Marcus took her arm. 'There is much to discuss, Lady Rose. Shall we retire to the study?'

'Where, when and who are three pressing items on my list of topics for discussion,' Rose said the moment the door was closed. 'But the question of my wardrobe is the priority.'

'Wardrobe?' It was almost amusing to see Marcus look confused for once.

'I assume you would prefer me to be married in something other than my breeches or the old gowns I wear to feed the chickens?' She did have a trunk of gowns from her time in London, but they would be sadly out of the mode now. The walking dress she was wearing had been chosen as the one least likely to make her noticed.

'Lord, yes,' he said with some feeling. 'Gowns, shopping… You are going to need a chaperon in residence here. One who can lend you countenance and who knows her way around all the right shops. Do you have a female relative who is not in your brother's camp?'

'There's my aunt Sylvia—Lady Dutton, the widow of the late Earl. She is my maternal grandmother's youngest sister, so is actually my great-aunt, but she hates being called that because it makes her feel old. She does not approve of Charles. Or of me, unfortunately. I threw away my chances, she will tell you. At length.'

'She will approve now, I imagine,' Marcus said wryly. 'I suggest you write to her, tell her of our impending marriage and also that Charles is attempting to push Chloe into a disgraceful match—there is no need to link the two things. I'll wager she will leap at the opportunity to turn you out just as a duchess should look.'

'She is an interfering old bat…er…biddy,' Rose protested. 'Surely you do not want her here?'

'On the contrary. She sounds ideal and it will not be for long, after all. What is important is that you have someone of the utmost respectability living with you until we are married. When you have written to her, could you make a list of absolutely everyone you can think of to invite to the ceremony? It doesn't matter how remote a relative, or how distant an acquaintance; what we need now is publicity for the match. I will do the same. Aubrey will see to the invitations.'

'But where? And when?'

'St George's, Hanover Square,' Marcus said. 'It is fashionable and not too large. If we do not have a crowd of guests it will not be so noticeable there. Will that suit?' When she nodded, he added, 'Two weeks' time, do you think?'

Two weeks was no time to assemble a trousseau, let alone a wedding dress of suitable magnificence for a ducal wedding, but Rose had a shrewd idea that any London *modiste* would fall over herself to dress a future duchess.

She took a deep breath and tried to sound assured as she said, 'And the wedding breakfast here, I assume?' It seemed a very long time ago that she had felt assured about anything, yet until she had met Marcus she had never been in any doubt about her own capabilities.

It was the threat to Chloe that so unnerved her, she realised. That and the fact that she had no right in law to protect her sister. She had to have Marcus's help, but that did not mean she could afford to become helpless and dependent. They must be partners in this marriage, she resolved.

'I will write to Aunt Sylvia at once.'

'There should be a writing table and stationery in your sitting room. Ring if you need anything.' Marcus already seemed to have his mind on the next item on his agenda.

I am marrying a man of business, she thought wryly. *And it seems as though he is regarding me as something akin to his clerks and secretaries.*

Oh, well, at least he was involving her.

Chapter Nine

The next day was Sunday, but Marcus said that attending church when she did not have a chaperon would be unwise, so they all stayed inside.

Lists and letters proved exceedingly time-consuming, Rose discovered when she continued with the task Marcus had set her. She found she was spending most of her time with Aubrey Farthing. Chloe seemed even quieter and more self-contained than usual and Kat had her head bent over the stack of paper that Mr Farthing had found for her, scribbling busily and distributing ink blots over herself and the table. There was no sign of Marcus, who was out all day.

'Being seen,' he said, when she remarked at dinner that he had hardly been home. 'And, apparently, becoming exceedingly popular. Men I would exchange nods with if I saw them other than in taverns, theatres or card rooms now want to chat, to suggest that I might like to join their clubs or buy a racehorse from them.' His smile was rueful. 'The way of the world, but it allows me to spread the news of our marriage. I have not mentioned that you are in town— that can wait until your aunt arrives.'

'There is no sign of Charles?' Rose asked, when the two girls had left the room and she and Marcus lingered over the dessert. As they had not yet been out of the house, other than to visit Lambeth Palace, it was unlikely the news had spread yet.

'No. But I know where he is now—at a house party in Bedfordshire composed of just about every man I would not like to see within range of a respectable lady. Including, of course, Soames Marlowe. It will be interesting to observe what happens when you fail to respond to his demands to bring Chloe to London.'

'Or when he discovers that we are here,' she said with a shiver. 'Aunt Sylvia is coming— I received a letter by the evening post. She says to expect her to arrive tomorrow morn-

ing. I have told Heathcote and Mrs Manville.'
The housekeeper had nodded approval at the
news and was preparing an impressive suite
designed to appeal to a dowager of exacting
tastes.

Rose had no intention of showing Marcus
the letter which ranged from expressions of
amazement that such a foolish chit as she was
had managed to 'snare' a duke, to remarks
about her step-great-nephew that showed
clearly she had few illusions about Charles's
character or morals.

'Of course I will come. I cannot imagine
how you will manage otherwise,' she had written from her mansion overlooking Green Park.

'I will leave you to your port and go and
make certain Kat has gone to bed,' Rose said.
'No, don't get up.'

She had reached the hall when there was a
loud thudding on the front door, even louder
than the sound of a footman showing off his
employer's importance with the infamous
'London knock'.

Peter the second footman hurried past her
with a murmur of apology and went to answer it.

'Good evening, sir—'

'Where the hell is my sister?'

Rose froze, one hand on the newel post, and stared at the tall figure that thrust past the footman, sending him reeling back against the panelling.

'Charles.'

'Sir, I must—' Peter straightened up, tugged his coat into order and placed himself firmly between Rose and her brother, who towered over him.

Charles had their father's strong build and, until recently, had kept fit with his various sporting activities. Now he seemed blurred, softer about the jaw, puffier under the eyes. Or perhaps it was her vision, unfocused with the shock.

From somewhere Rose found her voice. 'Peter, neither His Grace nor I are at home to Lord Wighton, now, nor at any other time.'

'My lord, I must ask you to leave.'

Charles stuck out an arm to push the footman away. Peter, sliding on the marble floor, pushed back, but he was no match for the larger man. As he staggered, Charles kicked his feet out from under him and then simply stepped over his prone body to grab Rose's wrist.

'What the devil are you doing here and

where is Chloe? Didn't you get my letter? What's this nonsense about you marrying Northminster?'

The smell of brandy on his breath made her want to gag, but she pulled hard against his grip, swinging away from the foot of the stairs. Chloe was upstairs, she had to keep him from her.

Rose felt the thin bones in her wrist would break at any moment, but she kept pulling. 'You'll never see her again. Leave us alone.'

Her brother tugged her close, so close she could see how bloodshot his eyes were, how tiny red veins were beginning to show on his nose. 'You'll tell me or I'll—'

'Get your hands off her.'

For a moment Rose did not recognise the voice, as calm and cold as a blade of ice. Marcus stood in the doorway to the dining room and she hardly recognised his face either. It was as though flames flickered for a moment in his grey eyes. Frost flames.

'It's true then,' Charles said, looking from her to Marcus and back again. He seemed to have drunk too much to recognise what danger he was in. Or perhaps he was simply too angry. 'I couldn't believe Cass when he came oiling in this morning, bleating about how I ought to know my sister had snared the Duke of Northminster. He even expected me to pay for his post chaise. You clever trollop—opened your legs for the Merchant Duke, have you? I expect he can't get another bride of any rank, not with him smelling of the shop—'

Marcus moved fast, so fast that he was beside them before her brother could react. 'I said, let her go, you sorry excuse for a man.'

'You've got no right to keep my sisters here!'

'No? This says I have.' Marcus hit him, a solid punch to the jaw that sent Charles reeling back.

He let go of Rose as he staggered and she half fell, half sat on the bottom step, holding her wrist as Charles reeled into Peter, who was hauling himself up off the floor. Her brother fell right over him and slid back until his head collided with the front door. It was all so fast that she could hardly comprehend what was happening, only that Marcus was between her and Charles, barring the way to the stairs and to Chloe. *Keeping us safe.*

There was a clamour of voices from the back of the hall as servants burst in through the baize door under the stairs. From the landing above she heard Chloe calling her name and then Kat, her voice shriller, frightened.

Marcus gave the footman a hand to get to his feet, then hauled Charles upright. 'Door,' he snapped at Peter, then, as it opened, he shoved Charles out into the night.

Peter slammed the door, shot the bolts and leant against it as though prepared to withstand a battering ram.

'Good man,' Marcus said, resting one hand on the footman's shoulder for a second as he passed. 'Heathcote, send for Dr Lawson.' He kept walking as he spoke, reached Rose, scooped her up, then started to climb the stairs.

'I'm all right, Marcus. I don't need the doctor,' Rose protested. 'My hand is perfectly unharmed. See? I can wriggle my fingers.' It hurt to do it, but she wanted to get that look off his face.

'Don't argue. Chloe, look after Kat,' he said as he passed the white-faced girl at the top of the stairs and Rose heard the chill melt from his voice as he spoke to her. 'You are all quite safe, but she is frightened and she needs you. I will take care of Rose,' he added as he shouldered open her bedchamber door.

* * *

Marcus kicked the door closed behind them and leaned back against it, suddenly unable to move. He waited for the pounding of his heart to subside. In his arms Rose lay motionless, as if sensing that he needed stillness, just for a moment.

When he saw Wighton's hand clamped around Rose's wrist, saw the pain on her face, he had wanted to kill the man. Tear him apart, wrench off that hand. He was not quite sure what had stopped him—Rose's eyes, perhaps, fixed on him, trusting him to free her and trusting, too, that he was in control of the situation. Which he had been...by a thread.

Mine. That was what he had thought when he had seen Wighton with his hands on her. *Mine.*

It hadn't been civilised: it had barely been a coherent thought, more blind possessive instinct. And it was wrong. Not to want to stop the lout of her brother hurting her, bullying her, but to feel like that about her. He didn't own Rose; he didn't *possess* her. She was her own woman and she had only agreed to marry him to keep her sisters safe. It would be an alliance, not a surrender, and to find that he was capable of that kind of violently possessive emotion was a shock.

Yes, he had a temper and he had fought enemies before, but never with the sensation that at any moment he might lose control. That he might maim, or worse.

'Marcus?' Rose whispered.

'It's all right,' he said. 'Just getting my breath back after lugging you up all those stairs. Goodness, woman, I had no idea you weighed so much. It must be all the muscle you developed earthing up potatoes.'

It was a feeble joke, but it provoked a shaky laugh.

He carried her to the bed and set her down. 'Let me see your wrist. Did he touch you anywhere else? Did you fall awkwardly?' He took her right hand in his, moving it gently. The skin around her wrist was red and the bruising was already coming up, but she was right, nothing seemed to be broken. He set the hand down gently on the counterpane.

'No, and, no,' Rose said. Her voice was very calm, but he recognised the tone she used when she did not want to frighten Kat. He did not want soothing, he wanted her to tell him everything, throw herself into his arms and ask him to set it all to rights.

'All I need is some arnica to bring out the bruising.' She looked down, then made a small sound of distress and took his right hand in her left, lifting it so she could look at his knuckles. 'You are bleeding,' she said.

'It's nothing, I just skinned them on Charles's chin. It looks worse than it is,' he said and dug a handkerchief out of his pocket to wrap around his hand to hide the blood.

'Nothing?' she said indignantly and took hold of his fist again, lifted it and touched her lips to it.

'Kiss it better?' Marcus said, forcing a laugh, because otherwise he was going to snatch her into his arms and put his mouth on hers, stop her biting her lip in distress. 'Is that what you would do for Kat if she hurt herself?' He tugged gently and she let go, leaving him feeling oddly bereft.

What the devil was the matter with him? Reaction, that was all.

'I'll send your maid in to bathe your wrist.'

'And Chloe and Kat, please, so they can see I'm all right,' Rose said. 'And can you make sure that Peter isn't hurt?'

'Yes, of course. You'll rest now?'

'I will,' she promised. Yes, that was the kind of brave smile he had seen her produce to reassure Kat.

But he wasn't a child and he was not reassured.

Marcus found the sisters outside the door with Frost and sent them in, then ran downstairs to find the housekeeper ordering Peter to go downstairs so she could do something about the bruise that was coming up on his forehead while the footman was refusing to leave the front door unguarded.

'Thank you, Peter. You did well, but go with Mrs Manville. Heathcote, I want all the doors and windows secured and someone on guard all night. We fear an attempt to remove Lady Chloe. I suppose it is too much to hope that no word of this gets out, but if you could ask the staff to exercise their discretion, I would be exceedingly obliged.'

'I trust that the entire household is aware of what is expected of them in a duke's employ, Your Grace. And, even if they were not, Lady Chloe is, if I might be so bold, already a favourite among them.'

'Thank you, Heathcote,' Marcus said, rather

shaken by the concern he saw in the butler's expression. It seemed that in the eyes of the staff, at least, he was not simply acquiring a wife and two sisters-in-law, he was forming a family.

Rose cut her toast into triangles using her right hand. She concentrated on not letting the discomfort that caused be visible to the three pairs of eyes all pretending they were not watching her every move.

More than three, in fact. Peter was hovering with the coffee pot, ready to refill her cup every time she put it down and Heathcote had been positively avuncular.

Frost applied more arnica that morning and bandaged the wrist neatly, so that only a thin edge showed beneath her cuff. The pain was more of a dull ache now, although the bruised areas were tender. What had taken most time that morning was trying to disguise the dark shadows under her eyes that a sleepless night had produced.

When they had finally got Kat to sleep she had told Chloe the truth about the man Charles schemed to marry her to and why. She had feared the reaction, but Chloe surprised her with anger, not fear.

'You and Marcus will stop him,' she said stoutly. 'And even if you couldn't, I would never say *yes*. And if they drugged me, or bribed a clergyman, then I'd cut off the man's privy parts with my embroidery scissors.'

It was the only part of the evening that made Rose smile and she saved the threat up to tell Marcus.

'Is Great-Aunt coming today?' Kat asked. She was a little subdued, but not as much as to worry Rose. Everyone was behaving so normally that Kat seemed reassured.

'She doesn't like us to call her Great-Aunt,' Chloe said. 'She says it makes her feel ancient, so remember to call her Aunt Sylvia.'

'There's someone at the door,' Marcus said as Heathcote went out.

Kat bounced up and peeped around the edge of the door. 'It's her.'

'It is she,' Rose corrected automatically. 'She's arriving early to catch us all off guard, no doubt. Thank goodness we have finished breakfast. I only hope that Mrs Manville has her rooms ready. Remember, girls—best behaviour now. I am afraid she has a number of exceedingly old-fashioned notions, Marcus.'

He had appeared very calm and unconcerned that morning, with no sign of the icily dangerous man of the night before. She had tried to thank him again, but he had brushed that aside and showed no sign of wanting to talk about it. His raw knuckles were hidden by a strip of bandage, but he was using the hand freely.

Rose tried not to think about the feel of it in her hand when she had kissed it, the thud of his pulse under her fingers, the way he had gone still when she touched him. He was a man and they didn't enjoy a fuss, she supposed.

Marcus got to his feet and tossed his napkin on the table. 'We will receive Lady Dutton in the drawing room,' he said to Peter as he led Rose and her sisters through the connecting door from the breakfast parlour. Mr Farthing murmured something about attending to the post and went out to the study.

For some reason, the sight of her great-aunt in Marcus's house brought the reality of her planned marriage home to Rose in a way that even the visit to the Archbishop had not. There was something about Aunt Sylvia that could only be real; she was so solidly grounded in her own belief in herself and the rightness of her opinions that it was impossible to believe she was part of a fantasy or a dream or even a feverish hallucination.

'Well, Northminster!' The Dowager advanced across the room, extended her hand and raised her eyeglass when Marcus shook it instead of kissing it as she obviously expected. 'You have abducted my great-nieces, have you?'

'Hardly abducted, Lady Dutton. Will you not take this seat?' He waited until she sank into the armchair, casting aside her furs, arranging her lilac draperies and setting her famous pearls straight on her imposing bosom.

'My intention is to offer shelter to Lady Chloe and Lady Katherine. Lady Rose has already done me the honour of accepting my proposal of marriage. They have all come willingly, I assure you.'

'And what you wrote to me is true, without exaggeration, Rose?'

Rose, thankful that she had explained the situation to Chloe, nodded. 'It is all true, I am afraid, Aunt Sylvia.'

'The boy's a disgrace to the family name; I can only be thankful that it is not mine. But we have a fine kettle of stinking fish here, Northminster. The rapscallion is of age and Chloe and Katherine's legal guardian, even if he has no control over Rose.'

'But I have the resources to fight him in court on the grounds that he is an unfit guardian and that their half-sister, who will be my duchess by then, is the fit and proper person to nurture two young ladies.'

'Hmm.' Her aunt lifted her eyeglass again and surveyed Marcus through it, her right eye alarmingly magnified. 'You will spend your money made from trade on lawsuits, will you?'

Rose bit her lip. Far from showing any gratitude for rescuing them, Aunt Sylvia was being exceedingly rude to Marcus. It was a miracle that he didn't wash his hands of them there and then.

'Yes, ma'am. Money made in commerce has exactly the same purchasing power as your inherited, unearned, wealth,' he said, his tone cool. One finger tapped slowly on the arm of his chair, the only sign of impatience.

The Dowager nodded, her lips pursed. Rose had noticed before that she liked people who stood up to her. 'It does. And why should you want to marry my niece?'

'Now I have this position I must marry. That is my duty. And you cannot deny that Lady

Rose is eminently eligible and will make me a charming wife.'

'Hah! That's a cool declaration for you, Rose my girl.'

'You are an advocate for romance, ma'am? For love matches?' Marcus said.

'Romance? Certainly not! Fit only for dangerous novels designed to turn girls' heads.'

Rose held her breath while her great-aunt and Marcus held each other's gaze, then the older woman gave a bark of laughter. 'You'll do. I can see why you want Rose, but why should you trouble yourself with the girls though? Tell me that? You could have packed them off to me.'

'Any gentleman would act as I have, under the circumstances.'

'You know Charles?'

'We met—briefly—last night. Prior to that I have played him at cards once, ma'am. When he was winning he had no problem taking my money, but when he began to lose, and lose badly, he found the stink of trade at the table too much to bear and walked away.'

'I wonder you did not issue a challenge. In my day no gentleman accepted an insult so meekly.' Her lip curled.

'Challenge a spoilt brat like that? I wouldn't waste my powder, let alone turn out of bed at some unearthly hour to put a bullet in him.'

Aunt Sylvia snorted. 'He might have chosen swords.'

'Not if he had heard of my reputation with them.'

'Aha! You have a fire-breather here, Rose. Yes, he'll do very well. Now, we must decide how to manage this for the best. What tale shall we tell? I have it: Northminster, I believe you went to Chalton with a message on my behalf, fell for Rose at first sight and I decided they would all be safest here, with my chaperonage, of course. I will tell all my friends it is necessary to keep the girls from Charles's corrupting influence—word will soon spread. Now we must decide on the wedding.'

'St George's, Hanover Square, in two weeks, with the wedding breakfast here, I thought,' Marcus said. 'I obtained a special licence in case we find it necessary to marry elsewhere and in haste, but I doubt Wighton will recover from our encounter and form any kind of plan before then.'

'He was here, you say?'

Marcus raised his right hand. 'Briefly.'

'Ha! Good for you. I trust you spoiled his not-so-pretty face for him. And now you expect me to assemble a trousseau fit for a duchess in just fourteen days, I suppose?'

'I have every confidence in your powers, ma'am.'

'Turning me up sweet, are you? I will see what I can do. And invitations—I'll give your secretary a list of those I can be certain will attend if I give them the nudge. We'll have the church filled and a dining room full of guests for the breakfast—that will make a fine notice in the newssheets.'

'Thank you, ma'am.'

'Pshaw, no more than my duty to the girls. Now, Rose, you've not got much to say for yourself.'

'I am very glad and grateful that you are here, Aunt. May I show you to your suite?'

'You may. And I'm not so old that I need hauling from my chair either, young man,' she said as Marcus rose and offered her his hand to rise.

'No, ma'am,' he said with suspicious meekness. 'I'll ring for the housekeeper.'

Chapter Ten

Marcus watched Rose show the old battle-axe out and gave a sigh of relief. The Dowager was going to be an uncomfortable house guest, but a formidable ally. Chloe and Kat sat silently side by side on the sofa, watching him. 'Well?' he asked them.

'She scares me,' Kat admitted. 'Last time I saw her she said I should be strapped to a backboard and made to walk around the room with books balanced on my head until I could glide like a lady.'

Chloe seemed about to speak, then fell silent.

'Go on, Chloe,' Marcus said, sitting down.

'I am sorry. You really do want to help us,' she said, all of a rush. 'I wasn't sure about you before because I couldn't think why you

should, because you aren't in love with Rose. I
thought you wanted the castle, but she says she
was going to sell it to you one day, so it cannot
be that. But then you fought Charles and you
sent for Aunt Sylvia and you really are going
to marry Rose.'

'I do not like to see people treated badly by
their own family, the ones who should care
for them most,' Marcus said, the all too personal truth of that twisting in his gut even as
he spoke. That, and the castle and a convenient
bride and the impossibility of turning away
from females in distress, of course. The problem was, one of the females happened to be
Rose, who increasingly made him wish that
this wasn't simply a matter of convenience.

'But I still worry.' Chloe stared down at her
own fingers pleating the skirts of the girlishly
simple gown.

'Do not. Your sister and I will look after
you.'

'No, I mean about Rose. She wouldn't marry
anyone, even though she had proposals before
and even though Papa was furious with her for
refusing. And when I asked her why, she said
it was because she did not love any of them
and that was important and she would not set-

tle for less and neither should I when the time came. I suppose that after Chr—' She broke off abruptly. 'So she is only marrying you now because of protecting us from Charles.' She raised anxious brown eyes. 'I worry that she will not be happy.'

'I will do my utmost to make her so,' Marcus said stiffly. What had Chloe meant by 'Chr—'? Christmas? What had happened then? Or was it Christopher? That made more sense. Someone she had been in love with, but had not married. Who, presumably, had not asked her, or surely she would have accepted him, unless he had been utterly ineligible—married, perhaps. Or a soldier or sailor lost in battle.

He told himself it did not matter in the least, that many people had old romances in their past: lost loves, passing infatuations, sad bereavements. They moved on with their lives and many married happily. He would ignore that little mystery because it was none of his business, even if it was a sad tale of lost love. This was a marriage of convenience and therefore Rose's past was certainly nothing to feel jealous about—not, of course, that he was prone to such an unpleasant emotion. Possessiveness, though… He recalled the blazing anger of last night, the word in his head. *Mine*.

There were more important things to be focusing on than his feelings—a church to book, wedding invitations to send—he must warn Aubrey to expect a lengthy list from the Dowager. He must speak to her about Rose's trousseau and effectively give her carte blanche to spend whatever she saw fit. He must decide on a best man, plan the wedding breakfast…

At least one thing could be ignored for the moment. A wedding journey, or any kind of honeymoon, was out of the question. They had to keep the girls close and begin the legal proceedings to give him their guardianship. And that was a battle he looked forward to fighting. Marcus caught sight of himself in the mirror hanging opposite and almost failed to recognise the man with the almost feral smile on his lips. He adjusted his expression before he scared the girls into fits and stood up. 'Shall we talk to Mr Farthing about wedding invitations? He might welcome your ideas about the design of the card.'

Not that there was much scope for imagination—cream or white for the card, plain or deckle edge, the quality of gold leaf, the position of his crest—but anything that made Kat and Chloe feel involved would help their morale, he thought.

'Marcus!'

He looked up as he closed the door to the drawing room and saw Rose coming down the stairs. Her cheeks were flushed, her expression anxious and with the speed of her descent her pale skirts billowed out around her so that she looked like a worried angel descending through clouds.

He stopped at the bottom of the flight and thought how lovely she looked, even lovelier than when he had first seen her in her shocking breeches and with her long plait coming undone.

'Steady!'

Even as he said it she slipped, her foot sliding over the polished edge of the stair. With a cry she pitched forward, desperately reaching for the handrail, but the stairs were too wide and she was in the middle.

Marcus went up four steps and caught her, the force of her fall knocking him backwards and off balance. He twisted and came down with a thump to sit on the bottom step, his arms clasped firmly around Rose.

'Oh!' she said, her voice coming from somewhere in the middle of his waistcoat. 'Are you injured?'

'No at all. Are you? Your wrist?' Marcus shifted her in his arms so that she was sitting on his knees and resting against his chest. He felt sick at the thought of her hurt any more than she was already.

'No. No… I think I am perfectly all right.' Rose struggled to sit more upright, to stand, so he opened her arms, but she gave a little gasp and sat down again. 'Oh! I'm dizzy. How foolish.'

She tried to stand again and this time he held tight. 'Stay still a moment or you will fall and hurt yourself again and we will have to send out to the pharmacy for more arnica.'

She did not appear to notice his attempt at a feeble joke. 'So ridiculous to fall here. I have been running up and down twisting, worn stone stairs at the castle and never a slip.' She sounded breathless.

'There, you knew to take care. This staircase looks safe, but it is deceptively treacherous with those highly polished treads. I must have it carpeted, I think.'

'That would be a pity, it is very fine.' She

twisted in his hold to look, creating a delightful friction.

Marcus made himself concentrate on stair treads, not on the sensation of warm female curves pressed into his lap. 'I suppose it would. Perhaps less enthusiastic polishing would make it safer.'

He did not want to talk about floor polish. He wanted something else entirely. 'Why were you in such a hurry?'

'I was coming to apologise about Aunt Sylvia. I think I had forgotten just how outspoken she is.'

Rose twisted back to look at him and Marcus bit off a groan. He must have done something quite dreadful to deserve this torture. 'She is magnificent and just what we need. But she frightens Kat.'

'Yes. I shudder to think what her reaction would be if Kat started describing the plot of her novel.' She relaxed a little, leaning against him, making Marcus aware of even more soft curves. 'They will get used to each other soon. It is such a relief to have her here, though, even if I am doing nothing right in her eyes.'

'Not even by marrying me?'

'Oh, that is the one thing she does approve

of. That and making certain the girls are safe. No, my hands are a disgrace, my deportment worse. I am far too outspoken and my lack of musical skills are deplorable. She shudders to imagine how much work it will take to turn me into something approaching a lady again, let alone a duchess. And Bassett, her maid, looks even more disapproving.'

'Lady Dutton will love the whole thing. She will find fault with all of us and lecture to her heart's content. She will wallow in shopping and new gowns and pretend to herself that she is an absolute martyr for doing it,' Marcus predicted. 'She will brag to her friends about her great-niece the Duchess and take the credit for every one of your successes. To say nothing of being worth a regiment of dragoons against your half-brother. If she had been here last night, she would have probably disembowelled him with a soup spoon.'

'Yes, I suppose you are right.' Rose's soft sigh caressed the line of his jaw and he clenched his teeth.

'I hadn't thought of it like that,' she said after a moment, sounding more cheerful. 'She is grumbling about all the shops we must visit and at the same time producing the most awe-inspiring list of things to buy. She is positively gloating over it. Thank you—I was letting it all get out of proportion.' Rose sat up straighter and smiled at him.

Marcus kissed her.

He had not meant to, but her face was only inches from his, her lips were the colour of her name, her shape seemed imprinted on his body and most of the blood that should have been in his brain appeared to have gone somewhere else entirely.

He knew the moment that his lips touched hers that this could only make things more complicated, more difficult. He had given his word not to touch her and now, before they were even married…

And yet he was still kissing her and her mouth was warm and yielding under his and her heart beat against his chest while her scent filled his nostrils so that his senses were drunk with her. His hands shifted, one to the curve of her hip, one to the swell of her breast.

Rose gave a little shudder, a rejection as effective as a bucket of cold water.

Hell.

There must have been more difficult things that he had done in his life, but just at that moment he could not have named one. Marcus stood up, setting Rose on her feet as he did so, and stepped back.

'I apologise,' he said, making his voice as cold and formal as he knew how. It was bad enough to take advantage of her after that tumble, but at least he need not sound as though he was panting to pounce on her again.

Rose knew she was blushing. Her face was on fire and as for her mouth… Thank goodness it felt so swollen and strange or she would have blurted out, 'Don't stop!' Her body still seemed to be racked by that sensual shiver from the touch of his hand on her breast.

Marcus looked furious, as well he might. He had saved her from a nasty fall and she had indulged herself by staying in his arms long past the moment when she was capable of standing on her own two feet. She had wanted his arms around her, needed to feel his heat and his strength. She had even felt flattered by the change she had felt in his body as he held her close, when she was quite well aware that any man would respond like that to any female pressed intimately to him.

And then she had smiled up at him, positively inviting a kiss, she now realised. Marcus was only human. Men would kiss, and far more, when some foolish female offered. They did not have to feel anything other than physical desire. Which in this case had rapidly turned to something else.

'I…' She turned and fled up the stairs.

Idiot, idiot, idiot.

She had understood, with her head, what Marcus was offering when he suggested they marry and it was not any exchange of emotion. A marriage of convenience for both of them was what he had proposed. Yes, sooner or later the marriage would be consummated—he needed an heir—but until then she was sure he had *that* side of his life perfectly well under control.

She had thought about it, she remembered, but the idea of Marcus in some other woman's embrace—a beautiful, sophisticated, skilled woman—hadn't seemed real. Now it did and she felt even more of an idiot not to have come to terms with it from the start, she thought as she shut her bedroom door, turned the key in the lock and leaned back against it for support.

Most men in society kept a mistress—it was no secret. Papa had had a string of them and very expensive they were, too, she had gathered from comments she had overheard her stepmother making when the two of them had their frequent arguments. Well, Marcus could afford an entire string of exotic opera dancers, actresses and scandalous widows if he wanted them.

He must think she was trying to seduce him, she thought miserably through a fog of embarrassment. And he did not want to be seduced. If he did, then he would never have dumped her out of his arms so unceremoniously. What if he thought she had tumbled into his embrace on purpose?

Rose pushed away from the door and walked to the dressing table. What must she look like! Red in the face still, no doubt. Tumbled from the fall and from writhing in Marcus's arms like a wanton.

She sat down on the stool and made herself confront her own image. Yes: pink cheeks, pink nose—just to add to her general humiliation—and her hair half-down. And yet her mouth, which felt so tender and swollen, looked perfectly normal.

And then an even worse thought stuck her. What if Marcus thought she was falling in love with him?

* * *

Marcus escaped to his club for luncheon and dinner was dominated by Lady Dutton, who provided the perfect excuse not to have to talk to Rose. Not, he suspected, that she much wished to speak to him. He made an excuse and went out again afterwards, telling himself it was to save Rose from embarrassment and knowing full well that he was dodging an awkward encounter.

The next day Lady Dutton, whom Marcus had hoped would take a breakfast tray in her chamber, swept into the morning room like a galleon, all sails set to do battle, presumably with the modistes, milliners, cordwainers and haberdashers of Mayfair. Chloe and Kat, subdued in the presence of their great-aunt, ate in silence, both of them visibly careful of their deportment and manners.

Rose entered just behind Lady Dutton, her expression unreadable. She greeted him pleasantly enough, although without a smile, and her eyes were wary—when he tried to hold her gaze it shifted at once and she began to talk over-brightly to her sisters about the shopping that they needed and whether they wanted to accompany her that morning.

Both shook their heads decisively. Kat, Marcus suspected, because the last thing she wanted to do was to drag around shops on her best behaviour and Chloe because she felt safer in the house.

But Rose… He watched her as well as he could without being caught staring and cursed himself all over again for that kiss and for not confronting the situation at once. He should have apologised and told her that it was relief that she had escaped uninjured that had made him…over-affectionate.

He remembered his businesslike proposal and how very quickly she had agreed to his promise not to press her to consummate the marriage at once. That should have told him that she dreaded the thought. The fact that she had been so easy in his arms the night before was due to shock and innocence—the innocence that had led her to smile up at him so confidingly.

He was going to have to seduce his own wife, Marcus realised. But what if, even after they were wed, she did not want to be seduced? He recalled the little shudder that she had given when he had touched her breast. Was he so dislikeable?

No, he told himself, it was not dislike. Nor was she afraid of him as a person. She trusted him with her sisters and with her own future. It must be that man, the one whose name Chloe had so nearly blurted out. Christopher, Christian, Crispin… She had loved him, lost him and now she could not bear the thought of being in another man's embrace.

Sooner or later Rose would come to his bed, he knew that. She had a strong sense of duty and honour and she knew that by agreeing to marry him she was also agreeing to give him children and to be a wife to him in every sense. Rose would give herself a week or so to become accustomed after the wedding, he was certain, and then she would dutifully make it clear that he might come to her bed. And she would do her level best not to show her true feelings when he was there.

And that was more than enough to dampen a man's desire, Marcus thought bitterly. For a moment he wished he was keeping a mistress, but he had parted from Annabelle, the dashing widow from Finsbury, when he had learned of his inheritance. He had not wanted to raise expectations, but she had understood well enough and the parting had been amiable. Not that he wouldn't have broken off a liaison once he was engaged to be married—

'Northminster? Are you in a trance? I have twice asked you to pass me the orange conserve.'

'I do apologise, Lady Dutton.' He placed the silver dish in front of her. 'I was making lists in my head. I am afraid that there is a great deal to consider.'

'There most certainly is. Do you wish me to order Court dress for Rose while we are selecting her trousseau? She will have to be presented at the first Drawing Room: it would give a most peculiar impression if someone of her rank were not.' She fixed him with a beady stare. 'You have made your own bow, of course.'

'Not yet.'

He was clearly not living up to expectations. Or perhaps he was living down to them... He would have to purchase Court dress himself because, although his wardrobe was extensive, it did not include a dress sword, a chapeau bras or whatever type of tailcoat covered in bullion lace that a duke was expected to wear at Court.

There was always his late cousin's wardrobe to explore, he supposed. He was taller and more broad-shouldered than William had been, but there should be the hat and the sword somewhere.

He pulled his thoughts back to more immediate and important concerns. At least he felt confident that the house was properly secure and had discussed it with the butler before he came down to breakfast.

'I want two reliable footmen close to Lady Chloe at all times,' he had explained. 'All the doors are to be kept locked and we are not at home to any gentlemen unaccompanied by ladies. No tradesmen are to be allowed through the area door—we'll need another footman, or one of the grooms, down there at all times.'

'Indeed, Your Grace. I have already worked out a rota and I believe we have adequate staff if the grooms are also involved. I do not believe that adding new footmen would be wise. Two men will be on hand before any external door is opened and all the ground floor and basement windows will remain closed, other than the basement windows with grills on them, which should be adequate for ventilating the kitchens.'

'Thank you, Heathcote. You appear to have thought of everything.'

The butler inclined his head. 'I regret to say, Your Grace, that we became accustomed to dealing with, shall I say, difficult gentlemen, during your predecessors' time. Parties became rather too lively, gentlemen imbibed too lavishly.' He left with just the hint of a smirk, leaving Marcus to wonder now just how his butler dealt with difficult gentlemen. With a poker, perhaps.

'Cat got your tongue?'

Marcus realised that his attention had strayed again and that Lady Dutton was now frowning at Rose.

'I am sorry, Aunt Sylvia. Like Marcus, I was also making lists in my head.'

'There is no need for that. Having launched three daughters and five granddaughters into society, and married them all off well, I am perfectly *au fait* with every detail of what is required.' She narrowed her eyes. 'And one of the first of those is your hair. It needs at least six inches off it and shaping so we have some hope of producing ringlets. I know just the coiffeur, Monsieur Troufaut. I will send for him to come this afternoon.'

'No.' Marcus realised that he had spoken out loud and that four pairs of female eyes were regarding him in amazement. 'Unless Rose wishes it cut, of course. But I think it is beautiful as it is.'

'You do?' Rose sounded amazed.

It was a good thing that she could not read his mind and see the erotically charged image that had flashed into it of her, quite naked except for her hair loose around her shoulders; how she would look kneeling over him, those long tresses falling to caress his bare chest. Or lower…

Then he saw her eyes widen and guessed that something of his thoughts must be visible to her. That, on top of last night's unwise kiss, would be enough to alarm any virgin on the point of marrying a man who was a virtual stranger to her.

'I dislike fussy, over-elaborate hairstyles for young ladies,' Marcus said, making himself sound as disapproving as possible. 'Most unsuitable. Simplicity is always best to my mind.'

'I am greatly of your opinion, Northminster, but a balance must be struck between modesty and fashion when one is of the rank Rose will occupy.'

'Perhaps a trim and some shaping,' Rose said colourlessly. Yes, he had shocked her again.

'The coachman has sent round to ask when you require the carriage, my lady,' Heathcote announced.

'In fifteen minutes. Come along, Rose. Chloe, Katherine, how do you intend to spend the morning?' Without waiting for an answer, she swept on, 'Chloe, I suggest you practise on the pianoforte, if it is in tune. Katherine, I assume you have schoolbooks to which you can apply yourself.'

'I will write my nov— Er…essay, Aunt Sylvia,' Kat said, looking so innocent that Marcus almost laughed out loud, despite everything.

'Excellent. Come along, Rose. This afternoon we will pay calls upon all of my acquaintance who are in town. It will not take long for news of your betrothal to spread.'

And that will inflame Charles Trafford even further, if nothing will, Marcus thought.

This morning he would leave Aubrey to wrestle with the wedding preparations and visit his lawyers, Marcus decided. He had sent them a detailed account of how matters stood and was expecting a message asking when they might call with their conclusions, but now he felt he should not risk Chloe or Kat overhearing a frank discussion of their brother's plans. They were unsettled enough. It was best he go to the legal chambers himself and not stand on his new-found ducal dignity.

Marcus studied the murky coffee dregs in the bottom of his cup, wondering if he could read his future there, or whether that was only with tea leaves. For a man who could hardly remember being part of a family he seemed to have pitched himself headlong into domestic life with more than its fair share of complications. He thought he could see his way through those, but there were other dangers, such as becoming a jealous husband before he was even married.

'More coffee, Your Grace?'

Marcus was so deep in thought that it took him a moment to realise he was the person being addressed. 'Yes, thank you.'

Could he have done anything differently and avoided ending up in this situation?

Of course he could. He could have taken Rose's word for it that she would eventually sell him Chalton Castle and then gone nowhere near the Trafford sisters again. He lifted his cup and looked across the rim at two pairs of watchful brown eyes. Even Chloe's were trusting now. Both girls smiled tentatively and Marcus found himself smiling back. There was no hope for it: he was doomed.

Chapter Eleven

Rose arrived back at Grosvenor Square for luncheon feeling dazed, confused and as weary as if she had spent the morning digging the vegetable garden. Her aunt Sylvia, almost three times her age, appeared to be entirely invigorated by the expedition.

Rose had been stripped to her chemise, measured, prodded and draped in fabrics. Her corset had been criticised and her figure analysed in mortifying detail. She had been talked over and around until she had recovered herself enough to start expressing opinions. Forcibly.

No, she did not like pink, or frills or satin. She wanted walking dresses that she could actually walk in, evening gowns that she could breathe in and ball gowns that she could move in.

She could see that Madame Blanche, the

modiste, was treading a fine line between pleasing a future duchess who could be a most valuable client and obeying the demands of one of her most domineering existing customers. Rose felt some sympathy, but it was she who would be corseted, laced and trussed into these gowns, and she was prepared to fight for her liberty.

By the time they returned to Grosvenor Square she thought she had prevailed, but apparently this morning's orders were only the tip of the iceberg. Tomorrow, Aunt Sylvia announced, they would be shopping all day, but this afternoon it was vitally important to make the rounds of the most influential matrons who were in London and not sea bathing, recuperating their strength on their country estates or stalking suitable husbands for their daughters at house parties.

It was essential that she created the right impression, not only because she could not let Marcus down, but also because it was necessary to garner as much support for their position when it came to a battle with Charles. Perhaps, she thought, he would back down if he was faced with strong opposition. Could he afford a legal battle?

Charles had encountered Marcus before, she remembered. He had lost money to him at cards and had insulted him. Would that make him more wary, or more arrogant? The worry of it was almost enough to eclipse her own humiliation of the evening before. Marcus was marrying her for convenience and out of chivalry: she must not forget that and allow herself to grow to like him too much, to desire him more than it was her duty as a wife. He had been cool and polite at breakfast and she must be the same.

The trouble was, she was too vulnerable to him and it had only taken his remark about her hair to have her in a glow of pleasure, dashed immediately by his remarks about simple, modest styles.

Once before she had mistaken a man's feelings quite disastrously, but she was not going to do so again. So, when they met over the luncheon table she smiled and chattered about gowns and shops and how she had brought some sketches of outfits that Madame Blanche suggested might be suitable for her younger sisters and thought she saw Marcus relax a little. The incident on the stairs had been forgotten, it seemed.

* * *

She was wrong, Rose discovered as she went into the drawing room to find her reticule before going up to change for the afternoon's round of visits. Marcus followed her in and closed the door behind him.

He looked tall and dark and immovable as he stood in front of the heavy mahogany panels.

This is the man who will be my husband, she thought with a shiver that was only partly apprehension.

'I wanted to reassure you,' he said abruptly, and she was certain he had seen that involuntary movement. 'I gave you certain undertakings when we agreed to marry and I fear you may have reason to doubt my word after that… incident on the stairs last night.'

Incident?

'In the alarm of your fall and the unexpected proximity, I fear I was distracted and not thinking as clearly as I should have been.'

Distracted? Not thinking clearly? So kissing me is something that happens when you haven't got your mind on what you are doing, is it?

He hadn't thought her forward and begging to be kissed at all. She had been right to wonder if it was simply an instinctive male reaction. Her embarrassment vanished in a flash of anger. Marcus had found himself with an armful of warm female and he had kissed her. Presumably he would have done the same if any moderately attractive woman had tumbled into his embrace. Then he had recalled who she was and dropped her like a hot coal.

'Please do not give it another thought,' Rose said, fixing a smile of understanding tinged with condescension on her lips. 'I am quite well aware of how men react if offered such…proximity. I admit I was flustered, but after three Seasons I really should have known better. I assure you, I do not regard it.

'Now, if you will excuse me, I must go and see if Aunt Sylvia's maid has managed to make one of my gowns fit to make calls in this afternoon. She assured me she can work wonders, but after all my good clothes have been packed away for months and have grown sadly out of fashion, it will take a miracle, I am sure.'

He was standing in her way and she was almost toe to toe with him before he moved. Then Marcus stepped aside and opened the door for her. 'I hope you have a pleasant afternoon.'

'Oh, I doubt it!' Rose was quite pleased with her sophisticated little trill of laughter. 'But duty calls must be made—and I know my duty.' Then she was past him with a flick of her skirts and halfway up the stairs before she realised she was holding her breath.

Foolishness! Did you think he would take advantage of that closeness to snatch another kiss? You flatter yourself, Rose Trafford.

Marcus was waiting in the hall when Rose came downstairs with her aunt.

'I have decided that I shall escort you.'

He must have changed with remarkable speed, she thought, reluctantly admiring the biscuit-coloured pantaloons, the Hessian boots with their silver tassels and the cut of his swallowtail coat. Heathcote held his tall hat, gloves and silver-topped cane and looked, for once, as though he thoroughly approved of the proceedings.

'That is very good of you, Northminster.' Aunt Sylvia, surveying him through her eyeglass, also appeared to be impressed.

'My pleasure, ma'am. It will also be useful to meet the ladies. I have not moved in their social circles previously, although I am probably acquainted with their sons and husbands.'

They took their places in the barouche, the ladies facing forward, Marcus opposite them. The hood was folded down creating an elegant open carriage.

'A very suitable equipage,' Aunt Sylvia observed, setting her parasol at an angle to protect her cheeks from any ray of sunshine. 'Parasol, Rose,' she commanded. 'Although how we are going to return your complexion to what it should be in the time available is a worry to me. Ottaway's Cream of Pearls, perhaps.'

Marcus came to Rose's rescue before the lecture could continue. 'The carriage was a purchase of my late cousin. His taste in most things—other than horses—was for the highest quality,' he added drily. 'The team, however, are mine, so we may be certain of a safe passage through the streets.'

'What will you do with the late Duke's horses?' Rose could not help but smile at the memory of the badly schooled chestnut and how skilfully Marcus had controlled it, the first time he had come to Chalton Castle. He had clearly not been pleased to be mounted on such an animal, but she had secretly thought him rather magnificent. And had tried, very hard, not to show it.

'Sell the entire stable, I imagine. I haven't inspected all of them and there may be some suitable for ladies, but I doubt it.' He seemed to notice her disappointment. 'I imagine you would prefer to choose your own horses in any case, Rose. Do both of your sisters ride?'

'Chloe is a good rider, but Kat has never been on a horse.' She smiled at the thought of her little sister learning to ride, although part of her could imagine just what terrifying adventures Kat might have if she ever got off the leading rein. She would probably want to learn to joust.

'After the wedding I will go to Tattersall's and see what I can find for all three of you. It is not somewhere I could take ladies, I'm afraid,' he added when she opened her mouth to protest that she wanted to select her own horse. 'But I can have a selection brought to you on approval.'

'Thank you.' For a second their eyes met and they shared a smile of genuine pleasure, then Rose turned her head to look at the passing traffic. It was best to maintain a slight distance in case Marcus thought she was being too forward.

It was hard not to show her excitement at the prospect of having her own horse again. She had enjoyed riding, but selling his sisters' mounts had been one of Charles's economies and she could not afford to buy even a pony for herself. There was Pudding, the little donkey they kept at the castle—named by Kat, of course—but she did not consider perching on his back to be the same thing at all.

'We will begin with Lady Melford,' Aunt Sylvia announced. 'We may well find several of the ladies on my list at her house in Hill Street, which will save time.' She lifted her eyeglass and ran a critical eye over Rose's attire. 'A pity none of your new clothes are ready, but I do not think we should delay and Bassett has worked wonders on that gown and bonnet.'

Rose, who hardly recognised her out-of-date blue afternoon gown with its new rows of braid around the hem, changes to the neckline and a ruffle of Brussels lace at bosom and wrist, agreed. Bassett had replaced the bonnet ribbons, added a sprig of artificial flowers and somehow managed to straighten the brim where Kat had sat on it.

The coachman drew the carriage to a halt and she took a deep breath. Now it began—she had another battle she had to fight. Marcus would help her defeat Charles, but she must win society's approval herself, just as he must.

Lady Melford was clearly entertaining several visitors, to judge by the sound of female voices from the first floor that greeted them as they entered the hallway of the elegant terrace house.

The butler showed them straight up. 'The Countess of Dutton, His Grace the Duke of Northminster, Lady Rose Trafford, my lady.'

Their entrance caused a considerable stir and Rose was grateful that Marcus was drawing most of the attention. The arrival of the slightly shocking new Duke—she could almost hear the whispers of *Trade, my dear!*—was clearly exciting for the four ladies who were seated around their hostess's tea table.

They did not seem hostile, more intrigued. Marcus presented such a picture of well-bred, well-dressed respectability that he must seem very different from their mental pictures of a vulgar self-made merchant flaunting wealth and bad taste. Rose wondered how many of the ladies had actually encountered someone from the wealthy merchant classes before. There were men who had made fortunes in India—the nabobs—of course, but they tended to return home to England to retire to country estates, not to plunge into the world of the fashionable *ton*.

Rose remembered three of the ladies from her London Seasons—Lady Spooner, Lady Ffrench and Mrs de Villiers—and committed Lady Wilmington to memory.

When they were seated Aunt Sylvia diverted their attention from Marcus by announcing, 'My niece has come to London to be married.'

'Married? My dear Lady Rose! How wonderful. And who is the fortunate gentleman?' Lady Melford said, with a sideways smile at Marcus.

'The Duke, ma'am,' Rose admitted.

That caused a flurry of exclamations and congratulations, then Mrs de Villiers said, 'Your brother is Lord Wighton, is he not?'

'He is.'

'Indeed.' There was a decided edge of disapproval.

'Dear Rose has been living in the country, very quietly, with her two younger sisters,' Aunt Sylvia said, with an approving nod in her direction. 'She did not feel that her brother's house was at all the place for two impressionable young girls, so at considerable sacrifice to herself has been quite out of society.'

'As it turned out, Chalton Castle, where the ladies have been living, is close to Northminster,' Marcus said, making Chalton sound rather more impressive than it was. 'As we were neighbours, it was almost inevitable that we should meet, and, well, as you see, I fell for Lady Rose and she honoured me with her acceptance,' Marcus said with a modest smile.

The unspoken words, *She would be a fool not to!* hung over the little group, then Mrs de Villiers, a plump beauty who was holding off the ravages of middle age with some success, asked the question the others were probably dying to have answered.

'But you are living with your brother now?' Mrs de Villiers asked. 'I had understood he was out of town.'

'My aunt and I, along with my sisters Chloe and Katherine, are staying at the Duke's house in Grosvenor Square.'

Five pairs of immaculate eyebrows rose with the unity of the front row of opera dancers performing a high kick.

'We thought it safer to have the girls under my roof and I prefer not to leave them unprotected,' Marcus said.

'Unprotected?' Lady Wilmington gasped. 'From what?'

'My brother, who has now returned to London, wishes Chloe to marry a…a friend of his, although she is scarcely out of the schoolroom,' Rose said. 'The man in question is not at all the thing, most dissolute, in fact. It is very regrettable, but we do not think this will be something that can be hidden. We—my aunt, the Duke and I—do not feel that Charles is a fit guardian for two very young girls and this only goes to prove it.'

'I most certainly agree,' Lady Melford said robustly. 'I would not dream of saying so if you had not raised the matter, Lady Rose, but I, for one, would not entertain Lord Wighton, or any of his set, under my roof.'

'There will no doubt be repercussions when he understands that we are firm in our refusal to allow him access to the girls,' Aunt Sylvia said. 'It may even come to a court case. There will be much talk and I would not wish Rose's position to be misunderstood. Nor that of Northminster, either.' She looked around the semicircle of ladies. 'I knew I could rely upon your support.'

'But of *course*,' Lady Ffrench said. 'A most distressing way for you to begin married life, Lady Rose. When is the wedding to be?'

'In ten days,' Marcus said. 'St George's, Hanover Square. Invitations should reach you shortly, ladies. My acquaintance with London society is somewhat limited at the moment—largely to the gentlemen. I am hoping that you will spread the word among your friends who may be somewhat surprised to be invited.'

'But of course. Do you expect Lord Wighton to, er, make trouble?'

'He is certainly not going to be giving the bride away! You think he might disrupt the wedding?'

Marcus sounded amused and Rose had a horrible suspicion that he might actually welcome another confrontation. But not in church, surely?

'Lady Rose is of age; Wighton has nothing to say to the matter,' he added.

The ladies all looked dubious, but Rose wondered if they were not finding this whole situation rather titillating. A merchant duke, a rakehell earl, three young ladies—a perfect scandal broth of delightful gossip.

Delightful, that is, if one is not embroiled in it.

They stayed rather longer than the usual half-hour, but nobody seemed to feel they had outstayed their welcome. The other hostesses on Aunt Sylvia's list that they found at home proved equally welcoming, although Rose was not convinced of the good-heartedness of all of them. Many, she was sure, would have accepted a three-headed sea monster if it had been wearing a ducal coronet and some of the others were simply thrilled to be hearing such delicious gossip which they would lose no time in retelling. Her aunt seemed satisfied, though, and Rose felt she must trust her judgement.

When the barouche drew up outside the Grosvenor Square house Marcus held up one hand to stop the footman who had run down the steps to open the carriage door.

'Would your sisters like to take a turn around the park?' he asked Rose. 'I imagine it will take Charles a while to decide what to do, but when he does, then driving about in an open carriage might then become somewhat awkward for them for a while.'

'Thank you. Yes, that would be very pleasant.' She had been worrying about Chloe, cooped up inside—a change of scene would do her good.

'I will bring them out as quickly as possible,' he said as he helped Aunt Sylvia down, then followed her into the house.

Chloe appeared very promptly, shadowed by a footman who handed her up into the carriage and then lurked discreetly on the front steps once she was seated next to Rose. 'Marcus is trying to persuade Kat that she cannot bring the kitten,' she said.

'What kitten? There was no kitten this morning!'

'The kitchen cat has a litter,' Chloe said with a roll of her eyes. She glanced at the coachman, saw that he and the groom were discussing a loose buckle on the harness, and whispered, 'I think I have been unfair to Marcus.'

'I think so, too, but why have you changed your mind?'

'I asked him why he was helping us and he said that he did not like to see people treated badly by their own family, the ones who should care for them most. I think he must have had a difficult time with his own family, to feel like that, don't you?'

'He was happy at Chalton Castle as a boy,' Rose said, thinking of Marcus at the fishing pool, of how much he wanted to own the castle. 'It was so obvious in everything he said.'

'Yes, but why was he there?' Chloe mused. 'Where was his family? Shh, here he comes.'

'Marcus, where are we going to drive?' she asked as he got in after a word with the coachman and Kat—without a kitten—was safely wedged between her sisters.

'Hyde Park, I thought. It is a little late now for the fashionable parade, but it should be lively enough to be interesting.'

'Oh, yes, please.'

Rose sat back against the squabs, feeling relaxed for the first time in…how long? Since Charles's letter had arrived, she supposed. Although she had not been feeling entirely at ease ever since the Duke of Northminster had ridden into their lives. That had been a different kind of unsettled sensation, she had to admit. Charles's letter provoked anger and fear. Marcus left her feeling on edge in a way that was almost pleasurable.

Is it desire? she wondered, watching him while pretending to study the passing scene. Yes, that certainly, and no wonder it made her uncomfortable. And there was an edge of danger about him which was strange, given that she trusted him with her sisters.

'A penny for your thoughts, Rose,' Marcus said and she realised that she must have been staring at him for at least a minute. 'Or have I a spider on my nose?'

'I was just wondering whether I will see any outfits in the high kick of fashion,' she said, covering her confusion with a laugh. 'I am so far out of touch with the mode that I must rely entirely on Aunt Sylvia and her maid for advice and I would really prefer to form my own opinions.'

'Oh, gowns and bonnets are *boring*,' Kat complained. She had the air of a child who had been forcibly inserted into her pelisse and her bonnet was tied under her chin with rather more firmness than elegance. Neither she nor Marcus had explained how she had been persuaded to leave the kitten behind, but Rose was inclined to award him honours for firm persuasion.

He would make a very good father, she

thought, and then found herself blushing furiously. 'Goodness, it is warm.' She flapped a gloved hand to fan herself.

'Too much tea, I expect,' Marcus said. 'We could go to Gunter's instead of the park and have ices.'

'Ices!' Kat said, bouncing on the squabs.

'The park,' Chloe voted.

'Both,' Rose decided. 'Park first, then ices if everyone is good,' she added with a repressive look at Kat.

'I shall do my best to behave and be a good boy,' Marcus said with an entirely straight face.

Kat gave a hoot of laughter at the thought of an adult promising to behave himself, Chloe giggled and Rose met his mock-innocent grey gaze and swallowed hard. Was he flirting with her, despite the way he had reacted on the stairs? Really, she did not want Marcus to be 'good', but she found she could not understand him at all.

Chapter Twelve

The barouche passed through the gate from Park Lane and then turned southwards. 'Rotten Row is close to the edge of the park,' she explained to Kat, who had never been there. When she had last lived in London her outings were limited to walks in Green Park with her nanny.

'It's a very silly name.'

'From Route du Roi, the King's Road, because it leads to Kensington Palace and was the way the King would travel into London,' Rose explained. 'Now it is a very fashionable place for people to drive, or ride or walk and see their friends and show off their latest fashions. It is very busy—see?'

She recognised a few faces and exchanged bows with other ladies in carriages who obviously recognised her, but who could not place her. Marcus was hailed by several gentlemen who were either riding or driving phaetons or curricles and several stopped for a word.

Marcus introduced his party to them all in the same way. 'Lady Rose Trafford, to whom I am lately betrothed. Lady Chloe Trafford, Lady Katherine Trafford.' To some he added that they would be receiving invitations to the wedding.

All the gentlemen expressed their delight at the news and some sent flirtatious glances in Chloe's direction, but she kept her eyes on her clasped hands in her lap.

'How they do stare,' she said when one particularly bold officer in the uniform of the Horse Guards cantered off after winking at her.

'You are very pretty, so I am not surprised,' Rose said. 'But I am afraid we must discourage gentlemen for a while. It is important that you are perceived as being hardly out of the schoolroom.'

'Why, exactly?' Chloe asked. 'I thought we were going to say that Charles was not a fit guardian for me and that will be the case whether I am seventeen or twenty.'

'Yes. But we will gain much more sympathy from the leading ladies of the *ton* if they believe both you and Kat are very young. Certainly they must be left totally shocked that Charles is suggesting you marry a rakish friend of his.'

Chloe sighed. 'It would be very nice to have pretty gowns and to drive in the park and to flirt a little. In an unexceptional manner, of course.'

'We will see how matters progress,' Marcus said. 'Perhaps by the start of the Season things might be different and you can attend some parties.'

Chloe perked up at that and began to look around again. 'Oh, look! Rose, isn't that Captain Andrewes?' She waved energetically and the tall man in scarlet regimentals on a strapping black gelding reined in, stared and then trotted over.

The coachmen brought the team to a halt again and the newcomer made his bows. 'Lady Rose, Lady Chloe—and young Kat. Goodness, how you've grown!'

The need to make introductions gave something for Rose to do other than stare in consternation at her long-lost love.

'Marcus, may I present Captain Andrewes, a neighbour and old friend of ours in the country.'

'It is Major now,' he said, with a modest smile.

'Of course, I should have guessed. Major Andrewes: the Duke of Northminster. My betrothed,' she added, somehow keeping her voice steady.

The exchange of civilities between the two men, and Christopher's congratulations to Marcus, gave her a chance to look properly at him. He was older, of course, and thinner, as though he had been ill. And then she noticed the black armband.

'You are in mourning? Not… Jane?'

'Yes, I fear so. I was in Vienna, you know, posted as an aide to one of the ministers during the Congress. Jane accompanied me and then fell ill, very suddenly. Some virulent fever. The doctors could do nothing.' He broke off and was silent for a second or so, his jaw tense as he got his emotions under control. 'She died within the month. That was just over a year ago now. You had not heard?'

'We have been living very retired,' Rose said. 'I am so dreadfully sorry.'

'Thank you. I am coming to terms with it

now and my duties keep me busy, which is a blessing. But your happy news—I must felicitate you, Rose. Is this very recent, might I ask?'

'Yes,' she said, finding a smile and managing to look appropriately delighted with her situation. 'We must send you an invitation to the wedding. I do not think I have your direction.'

Christopher produced a card, said he must be leaving to go on duty and cantered off.

'How sad,' Rose said. 'He obviously still feels it very much.'

'Yes. Poor Jane, how awful to be so sick and away from home. You and she were very close once, weren't you?' Chloe said. There was something questioning in her expression and Rose felt a sudden uneasiness. Did her sister know how the news of Christopher's betrothal had affected her? Surely Chloe had been too young to notice any undercurrents. After all, Christopher had not realised how she felt about him and Jane had given no sign of suspecting that her best friend had fallen for the same man she had. But Chloe did look rather pensive, as though she had only just realised her actions might have created an awkwardness.

No, it was just her own sensitivity, reading meaning into every fleeting change of expression. 'Yes, we were very good friends once, but it faded, as is so often the case when people move apart. She was never a very enthusiastic writer of letters and I did not like to intrude. Besides,' she added brightly, 'I would have had nothing in common with the wife of a serving officer, I suppose.'

'It will be good for you to have a friend in London, one from your childhood,' Marcus remarked.

'Oh, I have several acquaintances from when I had my Seasons,' Rose said, seized with a horrible fear that Marcus would start to cultivate Christopher for her sake, thinking she might feel lonely and isolated. 'I have been writing to all of them and I am sure we will soon be receiving calls. Shall we go and have our ices now?'

Marcus directed the coachman to Berkeley Square as the Major's scarlet uniform was lost in the throng along the Row. Rose had been uneasy, he thought. Her responses had seemed brittle, but perhaps it was simply distress over the death of someone she had known and awkwardness over not having heard. It had certainly been unfortunate, putting Major Andrewes in the position where he had to tell her about his bereavement.

Chloe was apparently deep in discussion over the flavours of ice cream with Kat, but he noticed her shooting a quick glance at him, as though she, too, was uneasy about something. He rather thought he would have a look at the Army List when they returned home and see what Andrewes's first name was.

But even if he was Christopher or Crispin, it did not mean he was the man Chloe had been so indiscreet about. And if he was? Marcus told himself that it was none of his business. It was in the past, the man had married someone else and there had been no sign of anything between Rose and the Major other than an old acquaintance. Rose had agreed to marry him and that should be enough.

But she hadn't known that Major Andrewes was a free man again until just now. One who had been in mourning for over a year and who might, now, be considered...available.

Marcus told himself he was making bricks without straw, building a chance meeting between one-time neighbours into something of significance.

'Here we are,' he said with what felt like unaccustomed brightness. The carriage drew up under the great plane trees that bordered the central greensward of the square. 'I am sure Rose has eaten ices at Gunter's before, so she will know this, but it is the custom for you ladies to sit here in comfort in your carriage and for me to organise the refreshments to be brought out to you.'

A waiter ran up with boards on which were listed the ices of the day and promptly threw everyone—except Marcus, who could never resist the pistachio flavour—into a crisis of indecision.

'Strawberry, chocolate or lemon?' Kat almost wailed.

'Brown toast, parmesan or bergamot?' Chloe asked, displaying unusually sophisticated tastes.

'Cherry or orange or peach? I cannot choose,' Rose said.

'As the ladies said. Three flavours apiece, and three scoops of pistachio for me,' Marcus ordered recklessly and hoped that Kat was not prone to sickness in a swaying carriage.

He was rewarded with wide smiles and Kat's declaration that he would make a *very* superior brother-in-law. Their cries of delight when the ices were brought were enough to make him laugh and relax a little as he surveyed them: Kat more than a little sticky, Chloe eating with the daintiness that he had come to associate with her and Rose making no ladylike pretence that she was not indulging herself in a delicious treat.

Her eyes met Marcus's over their raised spoons and she laughed out loud. 'Look at you, Your Grace! I declare you are as bad as Kat. You both have an ice-cream moustache.' She leaned forward and ran one fingertip along his upper lip, then offered it to him.

It was as much as he could do not to draw the slender digit deep into his mouth, to caress it with his tongue, but Marcus managed to give it a quick lick and then made a business of excavating a clean handkerchief for all of them from the pocket in the tail of his coat.

'Time to go home now, I think,' Rose said, still smiling.

It took Marcus a second to realise that she meant Grosvenor Square, his house. She had called it *home*.

That word was still warming him when he went through to the library and took the Army List from the shelf. Yes, here he was: *Major*

Christopher Andrewes, he read. He pushed the volume back into its place.

Andrewes could not have been in love with Rose, he reasoned, or he would have asked her to marry him and she would have accepted him. She had told him wryly about the men who had proposed to her and whom she had refused and none of them sounded like a tall, handsome officer to him. The man had married Rose's friend, a good enough reason for her to hug her wounded heart to herself, and close enough to home for her young sister to have noticed something amiss and guessed the secret.

Marcus began to pace up and down the room in an effort to clear his thoughts. If Andrewes had wanted to contact Rose after the death of his wife, then he had had every opportunity to do so and with the greatest propriety, as they were old friends. But he clearly had not done so, even after a year had passed, and that argued that he had married the woman he loved at the time and Rose's hopes had been in vain.

So he could stop worrying about the Major, he told himself. This was not a case of two young lovers torn apart by circumstance and now able to reunite at last. But did he have to worry about Rose? Was she still in love with her childhood friend? And, if she was, what did that mean for their marriage?

Nothing, he told himself and tried to believe it. People failed to marry their childhood sweethearts all the time and then went on to have perfectly happy marriages to other partners. And yet, he could not put it out of his mind. It was one thing to make a marriage of convenience to a woman whose affections had never been engaged, but something else when she was perhaps still holding the image of another man in her heart. Who would Rose see in her mind's eye when she kissed him? Who would she think of when they were in their marriage bed? What had the sight of her lost love, so close now in London, be doing to her feelings?

Marcus had striven all his life not to be second best, not to let the actions of others hurt him. He had thought his hard-won carapace of confidence and success was thick enough to cope with any situation. He had long ago managed to forgive his father for dying without leaving adequate provision for his family, his mother for sending him away to uncaring relatives. In both cases he had come to realise it had not been their fault. The fact that it still hurt was simply his own weakness and must be ignored.

It was a waste of energy and emotion, he had learned, to hate his father's cousin, the Third Duke, for calling him 'the church mouse' and 'a parsonage charity brat' and packing him off to Chalton, then, at the earliest possible moment, to India as a small and frightened boy.

He had grown up tall and hard and rich, more than capable of making his own way in the world and, if he had been inclined towards revenge, what better vengeance could there be than to assume the title that his cousins had been so proud of?

But somewhere, deep inside, was still that confused and grieving child who had only wanted someone to love him, whose family had abandoned him and who had found a substitute in the serenity of an ancient, ruined, castle and the gruff affection of an old countryman.

Marcus flung himself into the depths of an armchair and brooded. Then he gave himself a mental shake. The reasons he had proposed marriage still stood. He would do his utmost to make Rose a good husband and he was certain she would do her best to be a good wife and duchess. They could be content and that was more than many people could hope for. If the image of another man was still imprinted on Rose's heart then she would be too thoughtful to ever let him realise it. And, in turn, he must never allow her to think he had guessed her heart had once been broken.

Only a coxcomb would demand that his wife fall in love with him under the circumstances. Especially when he was not in love with her. As, of course, he was not. More than a little in lust, yes. But love? No, of course not.

Rose sent Kat to have a thorough wash and change her dress before dinner. 'I think you have even got ice cream in your hair!' she called after her as Kat laughed and ran off to her own bedchamber and the long-suffering maid who was looking after her.

'I am looking forward to the first of my new gowns arriving,' she said to Chloe, who was sitting at Rose's dressing table repinning a curl. 'I had thought myself quite at home in my breeches and working clothes, but now that silks and lace are dangled before me I have to confess that I do not miss them at all.'

'Oh, never mind clothes!' her sister blurted

out, twisting around on the stool to face her. 'I haven't said *thank you*. I should have realised what a sacrifice it is for you to marry Marcus, just to protect me and Kat. You are being so brave about it.'

'Brave?' Rose blinked at her. 'That is non-sense. I am going to marry a kind, decent man. I will be a duchess. Charles will be out of our lives. We need never worry about money again. Whatever am I being brave about?'

'There isn't anyone else you wish you had married? Could marry?'

'No,' Rose said with complete conviction. 'Of course not.'

Thank goodness we encountered Christopher today, she thought.

There had been a corner of her heart that had ached for him, but now she realised that had simply been a romantic dream that had persisted because it had never had expression. If she had been able to weep and wail and tell someone about her broken heart at the time, she was sure she would have almost forgotten him by now. She was truly sad for him, but when she had realised that he was a widower there had not even been the flicker of a thought that now he was free they might one day be together.

'I had come to accept that I was never going to marry and I was enjoying my independence, not yearning for a lover,' she added when Chloe looked perplexed. 'And now I do believe I can keep a large measure of that independence, as well as seeing us all secure.'

'Can you? Marcus will want to make all the decisions, surely?' Chloe turned back to the dressing table and appeared to be engrossed in dabbing cream from a little pot on to her hands. 'That's what husbands do.'

'Not necessarily. Marcus respects my independence,' Rose said firmly and then wondered why she was so certain of that, because it was something they had never discussed. It occurred to her now that the fact that he had appeared to admire her resolution in escaping from Charles and managing their little farm did not mean that Marcus would tolerate her behaving with equal eccentricity once she was his duchess. Perhaps some frank discussion was called for.

Chapter Thirteen

Rose found Marcus in the library, sitting in one of the deep old armchairs, his eyes closed. He was frowning slightly, like a man lost in thought.

'You look as though you are wrestling with some deep problem,' she said teasingly. 'How to solve the national debt? The appointment of the market beadle? The Schleswig-Holstein Question? No, please do not get up.'

Marcus dropped back into the seat and she perched on its arm before she remembered it was perhaps not a good idea to get so close. But she could hardly bounce to her feet at once—it would be too pointed.

'What is wrong?'

'Must there be something amiss for me to want to come and talk with you?' She did not wait for him to reply, but pressed on before she lost her nerve. 'There is something I would like to discuss, however.'

Looking down at him from this position, Rose saw things she had not noticed before—how straight his eyelashes were, how his smile had made the dent beside his mouth deeper on the right than on the left, how the English climate was fading the tan sea voyages had given it and how thick his hair was.

'Your hair is beginning to curl,' she said and incautiously reached to tug one rebellious lock.

Marcus's hand came up and caught her wrist in a light grasp, bringing her hand down level with his mouth. 'Shall I tell my valet to cut it? How ruthless shall I ask him to be?'

'I was not complaining,' Rose protested. His breath was warm on the back of her hand. 'I should like to see the effect of curls, that was all.'

'Should you indeed?' Marcus threaded his fingers into hers.

'Yes.' It came out rather breathlessly. 'Let me go, please.'

'We can discuss your problem just as easily like this.' He made no other move to touch her and his hand stayed quite still, warm and big as it caged her smaller fingers.

Rose took a cautious breath, deciding it was safer—and more dignified—to stay where she was than to try to struggle up. 'We have not talked about how we should go on after we are married. I am accustomed to making decisions for myself, spending my own money—'

'Yes? I do not see the problem. You will have considerably more money, of course.'

'But what will you want me to decide upon? Or, rather more to the point, what will you expect me to surrender to you?'

She thought for a moment that his breathing deepened and she was so close it was hard to miss any movement that long hard body made, but it seemed she was mistaken, because Marcus said lightly, 'Surrender? In what way?'

'From what friends tell me, and from what I have observed, most husbands expect to decide upon everything except what their wives spend their pin money upon and the orders they give to the cook and housekeeper. They say who is and is not acceptable as a friend, where their wives may go, what they do. They read their letters and do not discuss any decisions beyond the purely household ones.'

'Do I appear to be a domestic tyrant to you?'

That was an interesting choice of words. Rose shifted so she could look at him, but Marcus seemed quite serious. 'Most men would not consider it tyranny, simply a husband's role.'

'But I am not most men, my dear Rose.'

Never a truer word... And then, *my dear Rose*?

She frowned a little, puzzled, but Marcus smiled back. 'Unless I know something to the discredit of one of your friends, then I would not dream of interfering, or of reading your private correspondence. I will make my own decisions about my political convictions, my spiritual beliefs and the management of my business, although I am perfectly open to an exchange of views on any of those points. Your own beliefs and convictions are, of course, your own.

'The domestic realm is entirely yours, although I reserve the right to make my wishes known—again, we can discuss the matter should you, for example, wish to paint the entire house purple or to stop serving fish at dinner.'

'What would you say if I did?' she asked, side-tracked into the ridiculous.

'I would say no on the grounds that I was saving you from yourself,' Marcus said. 'We will agree a housekeeping budget and your personal allowance and I would appreciate not receiving any sharp shocks come quarter day. If you need more, you have only to say.

'Your sisters are your affair, but I am fond of them both, so I hope I may be included in planning their future. As for our own children, the most important thing is that they are loved and secure and we must find a consensus on how to achieve that when it arises.' He quirked an eyebrow at her. 'Does that cover your concerns?'

'It does, thank you,' Rose said, feeling slightly winded. It was far more than she had expected and she had anticipated having to negotiate every point. She had not thought Marcus would be a domestic tyrant, but she had accepted the expected loss of many of her freedoms as simply the price she had to pay for their security.

'You do not seem very convinced of that,' Marcus observed.

'Oh, but I am,' she protested. 'If I did not trust you to keep your word, I would never have agreed to marry you. But the more you say, the less I understand why you would want to marry me. It seems that all the benefits are on my side.'

'Indeed?' He was looking very quizzical now, and amused, despite the fact that he was keeping a straight face. This close she could see the way the corners of his eyes crinkled and it made her want to smile back.

'It gives you the convenience of not having to hunt for a wife, but that is all,' she persisted, feeling as though she was poking a stick into a beehive that, at the moment, was quietly buzzing, but if disturbed might be positively dangerous. She wanted him to deny it, tell her there was more, that he desired her. But of course, if he did, she would hardly be sitting here beside him like this—he would be making love to her. 'Oh, and you come to own Chalton Castle sooner.'

'It seems to me,' Marcus said, 'that you are beginning to doubt my sincerity. Convenience is a valuable commodity to a businessman. You are saving me time and money and reducing the risk of a wrong choice of wife. You might argue that the nuisance caused by your brother and the concerns over your sisters' welfare might unbalance that,' he went on when she opened her mouth to protest. 'However, it gives me pleasure to thwart your brother and, other than an increase in domestic security for a while, it will give me little trouble. My lawyers will deal with it all.'

'No, I am not doubting you.' Rose stood up and he released her wrist without a struggle as she moved to another chair. She was conscious of faint disappointment. 'I am simply trying to…'

'To save me from myself?'

'I am not that unselfish,' Rose said tartly. Inside there was a flare of an emotion she couldn't name, but didn't like. 'It is greatly to my benefit to marry you, Marcus, and I should not have been so foolish as to come asking about decisions and your authority and money. Even if you had pokered up and informed me that from henceforth your word was law, I would still have married you.'

'Because of your sisters.'

'Exactly,' she retorted. 'Oh, I do not know why we are having this conversation, we have just gone around in a circle and now we are both thoroughly out of temper.'

'I think I know,' Marcus said slowly. He seemed intent on examining his knuckles where the grazes were hardly healed. 'You are an intelligent woman who has spent a great deal of time carefully assessing situations, weighing up costs and benefits, making hard decisions, and my approach to marriage was one more element to add to your calculations of profit and loss. It is a pity that there are so few women in business, because you would have excelled at it. Before you took that final, irrevocable leap, you wanted to be certain I was your best bet.'

'You make it sound so...so cold and calculating,' Rose said, aghast. 'We agreed that this would be an arrangement of mutual benefit, although I freely acknowledge I have most to gain. But I gave you my word that I would marry you and I am not going back on that, not when nothing that you told me about yourself has changed.'

'Nothing about me, no,' Marcus agreed.

He got to his feet as she was puzzling over what he had just said, so she stood, too, meaning to leave, because she had interrupted him while he was brooding over something here alone.

'I will go and leave you in peace, then.'

'Do not look like that,' Marcus said as she passed him. He sounded almost exasperated.

'Like what?' That hot little flame of something that wasn't quite anger, wasn't exactly hurt, flickered again.

'Patient and resigned. Faintly martyred, if you must know. If you want me to pretend this is a love match and protest my feelings for you and tell you I cannot live without you, then you only have to say so.'

'I… What? Oh, *you*…' She struck out, hitting his shoulder hard enough that he stepped back abruptly. 'Do you take me for an idiot? I do not expect you to have any feelings whatsoever, except for your precious castle.'

The study door banged behind her, but she ignored it in her flight down the hall.

'My lady? Is something amiss?'

Rose skidded to a halt. 'Oh. Heathcote. Er, nothing at all, I just recalled I had left something.' She walked briskly past him and managed not to run up the stairs to her room.

Frost, her maid, was not there, thank goodness. Rose turned the key in the door, plumped down on the bed and tried to sort facts from emotions, feelings from words.

What had gone wrong just now? What had possessed her to flare up and hit Marcus, for goodness sake? She supposed the flaring was obvious enough—nobody would like being told they looked faintly martyred. But something else was amiss. Marcus had been on edge, however well he tried to hide it. He had said that nothing about him had changed, implying that something about her had.

For the life of her she could not think what it might be that was disturbing him or what it meant for the two of them. One thing she did know: she had to apologise for hitting him. Nothing else, though, because he had offered severe provocation, but a lady did not hit anyone unless she was in danger.

But not just yet. She wasn't going back into that room.

He was jealous. Marcus made himself face the fact, unpleasant as it was. He was feeling insecure about Christopher Andrewes and that had led him to insult Rose to the extent that she had hit him.

It had been a good blow and his shoulder still felt it. Clearly digging the vegetable plot had built muscles. He tried not to think about Rose's muscles or anything else about her anatomy, because desire only fogged what was left of his functioning brain.

Not very much of it was functioning on the evidence, he concluded, throwing himself back into the arm chair. He, a wealthy duke who had every reason to believe women did not find him unpleasant to look at or tiresome to be with, was jealous of an untitled cavalry major. To be fair, the man cut a good figure and appeared decent enough, but if he was interested in Rose as a second wife, Andrewes was a master of disguising his emotions.

Jealousy was unpleasant, destructive and humiliating. It meant he was failing to trust the woman who had promised to be his wife and he had allowed her to see that something was wrong. He did not think she could have guessed what the problem was, but she knew there was one. No fool, his Rose.

So, what did a gentleman do under these circumstances? The mature answer was talk frankly to Rose. He could not confess he was harbouring dark thoughts about Major Andrewes, because that would betray Chloe, who had almost let slip his name. But he could apologise for turning what had been a perfectly civil, if exceedingly personal, conversation into something very close to a row. He could ask her whether, if there was some other way to protect her sisters, she would prefer not to marry him.

Marriage to him was the strongest defence, but it wasn't the only option. He could perfectly well afford to set her up in Brussels under an assumed name and to maintain the three young women there until Chloe came of age and Charles was no longer a threat, although she would find it a very lonely existence, he suspected. But it would allow her to get in contact with Andrewes, who she could presumably trust to keep her secret. If there was anything between them, it would have the opportunity to develop.

But he didn't want to do it. In fact, the idea gave him a pain under the breastbone. Marcus made himself face the fact that this wasn't simply a case of having to endure the inconvenience and tedium of spending next Season searching for a suitable bride or concern that it wasn't the safest option for the sisters. He desired Rose, he liked Rose—and he wanted to be married to Rose.

Skulking in here brooding was not going to mend matters. Marcus stood up and went in search of his betrothed.

He found Chloe practising her piano exercises and Kat occupying one end of Aubrey's desk, both she and his secretary with their heads down over their work. He could only hope that Aubrey's efforts were less fanciful than Kat's. There was no sign of Lady Dutton which was a relief, but Marcus was beginning to think he was going to have to ask one of the servants if they had seen Rose when he heard someone banging about in the flower room by the rear door to the garden.

He looked around the door and found her poking foliage into a large vase.

'Oh, for goodness sake! Stand up, will you?' She appeared to be addressing a sprig of myrtle. 'And you, go in there—and stay there,' she threatened some trailing fronds of ivy, which even to Marcus looked highly unlikely to remain where she was putting them. She jammed them in with the aid of some sprays of greenery he did not recognise and then picked up one of the roses that lay beside the vase.

In common with most gardens behind the houses surrounding central London squares, the plot behind Northminster House was not large and possessed only one rose bed. By the look of it his betrothed had plundered every bush in it.

'Ouch!' Rose dropped the flower and sucked her finger.

'Shall I strip the thorns off first?' Marcus offered, pushing the door wide and walking into the room.

Rose spun around. 'I didn't hear you there.'

'No, you were too busy abusing the foliage. I had thought flower arranging a gentle art for the refined female, not a matter of wrestling and cursing and spilt blood,' he said mildly, offering her a clean handkerchief for her pricked finger.

'I was in a temper, which is not a good state of mind for doing anything like this,' she admitted, her attention apparently fixed on dabbing the small drop of blood from her fingertip. 'I must also admit to picking your roses.'

'I had not been out to look at them before. Now we can all enjoy them,' Marcus said and began to strip the thorns off each stem. He held the first out to her and she took it with a faint smile and slid it into the vase.

'It is all staying in place now that you have come to fix it with a stern eye,' she said. 'How lowering.'

'I suspect it is simply that you had enough of the framework in place,' Marcus suggested, handing her two more stems. 'Not that I know anything about flower arranging.'

'But I am supposed to. Aunt Sylvia would be horrified to see this effort. It is one of the skills a young lady is supposed to acquire, like watercolour sketching, playing the piano and embroidering useless articles.'

'I came to apologise,' he said. 'That became a very scratchy conversation—much like this foliage—and I spoke without consideration.'

'Oh. Thank you.' Rose pushed the last flower into the arrangement and stepped back from it, her head tilted to one side as though assessing it. 'I was only doing this because I knew I ought to go and apologise to you, but I wasn't sure what to say. I am not at all certain what the matter was, or what we are both apologising for, to be honest,' she added, looking up at him suddenly with a rueful smile.

'It occurred to me that perhaps we have been too hasty,' Marcus said, feeling his way cautiously into what he was about to suggest.

'Hasty?'

'In agreeing—' He broke off at the sound of an autocratic voice from the hall.

'Rose! Where is the girl?'

'In here, Aunt Sylvia.' Rose pushed the door

wide and her aunt swept in, making the small room decidedly crowded.

'Whatever are you doing?' Lady Dutton raised her eyeglass and studied the flower arrangement. 'This is a dreadful effort. Surely you have been taught better than that?'

'I felt it was rather good, for my first attempt,' Marcus said. 'Now I am quite cast down.'

'*You* did this, Northminster? Tsk.' She reached out, tweaked several stems, gave the ivy a firm push and stepped back. 'There. Balanced. Elegant. This is not a pastime for a gentleman—you might as well take up knitting.'

'You were looking for me, Aunt Sylvia?' Rose asked, cutting across Marcus, who was about to tell the Dowager that he was quite capable of knitting, having been taught years ago by a sailor while becalmed in the South China Sea.

'Yes. For both of you. I have come to the conclusion that what is needed is a ball.'

'A *ball*?' Rose stared at her.

'Yes. Music, dancing. A ball. I should have thought of it before—we must avoid anything that looks in the least hole-and-corner about your engagement. What would have been more natural than to celebrate Northminster's inheritance and your return to London and betrothal in such a way.'

Rose met his gaze and he read in her face an exact image of what his own must be showing: complete dismay.

Chapter Fourteen

'A ball?' Rose repeated. 'Here?'

'Of course not. At Dutton House. To welcome Northminster into the family.'

'But Charles—'

'Will not be invited, naturally.'

'Is there time, Lady Dutton?' Marcus had got his face under control now and no longer looked horrified. 'I assume you intend to hold this ball before the wedding?'

'Next week. Tuesday. I have already set the household to work cleaning the ballroom. We shall be a little short of company, I fear, as many people will still be in the country and it is short notice, so it will not be an absolute squeeze, but I am confident it will be respectably crowded. Now, come along, we must plan.'

They followed her through the hall into the

drawing room and sat mute, side by side on the sofa, while she held forth. One might as well argue with the tide, Rose thought and even Marcus would not be able to do that. What had he been about to say when her aunt interrupted them? Something about being too hasty? Too hasty in agreeing to marry? That would be dreadful.

'Grenadier Guards.'

'What?' she blurted out, startled.

'Really, Rose! I was saying that I am acquainted with the Colonel-in-Chief of the Grenadier Guards. I am certain we can secure their band.'

'That would be excellent,' Marcus said. Under cover of her skirts he slid his hand over hers and gently pinched one finger, silencing her instinctive protest. 'But I think I would prefer to save them for a garden party where they would be heard to the best advantage. A string ensemble for the ball, perhaps?'

Rose sat and marvelled at his self-control while her aunt outlined plans for the decoration of the ballroom—pale azure and white silk draperies in honour of the Northminster coat of arms—the supper—lavish—the arrangements for the ladies' sitting out room—luxurious—the gentlemen's retiring room—not so luxurious that they might be tempted to linger there—and the programme of music...

Marcus's hand remained over hers, big and strong and very calming. A ball *and* a wedding. Could she manage? It seemed so long since she had been out in London society that she had probably forgotten everything—the steps for the dances, the correct depth of curtsies for different ranks, the art of meaningless but pleasant small talk.

'Invitation cards?' she ventured when Aunt Sylvia at last paused for breath.

'They are already in hand. I have spoken to Mr Farthing. Such a helpful and competent young man, Northminster.'

And a very overworked one, Rose thought. Perhaps Chloe could help him. She wrote a very elegant hand and was neat and organised.

As she thought it her sister looked around the door. 'Oh, I am sorry to interrupt.'

'Not at all, my dear. Come in,' Aunt Sylvia said and patted the sofa next to her. She explained about the ball and Chloe's face lit up.

'Oh, may I have a new gown for it?'

'You are not out yet,' Rose said. 'If it was a small reception it might be acceptable, but not a ball, particularly when we are so concerned to fix in everyone's minds the fact that you are far too young to marry,' Rose said, feeling a brute when her sister's face fell. Chloe had worked so hard at the castle, had been thoroughly alarmed over Charles's plans. Now she deserved a treat.

'I presume you intend a select dinner party beforehand, Lady Dutton?' Marcus asked. 'Perhaps Chloe could attend that, suitably dressed as is appropriate for a girl not quite out of the schoolroom?'

'That might be possible, yes. A very simple gown—white, no jewellery, her hair down.'

'Oh, thank you, Aunt Sylvia.'

'I will write to the modiste and order it at once,' Rose said. 'Madame Blanche will be coming here to fit all our new clothes in the next day or so.' When Chloe smiled properly for the first time in days, she added, 'Do you think Mr Farthing might like your help, Chloe? He will have all those invitations to write and address and you have such a neat hand.'

'Yes, of course.' Her sister jumped up and went to the door. 'I will go at once.'

'What a dear child,' Aunt Sylvia remarked

as the door closed. 'So pretty. And so biddable,' she added with a meaningful glance at Rose.

Marcus's hand closed around Rose's fingers as she opened her mouth to protest that, of course, she was *perfectly* biddable.

'Now, I must return home for a few hours to see how preparations are getting on.' Her aunt rose and Marcus did, too. 'I shall return for dinner,' she added as he opened the door for her. 'Thank you, Northminster.'

Marcus returned to his seat. 'Thank goodness you are not *"perfectly biddable"*,' he said in a passable imitation of Aunt Sylvia's voice as he settled himself with one arm along the back of the sofa behind her.

'Really?' All well-bred young ladies were supposed to be meek and obedient.

'If you were, you would all still be trapped with Charles. Besides, a duchess needs to have a backbone.'

'I have one of those.' She put back her shoulders and tipped up her chin. As a child her governess had never had to threaten the use of the backboard to correct her posture.

'And a very graceful one it is, too.'

Something touched her back just in the gap between her hairline and the top of her gown where skin was exposed. A finger, tracing down the vertebrae. *One, two, three…* Then the touch was gone as quickly as it had come. Rose bit her lip to stop the instinctive protest. She wanted his hands on her, she wanted to get closer to him and inhale that elusive scent that teased her nostrils and which she was learning to associate with Marcus. A hint of leather, a hint of Castile soap, freshly ironed linen and, under it all, the intriguing muskiness of male skin.

'Thank you,' she said politely, as though she was unaware of the touch. Did he perhaps want her too, after all? More than any man naturally wanted an available female? No, it was only a fleeting touch to illustrate a compliment that was clearly meant to reassure her.

'And thank you for diverting Aunt from the regimental band,' she said, casting around for something less personal to talk about. 'I really think it would have been overwhelming, even if her rival Lady Yelverton did have the Grenadier Guards at her last ball.'

There was a companionable silence, but Rose could not relax and sit back. Aunt Sylvia's announcement of a ball had added yet another thread of worry to all the others that were knotting in her brain like tangled wool.

'Why hasn't Charles done anything?' she asked abruptly. 'I expected a letter. Or something from a lawyer, or for him to come back threatening us.'

'So did I.' Marcus sounded thoughtful. 'He may not be very intelligent, but Soames Marlowe most certainly is, and I would have expected him to have prodded Charles into some action by now. I have to confess that I wish that he would act, because this makes it difficult to do anything positive to counter him. At the moment all the evidence we have of his intentions are that letter he wrote and I don't think that's enough to go to court on.'

'Yes, and when he came here—which could simply be presented as making a normal social call—you hit him. It would have been better, I suppose, if he had attacked you first.'

'You would sacrifice me, would you, you bloodthirsty woman?' Marcus's snort of laughter made her smile. 'But I agree, a thoroughly irrational attack in a public place with plenty of witnesses would be very helpful.'

Ghastly visions of knives or pistols or hired thugs jumping out of dark alleyways assailed

Rose and she twisted around, reaching for him.
'I never thought. What if he hires men to am-
bush you? Or shoots you from some hiding
place?'

Marcus looked down at her hand that was
flattened on his chest. There was a moment
of stillness when all she was aware of was the
thud of his heartbeat, then, 'I didn't realise you
cared,' he drawled.

'Of course I—' She saw the amusement
warming those chilly grey eyes and pushed
away, using the momentum to stand up.
Wretched man. He was laughing at her, amused
by her concern. 'Of course I care,' she said,
managing to keep her voice steady. 'You are
of no use to me dead, are you?'

She sailed out of the room, not troubling that
the door slammed behind her.

It should have been no surprise that she
hardly saw Marcus in the days leading up to
the ball, Rose thought as she stood patiently for
yet another dress fitting on the morning before.
He had a business to run, all the new responsibilities of his inheritance to wrestle with and
a wedding to prepare for. The fact that when
they met they spoke only of practical matters

told her that they were both still unsettled from that strange day when they had so nearly lost their tempers with each other.

Rose was still not certain what that was all about and worrying about what life would be like with a husband she did not understand was keeping her awake at night in the intervals between fretting over Charles and his intentions.

At least she did not need to worry about her sisters, not while they were safe in the house. Kat was blissfully immersed in her epic story, provided with as much paper as she wanted and encouraged by Aubrey. The rest of the staff spoiled her, too, and the housekeeper had found a box of masquerade costumes so Kat was apt to appear at meals dressed as a Crusader knight swamped by a sagging coat of knitted mail, or as a Cavalier, peering out from under a vast wig. Everywhere she went she was trailed by a tiny bundle of ginger fur and the entire household was becoming used to needle-sharp claws fixing on their ankles.

Chloe spent most of her time, when she was not in dress fittings or driven to the piano by their aunt, in helping Mr Farthing. She seemed to enjoy it and he must have found her useful, because whenever Rose looked into his office she found them one each side of the desk, heads bent over their work.

Rose brooded as she turned, obedient to the dressmakers' murmured requests, or gentle pushes. *Perhaps Marcus and I have nothing in common and that is the problem.*

'There, my lady. The hem is finished.' The chief assistant stepped back, sliding the final pin into the little cushion tied to her wrist. 'Molly, turn the glass so that her ladyship can see.'

Oh. It had been so long since Rose had worn a ball gown that it was a shock to see the woman reflected in the long mirror. The gown was simple, but the effect was complex, she realised. The pale blue underskirt shimmered under the darker blue of the net and both enhanced her eyes. The soft white of the bodice and sleeves were kind to her still-tanned skin as a colder tone would not have been and the cut showed off her figure in a way that was more daring than a debutante's gown would have been, yet which would not seem unsuitable for an unmarried lady.

'That is so beautiful!' Chloe had come in without Rose noticing. 'The filigree gold set of Mama's would look perfect with it. And the high stand of the collar at the back means you

can put your hair right up, with just one ring-
let. And you can wear the pale blue satin shoes
with the little dark blue French heel you bought
the other day.' She sighed happily and Rose
slipped her arm around her sister's waist.

'We have your dress for the dinner,' she told
her. 'I was just going to call you to try it.'

It was pale, of course, and very simple, but
the creamy fabric was silk and the hem and
modest neckline were outlined in a twisting
embroidery of green leaves and tiny roses.

'Thank you.' Chloe beamed at the row of
three dressmakers. 'Now, Rose, we must take
them off and hide them before the men see
them.'

'Men?' Rose queried.

'Well, Aubrey—I mean, Mr Farthing—is
coming to both the dinner and the ball,' Chloe
said airily, but there was the faintest glow of
colour over her cheekbones.

Rose neither commented nor raised her eyebrows. If Chloe was developing a *tendre* for
Marcus's secretary, then comment or teasing
would only make matters worse. She was too
young to form any kind of attachment yet and,
excellent young man as Aubrey Farthing might
be, Chloe might well change her mind when
she came out, she told herself.

* * *

Marcus shifted on the seat of the carriage and ran one hand surreptitiously over the bump in the door pocket that contained the pistol. It was safe enough to be transporting Chloe the few streets to Lady Dutton's house, he concluded as they took a different route from the one he had used that afternoon when he had delivered Kat, who was also going to stay at her great-aunt's home overnight. Neither he nor Rose wanted to leave her at Grosvenor Square without them and Charles's continued, inexplicable, silence was making Rose uneasy.

Both Rose and Chloe sat opposite him swathed in their evening cloaks like a pair of particularly enticing parcels. For both of them—if only Rose could relax—this evening would be a rare treat and he knew better than to spoil the fun they would have revealing their new gowns.

Beside him sat Aubrey, turned out most elegantly thanks to the loan of Marcus's valet and the arrival of a package from his father containing a rather fine India sapphire stickpin for his neckcloth.

The entrance to Dutton House was lit by flaring flambeaux in holders either side of the door and a red carpet ran down the steps and across the pavement. The usual small crowd of gawpers had gathered to view the arrivals and there was a sigh of disappointment when the ladies were seen to be covered from head to toe with no glimpse of gowns or jewels.

Marcus delivered Rose and Chloe into the care of Pomfret, the butler, then lingered to speak to Philips, the head footman, who was by the front door. He had spoken to him and to Pomfret earlier and had warned them that Lord Wighton might try to enter, despite, as Lady Dutton had told them, not being received by her. He also described Soames Marlowe, as best as he could remember him. 'The man has an obsession with Lady Chloe,' he had explained. 'He is quite irrational, however plausible he might appear. No one who is not on the guest list may be admitted.'

Reassured that Philips was on the alert, Marcus went through to the drawing room to wait with Aubrey. As Pomfret put it, 'The ladies may well be some time, Your Grace.'

As it was, they arrived downstairs half an hour before the first dinner guests were due. Lady Dutton swept in first, magnificent in mauve and purple draperies, the famous Dutton diamonds, the inevitable eyeglass and an alarming toque topped with egret plumes. She offered her hand to each in turn, which must have been unnerving for Aubrey, Marcus thought, although he bowed over it with grace.

One eye, magnified by the glass, inspected them both from head to toe. 'Very good. I do like to see evening dress on a man with a shapely leg and a pair of shoulders that need no help from his tailor.' Lady Dutton turned to the door. 'Chloe, my dear.'

Chloe was a picture and Marcus said so, making her blush very prettily. The dress was a masterpiece and Rose had managed to turn her out looking very young, very charming and very much an innocent girl teetering on the edge of a come-out.

She turned from them and said, laughing, 'But you haven't seen Rose yet. Come in, Rose!'

A figure appeared in the doorway and Marcus lost the breath from his lungs. Ivory and periwinkles and a summer's sky wrapped themselves around a slender woman whose hair was confined in a fragile filigree tiara of gold like a Grecian goddess, all except one long curling strand that lay on her right shoulder and across the curve of her breast.

Eyes the colour of sapphires looked back at him from a face that he would have sworn was as familiar to him now as his own in the mirror, and yet had been transformed into something else entirely, because now she met his gaze with her soul in her eyes.

I have been taking her for granted, he thought through a feeling of mild concussion. *I have been working so hard at not desiring her, not alarming her, that I haven't looked. I haven't seen her. I see you now, Rose.*

Chapter Fifteen

Marcus took three strides across the room, took Rose's hand in his, lifted it to his lips and kissed it, wishing it was warm flesh he touched and not the fine kid of her gloves. 'You look ravishing.'

She blushed, the colour washing up under the faint golden glow of her skin, making him want to peel off the glorious silks that enveloped her to discover where the blush ended, or began.

This was Rose, the Earl's daughter, who'd had the guts to rescue her sisters—the woman who'd learned to earth up potatoes to feed them, regardless of blisters; the lady who consented to a marriage of convenience to safeguard the girls. And he'd seen her as a rather desirable female who came with a bundle of interestingly challenging problems and a ready-made family.

And, yes, she was all those things, but she was also Rose, who would be his wife and who looked at him now with something like hope in her eyes. And it wasn't simply that she was seeking his approval for her appearance, he knew that. She had happily ignored the effect on him of her breeches, muddy boots and out-of-date fashions.

Mine, Marcus thought. *Mine. And I believe she is looking at me and thinking the same thing.*

Whatever had made the pair of them scratch at each other had gone as if it had never been.

'Marcus?' she said.

'Yes.' He was not certain what the question was, but the answer appeared to be satisfactory, because her hand, still in his grasp, turned and she squeezed his fingers before he recollected that he was standing gazing at her in front of an interested audience. He let go and stepped back, clearing his throat. 'I expect the other dinner guests will be arriving soon.'

Before Lady Dutton could point out in her usual tart manner that this was a statement of the obvious there was a knock at the front door, the sound of footsteps in the hall, and she gestured them all to stand in a rough arc around her, ready to greet the first arrivals.

Rose was not aware of having eaten any dinner, but she supposed she must have done. She thought, too, that she had made suitable conversation with General Abernathy, an old flame of Aunt Sylvia's who was placed at the head of the table with her on his right, and with Lord Piper on her other side, because they both seemed perfectly happy as the dessert plates were removed.

She appeared to have spent the entire meal trying not to gaze at Marcus, diagonally across from her at the other end of the table, on Aunt Sylvia's right.

What had happened in the drawing room? It was as though Marcus had seen her for the first time and, in that moment, something had passed between them, some message she could not quite interpret. She had said his name, she was not quite sure why, unless it was to be certain that this *was* Marcus and not a figment of her imagination who was looking at her as though she was his heart's desire.

And he had said *yes*. What did that mean?

'Ladies.' Aunt Sylvia was rising to lead them out, leaving the gentlemen to their port.

Rose gave herself a little mental shake and smiled her thanks to the General, who was moving her chair back for her. Further down the table she could see Aubrey doing the same for Chloe. It was time to concentrate entirely on the impression she and Marcus made on the guests, not on whatever had passed between them earlier.

If he feels...affection for me, he will say something, she told herself.

She entered the drawing room as Chloe was obediently making her curtsies to the ladies and bidding them goodnight. She was dragging her feet a little and presenting a charming picture of a schoolgirl allowed to stay up for a treat, but now being sent back to her room. As soon as she was gone the half-dozen female guests gathered around Aunt Sylvia, assuring her of their dismay at the very idea of such a sweet innocent being married off to a dissolute rake.

'Especially one who is a close crony of Wighton's. The man's a disgrace,' pronounced Lady Wilshaw, who revelled in her reputation for saying exactly what she thought on every subject. 'It must be so trying for you, dear,' she added, catching sight of Rose.

'Very,' Rose agreed. 'It is most worrying, but the Duke assures me his lawyers have the matter in hand and we have every hope he will be appointed guardian for the girls.'

Some of the other ladies, with rather more tact, turned the conversation to the wedding and asked Rose about her trousseau and their plans for Northminster Castle. Other than Mrs Abernathy wondering innocently whether Marcus's trading company would be furnishing all the hangings in interesting Eastern fabrics at bargain prices, this proved a safe topic of conversation until the gentlemen joined them, just as the string orchestra could be heard tuning up in the ballroom.

With a glance at the clock Aunt Sylvia assured her guests that they would be perfectly comfortable where they were until they were ready to enter the ballroom and chivvied Marcus and Rose out to join her to form a receiving line. 'Because there is always someone who is unfashionable enough to arrive at the exact hour on the invitation,' she explained.

An hour later, released from their posts at Lady Dutton's side, Marcus and Rose entered the ballroom. He was feeling rather calmer now, probably, he told himself, because he was becoming used to this new, elegant Rose. Over dinner he had convinced himself that he had imagined the look she had given him earlier, because he kept catching her darting glances down the table at Chloe, not at him. Now she showed no sign of wanting to cling to his arm or gaze into his eyes while asking enigmatic questions. It had been a desire for approval of how she looked, that was all. This was the first large social event she had attended since before she had fled to Wiltshire and he hoped he had appeared suitably impressed.

Suddenly Rose clutched at his arm.

'What's wrong?'

'Can you dance?' she whispered urgently. 'I never thought to ask.'

'I can. Even merchants have the opportunity, you know. The East India Company insists all its young gentlemen have a bare minimum of social graces. I am not going to show you up.' He spoke more harshly than he meant, but the memories were just that—harsh—and jolted him back to the draining heat of a Calcutta evening and the dancing master rapping at his ankles with his long cane as he trod on the foot of his partner for the tenth time that lesson.

'Farm boy' the other griffins called him, mocking his lack of social graces after years spent happily running wild at Chalton. He was always the last to be picked as a partner when the whole group of them—gangling, spotty, sniggering adolescents—were forced to behave like little gentlemen. He had hidden his feelings at the sneers and coarse jokes when he had to play the lady's part and put up with the mock swooning from his partners when he took the male role.

And then Marcus grew into his feet and learned to use a combination of his fists and his intelligence to put an end to the bullying.

But the sight of a dance floor always brought back those memories until he could relax into the music and any suggestion that he could not dance well triggered an instinctive defensive reaction.

'Of course,' Rose said, but they were surrounded before she could finish whatever she had been going to say.

Young gentlemen begged Lady Rose for the honour of a dance, older men he had only met in the receiving line ten minutes before wanted to talk to him. It was amazing, he thought wryly, what a difference life as a duke was compared to his experience as a wealthy merchant with exactly the same pedigree. He could see his partners, Arnold Gregg and Aubrey's brother Richard, on the other side of the room and wished the three of them could retreat to the library and talk business.

Rose was already being led into a set, presumably by someone who didn't snap her head off when she asked about his dancing abilities. He set himself to circulate, making new acquaintances, greeting old ones, forging diplomatic links for the forthcoming battle with Lord Wighton.

As he circulated he kept an eye on Rose, whose own ability to dance elegantly had not been diminished by isolation in a crumbling castle, it seemed. She looked ravishing and was smiling up at her partner. Marcus might be keeping an eye on her, but she was showing no concern about where he was. He positioned himself where he could watch her and intercept her at the end of the set. As her betrothed it was perfectly respectable for him to dance more than twice with her and he fully intended to do so.

He wanted her in his arms where everyone could see them—*and* where they could not be seen, but that must wait. He wanted to hang a large notice around her neck that read *mine* and, even as he thought it, he smiled ruefully at himself for wanting to behave like a farmyard cock, wanting to strut his plumage in front of his favoured hen and quite willing to show his spurs to any rival.

Rose had agreed to be his and everyone knew it. And then, as he watched her laughing as she and her partner danced down the line, he remembered her questions the day they had that almost-row. She did not *want* to be his or any man's property. She had agreed to marriage for her sisters' sakes and she had questioned him, testing the boundaries of her freedom.

If he wanted her to grow to love him as he loved her, he was going to have to—

Marcus's thoughts juddered to a halt. *I love her?*

Beside him someone—what was his name? Ah, yes, Sir James Frogley—stared at him and Marcus realised that he had been able to carry on a conversation of sorts, watch Rose and wander into mental quagmires, all at the same time, but now he had lost the thread entirely.

'I beg your pardon, I've just remembered something urgent I have to speak to my secretary about,' he said, snatching at the first excuse that presented itself as he caught sight of Aubrey.

'We should start to take a regular walk around, as we agreed. Check that they are as watchful on the doors as instructed,' Marcus said when he caught up with him.

'Yes, sir. I will do that now, shall I? I'll check on the young ladies' rooms upstairs as well, just to be on the safe side, and then repeat it every half-hour. You will be wanting to dance with Lady Rose.'

That was true enough. Aubrey slipped away like an eel through the throng just as the musicians drew their bows across in a final flourish. Marcus moved swiftly, cut neatly in front of an officer in magnificent dress uniform and caught Rose as she came off the floor.

'My dance next, I believe.'

'Yes, of course,' she said, looking slightly chastened. 'I should not have accepted any before you had the opportunity to reserve the ones you wanted.'

He had not meant to sound as though he was rebuking her. 'Nonsense, you may dance with whom you choose.' Now he sounded merely condescending. What the devil was the matter with him?

Love, and you weren't expecting it, said an inner voice as he led Rose back on to the floor. People were watching them now After all, they were the betrothed couple, Lady Dutton's guests of honour.

'It is a waltz,' Rose said as he glanced around the floor to see whether country dance sets were forming.

She, at least, had had the wit to look at her dance card, Marcus though savagely as he gathered her into the appropriate hold, but presumably her brain wasn't addled by love. Or was it the fact that he hadn't realised how he felt about her that was addling him? Whatever it was, he needed to think about what he was doing now, with Rose in his arms.

Then the music started up and they began to move and everything slid into place. The perfect woman, here in his arms. Beautiful music, her scent drifting up to him, the perfume of warm female skin, jasmine blossom, Rose. She was the ideal height for him, Marcus thought as he drew her in a little closer and then swept around into a turn at the end of the ballroom. She was perfect.

He should talk, make polite conversation, of course, but this was too magical for words and he kept dancing in silence, Rose seeming to follow his lead without conscious thought.

Making love with her would be like this...

Marcus was angry with her, Rose thought as they swept around another turn, her skirts swishing against his legs. She had questioned his ability to dance and then she had rushed off with the first man to offer himself as a partner. No wonder he wasn't talking to her.

He could certainly waltz beautifully and, if truth be told, she didn't want to talk, only to be held like this and feel the way his muscles moved so smoothly, so strongly, inhale the scent of clean male skin, a spicy note that must be his soap and a certain something that she couldn't describe but which simply said, *Marcus*.

Falling in love when it was not reciprocated was a miserable experience, she decided, fastening an extremely bright smile on her lips. Worse, she and Marcus seemed to strike sparks off each other because of the smallest things now. Perhaps he was regretting his offer and the decent thing would be to withdraw from the engagement.

On the other hand, she would walk barefoot over broken glass for her sisters and humiliating herself by marrying a man who didn't love her couldn't be as painful as that. Could it?

'We have stopped,' Marcus said.

Rose blinked up at him. So they had. The music had stopped, too, and when she looked around she could see other guests looking at them with smiles on their faces, or doting looks, or, in the case of some of the younger men, expressions of faint nausea.

Marcus kept hold of her hand and walked up to the string ensemble, who were rearranging the music on their stands. 'Another waltz, if you please.'

'It's supposed to be a gavotte,' Rose whispered after a quick glance at her card, but the leader was already turning away and the musicians had raised their bows.

'It will confuse people,' she said as they returned to the centre of the dance floor. 'There will be young ladies who haven't been approved to waltz—'

'I am sure they'll work it out,' Marcus said. 'And if they don't and they want to be daring and carry on, they can always blame me.'

'But—'

'We need the practice, I'm sure,' he said vaguely, whirling her into a scandalously dramatic spin, then, as she was gathering her balance and her wits, he looked down and gave her a smile so warm and intense that she lost control of both balance and wits and tripped over his feet.

'You see?' Marcus said, gathering her up firmly and sweeping on. 'More practice required.'

The waltz was followed by the postponed gavotte, so they danced that, then, before Rose had the chance to protest that she was out of breath, a set of country dances.

'We really must stop and take other partners after this,' she said when they came to a halt at the top of a set and another couple danced down between the two rows of dancers.

'Must we?' How such a big, tough man managed to look wistful Rose had no idea, but it made her want to cry, even though she knew perfectly well he was teasing her and deserved a sharp rap over the knuckles with her fan.

'Yes,' she said severely, just as he took her hands and they sidestepped rapidly down the room. 'In fact,' she gasped as they reached the end, 'I am going to sit out the next set, drink a large glass of lemonade and—What's wrong? Look—over there.'

By the entrance there was a disturbance, people drawing back, exclaiming, staring.

'Hell,' Marcus said. 'Stay here.' He took a step and then stopped as the dancers parted to reveal the figure of Kat in her nightgown, feet bare, hair sticking out in tight braids, her face screwed up as though she was holding back tears with an effort.

'Rose! Marcus!'

'Here, darling.' Rose ran to her and fell to her knees. 'What is wrong? Did you have a nightmare?'

'No,' Kat said furiously. 'Don't be *silly*. It's a man and he's got Chloe and he's killed Mr Farthing up on the landing.'

Chapter Sixteen

'Stay here,' Marcus ordered and pushed his way towards the doors.

'Stay here,' Rose said to Kat as Aunt Sylvia hurried across the floor to them. 'Aunt, please keep her with you and have someone send for a doctor.'

'Sir Charles Willoughby's here.' Her aunt knelt down, draperies flowing around her, and gathered Kat up. 'Lord John, find Sir Charles and—'

Rose was running after Marcus and heard no more. *Chloe. And Aubrey. Surely not dead. Surely?*

She reached the foot of the main stairs in time to see Marcus stop abruptly at the top and then vanish into the shadows of the landing that bowed out to form a balcony overlooking the hallway. When she reached the same spot she saw him kneeling beside a sprawled figure, clearly male. There was no sign of Chloe, but there was a great deal of blood visible, even in the dim light.

'Is he dead?' Somehow she kept her voice steady.

'No. It's a head wound and they bleed like the devil,' he said, pulling out a handkerchief and beginning to bind Aubrey's head. You shouldn't be here, Rose.'

'Now is not the time to come over all protective,' she retorted as running feet came pounding up the stairs behind them. From somewhere below a voice cried, 'Come back here this moment, Kat!'

Her little sister arrived at the top of the stairs on the heels of Sir Charles Willoughby, physician by Royal Appointment. He had probably not had to deal with anything like this for years and he had no medical bag with him, but he went down on his knees in the gore alongside Marcus without hesitation. Marcus turned and said something urgently to a footman.

'Kat.' Rose pulled the child to one side, keeping between her and the sprawled figure of Aubrey. 'He isn't dead, but he can't tell us what happened. Can you?'

Kat took a deep breath. 'Chloe was out here, watching from between the banisters. I came out, too, but she told me I must go back to bed, but I hid in that so I could listen to the music.' She pointed to an elaborately carved camphor-wood cupboard near the start of the corridor leading off the landing.

'And then after a bit, Mr Farthing came up and saw her and laughed and they did a dance and then he said he had to go downstairs, so he did. And then this other man came. He didn't see me, but he asked Chloe if he could dance with her and she said yes, so they did, too, and then he tried to drag her back down there, towards the bedchambers, and she started to struggle and he put his hand over her mouth and I think she bit him, but I couldn't see because I came out and kicked his ankle very hard and shouted—'

She broke off as Richard Farthing, Aubrey's brother, came up the stairs, taking them two at a time.

'Breathe,' Rose told her, catching her hands. 'That was so brave of you. What happened then?'

'I kept shouting but the music was so loud and then Mr Farthing came running up the stairs and the man took something out of his pocket and hit Mr Farthing on the head very hard. And then he pushed me and I fell over and landed against the cupboard and all the breath was knocked out of me and by the time I could stand up again, they'd gone.' She looked at Rose, her eyes wide, her face screwed up with the effort not to cry.

'You have been *wonderful*, Kat. Did you hurt your stomach?'

Kat rubbed it. 'No. I'm all right, but he's got Chloe.'

'We'll find her.' Marcus came over and crouched down beside them. 'Thanks to you, Kat. Which way did he go?'

Kat pointed down the corridor. 'That way, the way he came.'

'Up the back stair? How the devil did he get in?' He shook his head, 'That can wait. What did he look like, Kat? Can you remember?'

'He was wearing clothes like you.'

'A gentleman, not a servant?'

'Yes.' Kat nodded impatiently. 'He had a silk waistcoat—I felt it when I grabbed hold of him to kick him.' She narrowed her eyes at

Marcus. 'He was shorter than you, a bit, and his hair was brown and he had a big nose, like the Duke of Wellington has in his pictures. He wasn't ugly but he wasn't very handsome. He sounded like a gentleman at first, when he asked Chloe to dance, but he used some dreadful words when we fought him.'

'Marlowe.' Marcus glanced at Rose, his lips tight. 'You, Kat, are a marvel and I am very proud to have you as a sister,' he said warmly. 'Mr Farthing is going to be all right, although he'll have a dreadful headache.'

Rose looked around and realised that footmen were carrying Aubrey towards a bedchamber, his brother and Sir Charles following. Her aunt's housekeeper, with maids in attendance, was listening to the orders the surgeon was giving and from the hall below she could hear Aunt Sylvia's voice.

'Yes, most alarming. It was a housebreaker who has stuck down the Duke's secretary. So dreadful, but the poor man is being taken care of and the criminal has fled. Supper is being served!'

'Aunt Sylvia's carrying on,' Rose said, startled.

'Of course. She doesn't want it known that

Chloe has been abducted. That may save a scandal when we get her back.'

'We will, won't we?' Rose saw her own maid waiting to one side. 'Frost, please take Lady Katherine to her room. I think she needs a warm drink and tucking up. Will you stay with her, please? Go with Frost, Kat, and we'll go and get Chloe back. Marcus knows who took her.' She gave her a hug and a kiss.

Kat looked miserable, but she went obediently. She was too intelligent not to realise she would only be in the way, Rose thought.

Pomfret, the butler, was talking to Marcus. 'The garden room door was forced, Your Grace.'

'Send to Northminster House. Have my tiger harness my best horses to the curricle and come here with an overnight bag for me. While I am waiting—' He broke off as Philips the footman ran panting up the stairs.

'Your Grace, I found a couple in the mews—they'd crept in for a bit of a… Well, they saw a man dragging a young woman out and he bundled her into a chaise and took off down Park Place. He says he *thinks* it turned north up St James's Street. A yellow chaise with dark panels—not black, the girl said—and a pair of greys in harness. I sent George running after to see if he could find anyone who saw them turn.'

'Good man. Where's Pomfret—?'

'He has gone to order your curricle,' Rose said and hurried down the corridor towards her bedchamber, catching one of the maids on her way. 'Quickly, I need help to change and to pack.'

She had brought a walking dress with her to wear in the morning. Now she scrambled into it while the girl ran to borrow a nightgown and a portmanteau from her aunt's room. Rose added the hairbrush and toilet things she had brought with her, flung her cloak around her shoulders and ran out again.

Marcus was still on the landing, keeping clear of the guests, she suspected, but Aunt Sylvia had joined him.

'Here, take this, you'll need money.' She thrust a roll of notes into his hand, then saw Rose. 'Good grief, where do you think you are going, child?'

'With me,' Marcus said. 'Rose can deal with anything and Chloe will need her when we find her. Tell people I have taken her home because of the incident.'

Aunt Sylvia gave an abrupt nod, then turned to Pomfret. 'Fetch Lord Dutton's duelling pistols and a supply of shot.'

'And the pistol from the door pocket of my town coach,' Marcus added as the butler hurried down the stairs.

It took surprisingly little time for the curricle to arrive. The tiger, a skinny youth, handed the reins to Marcus and scrambled up on to his perch behind, taking Rose's bag with him. 'All stowed safe along of yours, guv'nor.'

Philips, who had found the courting couple from the lane, ran up with a younger lad in livery. 'This is George, the under-footman, Your Grace. He says they did turn north. You tell, His Grace, George.'

'Found a gentleman sitting on the steps outside Brooks's Club cursing and swearing, Your Grace. Said the chaise took the corner so fast it knocked him into the gutter. Says it had maroon-coloured panels which he could see because of the flambeaux in front of the nearest house and there was a crest on the door. He said he was so mad he stared after it and it turned left along Piccadilly. I hailed him a cab, Your Grace, and got him in.'

'Well done.' Marcus sent coins spinning to both footmen and sent the pair of chestnuts off towards St James's Street. 'With any luck we'll find someone who saw them at the Hyde Park turnpike gate, but my money is on them turning northwards there and making for the Edgware Road.'

'It is Charles's chaise, I think.' Rose curled her fingers firmly around the side rail. 'They would be turning right and heading for London Bridge if they were going to Wighton. Is he taking Chloe to Gretna Green?'

'Anywhere across the border would serve Marlowe's purpose, but all he needs to do is keep her away from us for a night and that will have served his purpose of compromising her.'

'That isn't important, we can think up some story,' Rose said. 'But, Marcus, what if he… he forces her?'

'No time,' he said with a certainty she hoped she could believe. 'We're probably only an hour behind him and by the time he's stopped at an inn and taken a room and somehow dealt with a screaming, struggling female who is quite capable of taking his eye out, however demure she looks, he won't have the opportunity.'

He reined in as they reached the junction

with Oxford Street and leant down to call over
a link boy who was loitering outside a coffee
shop.

'Drivin' like the devil? Aye, guv'nor, straight
up the Edgware Road he went.' He snatched the
coin Marcus sent him out of mid-air as their
curricle took the turn.

'The traffic will be better soon if he keeps
heading north,' Marcus said.

'Unless it's a ruse?'

Marcus shook his head. 'They had no way
of knowing that they had been observed and
that the alarm would be raised so quickly. With
Aubrey unconscious they will think they've
got clean away, with us expecting them to take
Chloe to Wighton.'

The keeper at the first gate on the Edgware
Road remembered the chaise with dark panels. 'An hour ago, near enough. Bought a ticket
through to Watford, sir. Nice pair in the traces,
but in a bit of a sweat, though the postilion was
taking it fairly easy when they went off, sir.
Thank 'ee,' he added.

'You'll be out of small change at this rate,'
Rose said, trying to make a joke of it and aware
her voice was wavering all over the place.

'Harry will have a stash of coins,' Marcus said, raising his voice to reach the tiger perched up behind.

'Aye, sir,' said the lad. 'Enough to get us to Edinburgh if we have to.'

Rose gasped, then told herself not to let her nerves get the better of her. That had only been a figure of speech, hadn't it?

'We'll get them,' Marcus said calmly. 'You don't think I'll let anyone hurt my little sister, do you?'

'Is that how you think of her?'

'Of both of them. You do realise I'm only marrying you to claim Chloe and Kat, don't you?' She saw his smile as he drove, his gaze fixed on the road ahead, just visible in the dying light.

'You had sister of your own, didn't you? I remember you told me her name.'

'Yes, I did once. Penelope.'

He sounded quite dispassionate and Rose glanced up at his profile, although she could hardly make it out now they were clear of the lights of London.

'And you went to your cousin, the Third Duke?'

'My father's cousin. Yes.'

She could hear the door being closed on the topic very clearly, but ignored it. 'To Northminster Castle?'

'No. To Chalton. Out of the way, somewhere I didn't cost money to keep or require effort to look after.'

'That was unkind. You must have missed your family so much.'

'I did at the time. Now I do not remember them, not very clearly.'

'How did you learn, though, miles from anywhere, living with an unlettered countryman? You must have understood mathematics and have had a grasp of good English if you joined the East India Company.'

'The vicar at Chalton Magna. He taught me in return for produce from the castle smallholding—and quite a few poached pheasants and hares, I suspect. He knew my maternal grandfather was a clergyman, too, so I think he felt he should help.'

'How old were you?'

'Ten, when I arrived there.'

Rose thought of Kat at ten and had to swallow the lump in her throat. Boys might not show their feelings as much as girls, but that didn't mean they had none. Her heart went out to the child he had been, bereaved, parted from the remainder of his family, unwanted by his relatives and thrust into a strange world. But, by pure good fortune, Chalton had been a sanctuary. No wonder he yearned for it back and no wonder he needed a family.

Marcus wanted her castle and her sisters as his own.

And all he has to do is marry me. Well, I love him, so I will do whatever I can to make him happy and perhaps, one day, he will come to feel more than affection and some desire for me.

Thankfully, the June night was fine and clear and there was a moon, and the horses were intelligent and steady as Marcus drove on through the night, controlling the sick apprehension in his gut by concentrating on his driving.

He had promised he would take care of Chloe and Kat and he had failed because he had been complacent and had underestimated their enemies. Now Aubrey was injured and Rose frantic, however well she hid it, and Kat was frightened. He tried not to think about how Chloe, delicate, modest Chloe, was feeling.

Watford, and a change of horses was behind them and at the last turnpike the keeper reported the primrose and maroon chaise had a ticket that could take them through to Bletchley. They'd not make that tonight.

Beside him Rose was silent. She needed rest, he knew that, just as he knew perfectly well that she'd refuse to stop for more than a change of horses.

He made himself focus on the road ahead and, with the part of his mind left free, to contemplate the nature of their enemy.

Wighton was negligible. Spiteful, spoiled and weak, he wouldn't have the brain for elaborate plots or evasions. But Soames Marlowe was quite another creature. He was intelligent, cunning and without any morals that Marcus was aware of. His only weakness appeared to be his ambition to be accepted by the *ton* and to acquire the trappings of a gentleman.

Marcus steadied the pair as they took the hill up into St Albans so he could join the ancient line of Watling Street and then remembered something. He had been playing cards in a hell off St James's and Marlowe had been there, boasting to anyone who'd listen about the estate he'd just won at dice off some gullible mark.

'A very neat little place,' Marlowe had crowed. 'Just near Harpenden.'

And Harpenden was about five miles beyond St Albans. Marlowe didn't need to make a run for the border, he just needed to take Chloe to his house in the country and keep her there for a short while and she would be utterly compromised. They wouldn't even need to go to the trouble and expense of obtaining a special licence, they'd reason—Chloe would be only too ready to marry to save her good name.

Little did they know Chloe, Marcus thought. 'Rose, I think I know where he's taking her.'

Beside him Rose sat up straight from the doze he suspected she'd fallen into. 'Tell me.'

'The bay's pecking, sir,' Harry called as he was explaining what he had heard.

'Damn.' Marcus reined back and the tiger jumped down and ran to the horse.

'Stone, sir.' He produced a hoof pick and worked for a minute. 'That'll do until St Albans—not beyond, though.'

An hour later and they were driving north again, after a change of horses at the Peahen in the centre of St Albans.

'And a more ill-matched pair I've yet to en-counter,' Marcus said, checking yet again the tendency of the slightly smaller horse to drift off to the right. 'Still, not far to go now. I'll ask at the inns in Harpenden, someone will know where Marlowe lurks.'

It was all going well, despite the horses, and they crossed Harpenden Common at what Mar-cus estimated to be five in the morning, the glimmer of lights in the town just visible ahead as the inhabitants began to wake and go about their business.

There was no warning as a great antlered body flung itself out of bushes by the road, right under the noses of the horses. They pan-icked, although he could have held them if the smaller horse had not entangled itself with its partner. One of them had a leg over the traces and then they both went down, tilting the cur-ricle at an impossible angle into the ditch.

Marcus dropped the reins and whip, grabbed hold of Rose. 'Jump!' he yelled at Harry and launched himself off the seat.

Chapter Seventeen

'Rose?'

Rose opened one eye and peered hazily up at the face so close to hers. 'Ouch,' she ventured as Marcus came into focus.

'What hurts?' he asked in a voice that sounded unnaturally controlled.

'My…posterior. Otherwise…' She waggled one foot, then the other, then her hands. 'Pull me up, nothing's broken.'

Marcus got an arm behind her and pushed her into a sitting position, then when she nodded, stood and hauled her to her feet. She felt rather unwieldy, like a sack of coal, because nothing was working quite as it should, but nothing was very painful either.

'Are you all right?'

'By some miracle, yes.'

It was getting lighter now and she could see the tiger working with the horses, cutting free the entangling traces.

'And you, Harry?'

'Nothing broken, sir,' he called as he led both horses free.

'What *was* that?' Rose asked as Marcus prowled around her, checking her hands, making her raise her arms and bend her legs.

'A stag. Fallow deer. Can you ride? Now, I mean, and bareback, behind me.'

She would have ridden a giraffe if that was what it took to keep on Marlowe's trail. 'Of course.'

The wreck of the curricle was far enough into the ditch to leave the road clear, the tiger managed to scramble down to retrieve the valises and within ten minutes they were riding on, with the lad and the bags on one horse and Rose behind Marcus on the other.

The innkeeper at the Red Lion, the first inn of any size they came to, rubbed his eyes at the sight of them, but Marcus's card, passed over with a glint of coin, got his attention. Yes, he knew about young Mr Halsey losing Elm House to some London gent a while ago. Not that the new owner ever came there—word was he would sell it, which was a good thing because, as it stood, there was no employment for local people, not even a caretaker employed.

Yes, it was easy enough to find, he added when Marcus interrupted the lament about absentee owners. 'Just carry on along for half a mile and turn to the left by the big old holly tree, go past the horse pond with the bulrushes and the gates are on the right.'

And, yes, he'd get someone out to pull the curricle out of the ditch, soon as maybe, he called after them as Marcus urged the unhappy carriage horse on along the main street.

'That's good news,' he said over his shoulder as they went. 'No resident staff there and I can't believe he took anyone beyond perhaps your brother in the chaise—no room.'

'The chaise is Charles's, so I assume the postilion is, too. But he might have sent servants on ahead.'

'That's true. Harry, have you got the pistol from the carriage?'

'I have, sir.' He patted his belt.

'Try not to kill anyone.'

'Aye, sir.' This time Rose could see the lad

was grinning. He thought this was a great adventure.

They found the holly tree and the horse pond and then the gates, closed between tall brick pillars, but not locked, Harry found when he dismounted. He dragged one open, led his horse through and looked up. 'Open or closed, sir?'

'Closed. And see if you can find something to wedge them. If Marlowe gets past us, that'll hold him up.'

Rose shifted her position to ease her bruised bottom and wondered why she felt so calm, then she realised it was because of the man in front of her, whose strong back was shielding her. They were going to rescue Chloe because Marcus was determined upon it and he wouldn't let them down, either of them. She rubbed her cheek against his shoulder blade and, as if in reassurance, he put one hand over hers where she clasped his waist and said something.

'What did you say?' Rose leaned closer— they had to be very quiet now. She thought it was, *'Courage, Rose darling.'*

'Never mind,' he said, so low she hardly caught the words. 'It's not important now.'

Not important? *Men! This one in particular...
Darling?*

If he meant it, that changed everything, but
if it was just said to soothe her, reassure her,
then it was meaningless.

The drive curved and there was a glimpse
of chimneypots ahead through the trees. Marcus reined in, threw one leg over the horse's
neck and slid to the ground, then held up his
hands to help Rose dismount. No lingering, no
caress, she noted.

'Harry, take off your jacket, rumple your
hair up and then scout around, see if you can
find the stables and see what's there. Careful
now. If you're seen, you're just a local lad out
for mischief.'

The tiger shed his distinctive jacket with its
horizontally striped front, scrubbed one hand
through his hair and set off through the shrubbery.

'What did you say just then?' Rose whispered.

'No idea, I forget.' Marcus looked down
at her and she wondered how she had ever
thought those grey eyes cold. It was as though
someone had struck sparks from flints. What-

ever he was thinking, feeling, it was not un-important.

'One big old carriage and the chaise, sir. No riding horses.' Harry appeared as silently as he'd left and Rose swallowed the words on the tip of her tongue. This was neither the time nor the place for the conversation she wanted to have with Marcus, even if she could find the courage.

'There's smoke from a chimney at the back—I reckon it's the kitchen. Shall I get in a bit closer?' The tiger was clearly enjoying himself immensely, Rose could see, even through a wave of dizziness that made her want to sit down on the nearest log. She was so tired, so anxious and so confused.

'Yes, I think so.' Marcus watched the lad vanish, then turned back to Rose. 'I can't lie to you, Rose, I realise that now. You don't have to—damn, this is not the place for this.'

I don't have to what? Worry? Marry him?

Harry reappeared, looking decidedly pleased with himself. 'A cook in the kitchen and a maid and what looks like a groom and a vicar, would you believe. Looks sick as a dog, he does.'

'What's the betting that's your little friend Cass from Lambeth Palace? Charles said he was the one who told him you were in London. They've brought him along to perform the ceremony, no doubt.'

'The wretch,' Chloe muttered.

'There was someone in the stables this time, just the one,' Harry went on. 'I looked round the side of the house so I could see the front and there's another groom by the door, sitting on the step and smoking a pipe. Look-out, I reckon. So I went back and round the other side and there's those big glass doors and some paving and one of them was a bit open and I could hear voices. Two, maybe three. Gentry. No woman's voice.'

'Right. I'll go and listen at those doors. Harry, you come and keep an eye out. Rose, you stay here.'

Marcus, moving almost as silently as the tiger, vanished with him into the shrubbery and Rose stared after them.

The man she loved, the man whose feelings for her were completely impossible to discern, was creeping through the undergrowth armed only with a pistol and supported by one skinny lad and intending a rescue in the teeth of what—half a dozen or more men? And she was sitting here just waiting like a feeble little miss in a fret about her feelings. It was time that she found the backbone that had supported her when she had taken the girls away from Charles.

Rose checked that the horses were secure, then ducked under a branch and found the path the others had trodden through the undergrowth. After a few yards it went off to the right, but she kept straight on to where more light showed where the shrubbery met the carriage sweep at the front of the house.

When she peered through the branches, thankful for her drab-coloured walking dress, she could see the sentry at the front door. He'd made himself very comfortable and he did not look particularly alert, which was reassuring, but next to him, propped up against the wall, was a shotgun.

She stepped back and began to skirt around towards the side, blessing the absence of gardeners to keep the shrubbery in check. Above her head something creaked and she looked up through a lattice of branches.

Chloe. Chloe leaning out of a first-floor window.

Rose stepped out of cover and even at that

distance heard her sister's gasp. 'Shh!' she hissed.

Chloe leaned further out and whispered, 'Locked in. Safe so far.'

Rose almost sat down on the grass with the sheer relief of it. She had kept telling herself that Marlowe had abducted Chloe out of a desire to force the marriage, not because he was consumed with lust for her, but that didn't mean that a man so unprincipled wouldn't take advantage of a young woman in his power.

'How many men?' Rose whispered back.

Her sister held up one hand, fingers spread. Four. 'And the clergyman we saw at the Palace,' she whispered. 'A friend of Charles called Cass.'

'Be ready,' Rose mouthed and crept away, around to the back.

There were lights in the kitchen window and the back door stood open, but no one was outside. She skirted the yard on tiptoe, then turned the corner to find herself on a narrow terrace. Halfway along a door stood ajar. Then a hand beckoned to her from the bushes and she discovered Marcus.

'I've found her,' she murmured in his ear, so close that his hair tickled her nose and the awareness of him made her head spin with longing. 'Safe. First floor, other side. Four men and Cass.'

Marcus's hand clamped around her wrist as the doors were pushed wide and a man stepped out on to the terrace in front of them. 'Marlowe.' The name was the merest breath in her ear.

'I'm for my bed,' Marlowe said over his shoulder. Then, 'You'd better take her something to eat and drink. It'll keep her calmer if you do it—I'm not risking any more hysterics from her. Not yet. Take Bill up with you.' He went back inside, leaving the doors open, and Marcus crept forward until his back was against the wall, his ear to the hinge-crack.

'Gone,' he whispered after a moment and gestured for Rose to join him. 'Tell Chloe I'm coming. When Charles opens the door to give her food, tell her to distract him—weep, faint into his arms, anything—but to try to keep the door open.'

And then he was gone into the room before she could say any of the things that were tangling her tongue. *Take care, I love you, take care...*

'Come on, Lady Rose, the coast's clear.'

Harry appeared beside her, making her jump. 'We've got to tell Lady Chloe, like the guv'nor said.'

They found Chloe still looking out of the window and passed on the message. Chloe nodded, then looked around sharply. 'He's here,' she whispered and was gone.

'Watch the front door, as close as you can.' Rose hurried through the shrubbery, emerged on to the drive just out of sight of the front of the house, then staggered towards it.

'Oh, help!' she gasped as the guard on the steps jumped to his feet and started towards her. 'My carriage. Oh!' She subsided on to his chest, her arms around his neck. He smelt of sweat and horse and tobacco and his hands tightened around her alarmingly, but she clung, feigning sobs until he suddenly went still.

'Drop her,' said a gruff voice. 'Or I'll blow a hole in your back.'

'Tie him up,' Rose said, wriggling free.

'Nah,' said Harry. 'Too much trouble.' He reversed the pistol in his hands and clubbed the man on the back of the head. 'That'll keep him quiet for a while.'

Rose picked up the shotgun, pulled the hammers back to full cock and shoved at the front door. From upstairs there was the sound of a man's voice, raised in what sounded like exasperation, then a gasp and a thud as though a body had fallen, then rapid footsteps in the hallway as the door opened.

Marlowe was halfway up the stairs, another man at his heels. Rose pointed the shotgun at the ceiling and pulled one trigger. The recoil sent her back into the doorframe, and the shot brought down a chunk of ceiling, but it stopped both men in their tracks.

She pointed the gun at them, not troubling to stop it wavering in her grasp. 'I really don't know who I'll hit, but at this range it won't do either of you much good,' she said.

From the top of the stairs a deep, very familiar voice drawled, 'But I know exactly who I will hit, Mr Marlowe. You. I suggest you and your friend make your way downstairs, very slowly, very carefully, or I might be tempted to hand the gun to Lady Chloe and I really wouldn't vouch for her temper, just now.'

They all ended up downstairs. The cook and the maid both protested that they'd been hired from St Albans the week before and didn't know anything about a kidnapping and Marcus believed them. The maid was in tears and the cook belligerent, but her anger was directed towards Lord Wighton and Marlowe, not towards him.

He gave them each enough to cover what they said was owed, and for the stage coach back to St Albans, and the cook went off willingly to walk to Harpenden. The maid declared she'd earn another day's wages, if that was what was wanted, and joined Harry in the kitchen, where he was showing considerable skill in rustling up breakfast.

The dazed groom, whom he had knocked out, and the postilion, who turned out to be one of Wighton's grooms and whose initial bluster was soon reduced to whining by threats of prosecution for kidnapping, were tied up and locked in the windowless pantry.

Geoffrey Cass looked on the point of fainting when Marcus marched him into the drawing room where he had held him, Wighton and Marlowe at pistol-point while Rose and Chloe, who refused to be left out, sat in smouldering silence behind him.

'It will save time if I make it clear now that I have bought up your debts, Wighton. The lot. Marlowe has, therefore, no hold over you.

I, however, do. I can't have you imprisoned for debt, because you're a peer, which is a pity. I can, however, send you on a long sea voyage while you work out how you intend to repay me. I'm sure you will enjoy the Spice Islands, provided you survive the storms at sea and assorted fevers. Or you can surrender guardianship of your two younger sisters to me, in which case I will write off the debts.'

Wighton began to splutter indignantly.

Marcus regarded his blotched face and bloodshot eyes unsympathetically and wondered how it was possible for him to be related to his sisters. 'No, don't thank me. Just sit and make your mind up.'

'Now, Cass. I've had enough of you. Get out.'

'I can go?'

'Oh, yes. Go wherever you like. I will be reporting your activities to the Archbishop of Canterbury, who will no doubt deal with you. But perhaps I should add that if Lady Chloe's name passes your lips again I will personally make you eat your own cassock. Now, get out of my sight.'

As Cass scuttled out of the door Marcus

turned to Marlowe, who was slouched in his chair, a sneer on his face.

'Now, Mr Marlowe, you are coming back to London with me where I will hand you over to Bow Street on a charge of kidnapping and unlawful imprisonment.'

'That horse won't run. Lady Chloe's brother was with her the entire time.'

'No, he wasn't, were you, Wighton? You've been at home since yesterday evening. I don't think your sister has seen you for, oh, two years, isn't it, Lady Chloe?'

'That's right,' Wighton gabbled. 'I know nothing about it.'

'You—' Marlowe broke off when Marcus lifted the muzzle of the pistol an inch. 'You'll not take it to court, not and ruin the girl's name. She's been with me all night.'

'With her sister and myself on your heels all the way to—where shall we say? Edgware, I think. The landlord at the Bull and Gate is an old acquaintance of mine and he'll recall us catching up with you there and retrieving Lady Chloe, quite unharmed.'

There was a simmering silence, then Marcus added, 'Of course, it would save us all a lot of trouble and unpleasantness if you were to decide on a sea voyage instead of your friend Wighton, here. I've a ship leaving for the West Indies the day after tomorrow.'

'You've got to get me to London first.' Marlowe was still defiant.

Marcus shrugged. 'We've two vehicles. I've no qualms about hitting you hard enough to keep you quiet the entire way back.'

Nor had he, although he was rapidly reaching the point where he just wanted Wighton and Marlowe out of the way so that he could concentrate on Rose and all the things he wanted to say to her.

At which point he discovered that occasionally wishes did come true. There was the sound of wheels on gravel outside, male voices and Harry came in.

'Here's Mr Farthing and Mr Gregg. Shall I put some more bacon on to cook?'

His partners came in, grim-faced and clearly ready for almost everything except the sight of Marcus's tiger, frying pan in hand, Soames Marlowe with a face like thunder and Lord Wighton, slumped in a chair and looking perilously close to tears.

'I am more than pleased to see you two,' Marcus said. 'How is Aubrey?'

'He's got a sore head,' Richard Farthing said. 'But he's young and it's thick. It was as much as we could do to stop him getting into the carriage with us, so concerned about Lady Chloe he was.'

Chloe blushed, Marcus noticed. *Interesting.*

'As you can, see we are all safe and sound, although two of us are not very happy. Wighton, you were in the process of making a decision, I believe.'

'I'll sign the girls over to you.' All the stuffing seemed to have been knocked out of him.

'Excellent. Then I suggest you retrieve your postilion from the larder, where my tiger has stowed him, and return to London and an appointment with your lawyers to draw up the relevant paperwork.' He waited until Wighton was halfway to the door, then added, 'And I do strongly advise that you do as agreed and with the utmost dispatch, because you really do not want to discover what happens when I lose my temper.

'Richard—Mr Marlowe here wishes to take a voyage to the West Indies and I said we can oblige him with passage on *Maggie Louise.* Just tell the captain to let him off at the first port of call, will you? I'd suggest transport-

ing him in bonds and with a pistol to hand—
he seems a little disordered in his mind and I
would hate for him to escape you and be wandering around loose.'

'Oh, yes. I'll look after him, all right,' Richard Farthing said with a slight smile as the
door closed behind Charles. 'We can have a
cosy chat on the way about how he came to
club my little brother insensible, but I'll make
certain he gets on that ship.' And he knew as
well as Marcus that the *Maggie Louise's* first
port of call was French Guiana, a fever-ridden
penal colony. Getting himself out of there and
back to civilisation would give Soames Marlowe plenty to occupy him for quite some time.

They ate breakfast, which was a noisy,
slightly chaotic, meal, and it wasn't until he
was halfway down his third cup of coffee that
Marcus noticed that Rose and Chloe were no
longer at the table. Rose came in again as he
pushed back his chair to go and look for them
and he saw how strained she looked.

He had taken her resilience and courage
for granted, he realised, and, now her sister
was safe and she could relax, she must feel
exhausted.

'Rose, come and sit down. More coffee? Tea?'

'No, thank you. I have asked one of these gentlemen's grooms to drive into the town and hire a post chaise and the services of a maid. Chloe wants to go home and to be with Kat. She is worried about both her and Mr Aubrey Farthing. I hope you do not mind the liberty,' she added to Richard and Arnold.

'Only too happy to assist. Lady Chloe's vehicle can travel along with my carriage when we leave,' Arnold said. 'She will be quite safe with us.' He was tubby and genial and reassuringly avuncular in his manner and Rose visibly relaxed.

'You do not wish to travel back with Chloe?' Marcus asked, shifting his chair closer to hers so they could speak quietly.

'We need to talk. There are things to discuss and we are both weary. This is a pleasant house—Marlowe has not had the chance to leave his mark on it. We could rest here for a while.'

An optimistic man would find that suggestion encouraging, especially a man looking for privacy to say the number of things that were on his mind. Normally Marcus was an optimistic man—if things were not going his way he got a firm hold on them and bent them until they did—but now, looking at Rose's shadowed expression, he felt an unfamiliar and chilling sensation of pessimism deep inside.

Chapter Eighteen

It seemed to take for ever before everyone had left. Rose had managed to spend five minutes with Charles and had pointed out to him that he was now out of debt, free from the threats of violent moneylenders and the pressures of Soames Marlowe and no longer had the trouble and expense of his sisters to worry about.

He was so cheered by this dose of common sense that she added the warning that he still had to pay Marcus back, but he was still looking happier than she ever remembered him as his chaise left the stable yard.

Half an hour later Richard's partners bundled a seething Marlowe into their carriage and drove off in company with Chloe's chaise, complete with a competent-looking maid from the inn. Marlowe's groom was bright enough to make himself scarce. That left Rose and Marcus in possession of the house, alone except for the kitchen maid. Marcus gave her a sovereign and set her to clearing up the remains of breakfast and heating water.

Rose leaned against the frame of the open front door, rather blankly looking out at the overgrown garden when the sound of Marcus's booted feet on the stairs behind her brought her to her senses.

She had gone somewhere beyond tired. How long that would last she had no idea, but while it did she had to make things right with Marcus before matters between them went beyond saving.

'The chambers have been made up. It's clean and decent up there and the beds have not been slept in. Why don't you go up and rest now?' He sounded matter of fact and sensible, as though he was speaking to Chloe or Kat.

'Not yet.' Rose went into the drawing room, where the dust sheets had been dragged off the chairs and sat down. Then stood up when Marcus came in and closed the door, frowning. Best to do this on her feet.

'You saved Chloe,' she said before he could

speak. 'You have saved Charles from himself. You have secured my sisters' future. If you will buy Chalton from me, then we can live perfectly comfortably while I help Charles sort out his affairs and secure a dowry for Chloe and provision for Kat.'

'Buy Chalton? Help Charles? Rose, what are you talking about? When we are married there is no need for me to buy Chalton or for you to require the money from it. I can help Charles deal with his affairs.'

'The thing that there is no need for,' she said as steadily as she could, 'is for us to marry. At least, there is no need for you to marry me. I realise this will put you to the inconvenience of finding a bride during the coming Season, but it does mean that you will have a choice and the possibility of finding someone who is perfect for you.'

'And you are not?'

He did not appear as relieved as she had expected, but then, he had offered out of gallantry and perhaps did not like having that spurned.

'No, of course not. You can find a bride who is younger, less set in her ways, less managing. Less likely to do shocking things.'

Marcus went to stand in front of the cold hearth. 'You do not wish to marry me?'

He seemed to find it quite hard to understand what she was saying, but then, he must be exhausted and in no condition to have to deal with messy emotions. Hers certainly felt very messy indeed, but she would get through this somehow and fall apart later.

'There is no need, is there?' Rose tried an encouraging smile, although it felt very stiff. Not easy when your heart hurt. It wouldn't break, of course, hearts didn't, although if she had to live with him, loving him, while he kindly and gallantly made do with his 'convenient' wife, then it would surely crack. 'And it would be second best for both of us, wouldn't it—marrying someone we didn't love and didn't desire?'

'Second best. I see.'

'I don't mean…'

'I know what you meant.'

'I hope we can still be friends,' she said, aware she was talking too much now and it wasn't helping, but unable to stop herself. 'Chloe and Kat would miss you so much.'

'Yes, of course,' Marcus said with deadly politeness, as though they were sipping tea together in the course of some morning call. 'I believe there is hot water. Not enough for baths, but I will take a jug up and shave. Tell the maid when you want her to take some up for you, too. If we leave soon after luncheon—say at one o'clock—that will allow time for you to sleep and for us still to be back before dark.'

'Thank you.'

There was the click of the door lock, then silence. Rose's legs gave way at last and she sat down abruptly.

Her handkerchief was in her hand. How had it got there? Why? She could not afford to weep until she was safely upstairs in a bedchamber. She would go up in a moment, just a moment when she could think clearly, because just now her mind was blank. There was the sound of something ripping and she looked down, bemused to find she had torn the fine linen right across, twice.

'What are you doing to that innocent handkerchief?'

'You'd gone,' she said stupidly, staring at Marcus as he closed the door again and leaned against the panels, arms folded.

'And now I have come back again.' He was very pale and his eyes were dark and unreadable. 'You are a logical, intelligent, woman and it occurs to me that you do not normally make decisions based on inadequate information.'

'No,' she said blankly, although her heart was beating far too strongly for an organ in such a fragile state.

'I have a fact for you. I love you, Rose Trafford. I love you and desire you and I want you to be my wife. If you do not wish to marry me, then that, of course, is your decision, but I thought perhaps you should have all the facts.' Marcus pushed away from the door, turned and was gone, leaving her staring blankly at the space he had occupied.

A hallucination? A dream? She pinched herself: it hurt.

He loves me? He gives me no clue that he does and then he tells me as though he is keeping me updated on the price of milk?

Rose was out of the chair, through the door and halfway up the stairs without conscious thought about what she was doing or what she would say when she got there.

Marcus was standing just inside one of the bedchambers, a jug in his hand. Steam curled up from it, which perhaps explained why there was colour in his face at last.

'You infuriating man! How was I supposed

to know? Do I look like a mind reader?' she stormed at him, clutching the newel post for support. 'When you suggested we marry you said you wouldn't come to my bed even though I hadn't said anything about being worried about that. When we kissed at the bottom of the stairs that time you dropped me as if I was a hot coal. You never said a word about love, about feelings. You get cross and short with me and we end up arguing over nothing at all. You don't notice how I feel about you!'

'How you feel?' Marcus put the jug down at his feet and crossed his arms. 'I notice you are concerned, quite rightly, about the degree of freedom you will have after marriage. I notice that how I treat your sisters is of prime importance to you. I am aware that you will do anything, even contract a marriage of convenience, to protect them. Have I missed anything?'

'Only the fact that I love you, you...you *man*, you!'

At least she had the satisfaction of seeing his eyes widen before he had himself under control again. And she saw something there she had never seen before—hope and vulnerability—and something inside her seemed to melt away, leaving her hoping and vulnerable, too.

'I have to admit to being male,' Marcus said and took a step forward. And another and then she was in his arms and he was kissing her.

At last. And, oh, the taste of him, the feel of him, big and strong and real under her hands. No longer a dream, no longer a fantasy. He was kissing her as though their lives depended on it and Rose answered him, knowing she was untutored and clumsy, but learning with each shift of pressure, each touch of his tongue, until she was giving as well as taking.

They were pressed together so tightly that she could feel Marcus's heart thudding, feel the pressure against her belly from his arousal, relish the delicious sensation of power that gave her. But this wasn't close enough. She wanted to feel his skin, kiss it, lick it. She wanted him in her and around her and realised that however much she knew in theory about this act, she had understood nothing about the feelings it created.

One hand flattened itself on her back, pressing her close, the other slid down over the curve of her bottom and fastened there for a moment. Something rumbled in Marcus's chest and she realised he had growled his desire.

It was too much for whatever tattered remnants of ladylike behaviour she still clung to. Rose wriggled one hand between them and tugged at his neckcloth until it loosened, then down to the top button of his waistcoat.

So many clothes, so many layers, she thought as she managed to free the top button. Marcus's hand tightened on her buttock and she stepped forward, pushing against his chest.

Marcus freed her mouth and she blinked up at him, indignant.

'We must stop. Now, while I still have a functioning brain and some thread of self-control.'

'Why?' She wanted to climb him as though he were a tree. She wanted to push him to the floor and crawl all over him. She definitely wanted to tear off all his clothes and then hers and—

'We aren't married.' He took a step back.

'We will be. The Archbishop of Canterbury said we might.'

'You are a virgin.' Another step.

'But you can deal with that.'

'It isn't right.' And another.

'It feels very right to me.' And then she was inside the room and could aim a kick at the door. It closed with a thud. From the landing came the sound of breaking china.

'Oops. That was the jug.'

'*Rose.* Look at me.'

'I am.'

'I know and it is making it very hard to think. Don't you want to wait, have a proper wedding night? Talk to some married ladies first?'

'I know what happens. And marrying you is the icing on the cake, it isn't the cake itself—that is us loving each other. I thought you didn't really want me, I thought you were just being gallant and kind and…and infuriating. And my heart was cracking into pieces. Don't you want to mend it?'

She looked up at him from under her lashes and saw his mouth quirk into that familiar wry smile. 'Don't you dare try that eyelash-fluttering, lip-trembling thing with me, Rose. That isn't you. Yes, I want to love you, very carefully.' The smile had gone now. 'Very tenderly. There is only one first time.'

'Can't you be careful and tender here?' she asked, no longer frantic. This was important, she realised. They had to get it right.

Marcus looked around. And Rose did too.

It was a pleasant room, a little dusty, but the shrouding cloths had been removed and piled in a corner. The bed was made up with fresh linen, faded chintz curtains were drawn back and the sunshine streamed in through the window making the dust motes dance.

'It's a charming room,' Rose said. 'Not touched by Marlowe, he's never been here before, the maid said. I am yours now and for always. That is my vow. A ring and a licence and a wedding don't make any difference. This is the morning you told me you loved me. This is where the first time happens.'

Marcus tugged off the ruby he wore on the little finger of his left hand, lifted hers to his lips and kissed it before he slid the ring over her ring finger. 'With this ring, I thee wed.' His lips curved. 'I think I should begin the body worshipping now.'

Rose discovered that suddenly she was shy. 'I know the theory,' she said.

'So do I.' Marcus was disposing of coat, neckcloth and waistcoat, but he stopped to smile at her.

'Yes, but you've done this before. A lot, I imagine.' She was twisting around to try to get at the numerous hooks and tapes. 'I suppose you've got a mistress.'

'Let me do that. I have never been with a virgin. I have never made love to you. This is the first time for both of us, but we will work it out. Oh, and I do not have a mistress, not for some time.' He sat down, pulled off his boots and stockings, then stood, wearing only his breeches and his shirt, open at the neck to show the dark curl of hair she remembered from that day by the stream.

Her lungs were short of air, which should have been cured when Marcus freed her from her walking dress and unlaced her corset, but that only made things worse.

'Breathe,' he murmured from behind her, so close that his own breath stirred the tiny hairs around her ear. The corset slid down over her hips and there she was in chemise and petticoat and stockings. Behind her something flapped and Marcus's shirt was tossed on to the chair. She could feel the heat of him as he cupped her breasts with his hands and drew her back against his body.

Once she had seen a demonstration of a device for generating static electricity and had dared to touch her finger to the cylinder. The tingling shock from Marcus's caress did not make her laugh as that experience had done. This went straight from her breasts to her belly, low, low down and she arched up into his hands. He groaned, deep in his throat, and she felt him untying the strings of her petticoat, then he turned her around in one smooth motion, pulling her chemise over her head as her petticoat fell to the floor and Rose was naked in his arms.

'Let me look at you.' He lifted her, sat her on the edge of the bed, then stood unmoving.

Rose looked down. She seemed to be all one blush except for the paler pink of her silk stockings and the white garters. The stockings somehow made the nakedness even more shocking.

'You are the most lovely thing I have ever seen in my life,' Marcus said. He sounded as though he did not quite believe his eyes.

'My stockings,' Rose murmured.

His smile was positively wicked. 'I know. Shall I leave them? Or...'

He knelt, took her right foot in his hands and began to kiss his way from her toes to the instep, her ankle, up the swell of her calf until he reached her knee. His lips wandered over the curve of it while his fingers teased at the knot of the garter, then began slowly to roll down the stocking, following it with his lips.

Rose looked down at the dark head bent over her leg. One lock of hair fell and brushed her shin bone as Marcus worked his way down and she shivered, uncertain whether this was pleasure or torture. Perhaps both. She let her hand stray over his hair and he stilled, rested his forehead against her leg as she caressed him, then began to move downwards again. When one stocking was off he repeated the process, then kissed his way up again, lingering over the marks the garter had made on her left leg and then up. And up, his broad shoulders pressing her legs apart as he leaned in.

'Marcus?' Unbalanced, Rose fell back into the softness of the quilt. Then 'Marcus!' when he didn't stop and his mouth was…was… 'Oh…' She sighed as sensation swept through her, shocking, indecent, extreme. Wonderful.

He used his lips, his tongue, even, very gently, his teeth. She gasped and writhed and panted and yearned for something, for more. One finger slid between the hot, wet folds and on, into her, and the tight knot of torment burst apart in a shuddering wave of sensation.

Through it Rose was mistily aware of Marcus moving, lifting her up and backwards to lie on the bed. Then his warmth was gone and she opened her eyes, protesting, to find him naked.

It should have been frightening, her first sight of a large, naked, fully aroused male, and the last remnants of the old Rose were swallowing apprehensively, but this new Rose, the naked, wanton Rose, tingling with her lover's caresses, opened her eyes wide, breathed, *'Oh'*, and then smiled.

Marcus came up on to the bed, over her, lay between her spread thighs which were clearly designed perfectly to cradle him, and said, 'I love you. Shall I show you how much?'

She kept her eyes open for as long as she could, because she wanted to look at him, at the intent tenderness in his expression, at the heated desire in his eyes, the way his hair curled and the tiny imperfections that made him human and perfect. She found a small scar on his chin amid the stubble, one pure white eyebrow hair, a crooked eye tooth, a network of tiny lines at the outer corners of his eyes.

But the things he was doing to her body made it impossible to keep her eyes from closing with the sheer intensity of sensation. 'I love you,' she murmured and realised she had been saying it over and over.

Marcus shifted again and she became very conscious of him intimately close, of the weight on her pelvis and the size of his arousal. She swallowed hard and opened her eyes to find him looking down at her, his gaze intent and dark. 'Be mine,' he murmured and thrust into her.

There was a second of outraged protest from her body, but she had known what would happen and her body was fit and lithe and he had prepared her well. Rose closed around him in a tight embrace, lifted her head and said, 'I am yours', against his mouth.

Chapter Nineteen

Marcus woke with a feeling that the world had shifted on its axis. He lay, eyes closed, body tense, until he realised he was in a strange bed, in a strange house and there was a woman curled against his back, her warm breath on his nape, her arm heavy over his waist, her knees tucked up into the curve of his.

Rose. His love, who loved him. Who had made love with him that morning. Several times, his body reminded him smugly, even as it stirred and hardened into readiness to do it all over again.

Too bad, Marcus told the parts that were waking up so eagerly. *Rose was a virgin and you are not going to make love to her again. Not yet. She'll be sore. So stop making life difficult and behave.*

Predictably, they took no notice at all. He would just have to exercise some self-control, which was easier said than done when a soft, warm female was stirring into wakefulness, her soft, warm female parts pressing against his back and buttocks.

'Good afternoon, my love.' He rolled on to his back, gathered her against his side with her head on his shoulder and captured her free hand before it could go exploring.

'Good afternoon,' Rose echoed, the words muffled because she was nuzzling into his neck, down his chest. Then she found his left nipple and explored it with her tongue.

Marcus almost lifted off the bed. 'No!'

'No?' To his relief Rose looked up. 'I enjoyed it when you did it to me.'

'I enjoy it too much. I am lying here, trying to think about ice, snow, Latin grammar and everything I have been told about the Patronesses of Almack's so as not to leap on you.'

Rose pouted, rather unconvincingly. 'Well, if you don't want me—'

'You'll be sore. I am doing my level best to be considerate.'

The Royal College of Heralds, prunes, cold baths...

'Oh. Thank you. I'm sorry,' she said penitently. She gave an experimental wriggle. 'I am, rather.'

'That's my lack of experience with virgins showing. I was greedy.' He pulled her in closer, wondering if he would ever tire of holding her, of the scent of warm, well-loved woman, of the feel of her slender, body with its lovely long, sleek muscles honed by hard work she should never have had to undertake.

'We were,' Rose said with a naughty chuckle.

He did not know why he suddenly had to ask, and the voice of caution was almost shouting at him to keep silent, but he said it anyway. 'Rose, have you ever been in love before?'

'Oh, yes,' she said immediately. 'First love and heartbreak, of course. He wouldn't have been right for me, I can see that now. You know, the other day I was thinking that if I had told anyone about it at the time, had a good weep, plunged into gloom, then I would have outgrown it far faster.'

'The other day?' Marcus probed, wrestling with the little green-eyed imp of jealousy.

'After we met again. You've met him, in fact—Christopher Andrewes. Wouldn't it have been awful if he had wanted to marry me then? I would never have known you.'

With her smile the evil little imp vanished, leaving him feeling chastened for even entertaining it for a second.

'What is the time, do you think?'

Marcus squinted at the window. 'Mid-afternoon. Damn, we'll have to stay the night.' He let his head fall back on the pillows and grinned happily at the ceiling.

'No, we will not.' Rose sat up abruptly, a distracting sight as the sheets pooled around her hips and her hair tumbled over her naked breasts. 'The girls will worry if we don't come home. Chloe needs me and Kat has had an awful fright. And what about poor Aubrey?'

'Poor Aubrey is probably being fussed over by his fond mama, to say nothing of Chloe, I suspect. But you are right, we must get back for the girls and to sort out what remains of this mess your confounded brother has made.'

'I can hear horses.' Rose slid out of bed, pulling the sheet with her, and went to look out of the window, draped like a rather fetching classical statue of a chaste goddess. 'Harry has found a curricle and a good-looking pair of bays. I had better see if the girl can bring us hot water.'

* * *

Thirty miles in an open carriage with a sharp-eared tiger perched up behind was probably not the best situation for a new pair of lovers to carry on their courtship. Which was a good thing or they would never get home, Rose thought, smiling behind her veil as Marcus drove through the Hertfordshire countryside.

'It has just occurred to me that the Grosvenor Square house is "home" now,' she said as they changed horses at an inn on Radlett High Street.

'Really? That dusty mausoleum?' Marcus gave the new pair the office to move off.

'Dust can be defeated and it won't seem like a mausoleum when I have finished decorating it.'

'You've an entire castle to deal with,' Marcus pointed out. 'Northminster makes Chalton look like a potting shed.'

'What fun. Chloe will love helping. Are you *very* rich, Marcus?' she added innocently.

'Hussy,' he said with a grin, catching his whip point neatly. 'I'm rich enough to deal with Grosvenor Square and to have it in prime order for Chloe's come-out. As for Northminster, that's more a question of expelling the memories of the last two Dukes and rearranging what's there, I suspect.'

'Mmm…' Rose said absently, thinking about Chloe. 'Do you think Chloe and Aubrey are falling for each other?'

'They're on the way there,' Marcus said. 'But she's young to fix her interest, wouldn't you say? And society would say she could do a lot better for herself than the brother of a merchant and the secretary to a duke. He's a good man, though.'

They drove on in thoughtful silence for a while, then Marcus said, 'Once I have my affairs on an even keel I must take my seat in the House of Lords. That will give Aubrey a wide range of useful contacts—he might think about standing for Parliament.'

'Yes,' Rose agreed. 'He would make a conscientious Member and might do a lot of good. Still, as you say, they are both very young and one thing I can be sure of, Chloe would never do anything rash—she is the well-behaved member of the family.'

They arrived back in London just before seven, in time for dinner and, more importantly, to hug her sisters. Kat was inclined to cling until reassured that Marlowe was on his way out of the country and that Charles had agreed to them staying with Rose and Marcus, and then became over-excited and bouncy and had to be threatened with early bedtime if she didn't subside. Rose sweetened the threat with a promise that the ginger kitten, now named Marmaduke, could become an official Upstairs Cat.

Chloe, to Rose's surprise, seemed oddly cast down and she took the first opportunity to pull her into her dressing room and shut the door firmly on Kat and the maids.

'What is wrong, Chloe? You mustn't worry now—Marcus has it all under control.'

'Oh, I know.' She plumped down on the bed and blew her nose. 'I was so happy and when I discovered how well Aubrey is, I thought everything was perfect and he told me he loved me—'

Oh, Lord.

'But he says we can't possibly be betrothed, let alone married, before I have my come-out and that's at least eighteen months away. And he says he won't even ask Marcus until then and I told him I didn't care.' Rose's well-behaved sister sobbed. 'I told him I would run away with him—and he was shocked and told me off.'

'I am glad to hear it. Aubrey is an admirable young man, clearly, and he is quite right.'

Now what do I say?

Inspiration struck. 'I had not thought you so selfish, Chloe.'

'What?' Shocked, her sister stopped weeping.

'Aubrey has his pride. He wants to make his way in the world, have a suitable standing to offer for the daughter of an earl. Marcus will support him, but he will want to achieve this himself. You pressing him to do what he feels to be wrong is very unkind of you, Chloe. Besides, you will make him a much better wife when you have a little town bronze. Have you thought of that?'

After dinner, with Kat in bed and Chloe sitting beside Aubrey on the sofa looking through books of prints with the air of a young lady who would never dream of suggesting to a man that they run off together, Rose joined Marcus on the other side of the room.

'Oh, my goodness. I have had a glimpse of what motherhood must be like—one long worry. Will the boys be easier to raise than the girls, do you think?'

'Boys? Girls?' Marcus's expression had her stifling a giggle.

'Don't sound so surprised. That was why you wanted to marry me, wasn't it?' she asked, threading her fingers though his.

'It was not. That was the reason I wanted a wife, in theory. It was never the reason I wanted to marry *you*, even when I was telling myself how logical and convenient it would be.' Marcus's grasp tightened over hers. 'But the idea, now it seems real, I find very appealing. Girls who look like their mother with blue eyes and hair like spun gold and the courage and humour of their mama, too.'

'And boys who are tall and dark and will grow up to be knights in shining armour,' she teased.

'I don't know how good a father I'll turn out to be. I hardly remember mine and I was angry with him for most of my youth—he had no right to go and die and leave us so badly off that Mama and Penelope had to go back to her parents and leave me to the tender mercies of my cousins.' He shrugged when she made a little sound of distress. 'I learned to forgive and came to terms with it, but I have no model of family life to build upon.'

'Mine was no pattern book to be followed, either. But I think we know what *not* to do.'

'That is very true. Of course, we need the children to practise on...' His voice had become husky with promise, sending shivers through her. 'We have made a start, but I think we should apply ourselves, don't you?'

'Oh, absolutely.' Rose got to her feet. 'Mr Farthing, I believe you should be resting your poor head. Chloe, you and I must retire. After our adventures we need our beauty sleep. Good night, gentlemen.'

She urged Chloe out and as she passed Marcus he mouthed, 'One hour.'

Oh, yes. If I can bear to wait that long, my love.

If anyone had told Rose two months before that she would be sitting in a carriage opposite her brother Charles on her way to her own wedding she would have assumed they were delirious.

Charles had presented himself two days after they had returned from Hertfordshire and apologised to all three of his sisters. He was still inclined to try to find excuses, but it was clear that he was finally realising just how badly he had behaved. Whether the desire to regain social acceptability was his main motive, Rose was unsure, but provided he behaved himself, this new, chastened Charles was a vast improvement.

He had even managed to control himself when Kat, at the first sight of him, had kicked him hard on the ankle and told him that was for being a beast and for upsetting Chloe and for causing Aubrey—who was her fourth-favourite person in all the world—to be hit on the head.

But now Chloe and Kat, the bridesmaids, were in the carriage in front of them and the coach was approaching the pillared front of St George's Church and Charles, perfectly sober and beautifully dressed, was going to give her away.

She hadn't expected the crowd outside the church, which was foolish because Marcus was a duke and this was the fashionable church and a magnet for sightseers, but she managed to keep her composure—the veil helped—as Charles handed her out and her sisters and Frost, the maid, fussed her skirts into order and handed her the bouquet.

Through the west door, through the darkness of the lobby and into the church, which wasn't so very large and which seemed like the inside of a jewellery box to her eyes, dazzled by stained glass and candles and the shining brass on the altar—and there was Marcus, tall and imposing at the altar rail, Aubrey at his side.

His face was stark and remote and he looked, for a moment, like the dark and supercilious stranger who had ridden into the castle on the fiery chestnut that day, not so very long ago.

Then Marcus smiled and the sight and the sound of the congregation vanished. Rose threw back her veil, let go of Charles's arm and ran to his side.

There was a gasp and then a ripple of laughter, then the sound of a collective sentimental sigh from the throats of several hundred of the *haut ton*'s most cynical members as Marcus took her hand and raised it to my lips.

'I love you, my Rose,' he said. 'Shall we get married?'

* * * * *

SAME GREAT STORIES...
STYLISH NEW LOOK!

HISTORICAL

Awaken the romance of the past

COMING SOON!

We really hope you enjoyed reading this book.
If you're looking for more romance, be sure to
head to the shops when new books are
available on

Thursday 27th October

To see which titles are coming soon, please visit

millsandboon.co.uk/nextmonth

MILLS & BOON®

Coming next month

THE LADY'S YULETIDE WISH
Marguerite Kaye

Then Eugene saw her. Petite, with a wild tumble of curly black hair pinned up in a top knot, clad in a dark dress with a white apron tied over the voluminous skirt. He told himself that it was merely the resemblance to a nurse's uniform that made him think it could be *her*, but his instant reaction was too visceral for him to be mistaken. He would never forget that one, fleeting memorable night.

He remembered the silky, springy texture of her hair when it tumbled loose over her shoulders. He remembered the olive tone of her skin, the voluptuous curves of her body, the full breasts, the flare of her hips. He remembered the roughness of her calloused hands on his skin. The tangle of their limbs, slick with sweat. The scent of their lovemaking mingling with the all-pervading smell of battlefield mud. The soft, muffled cry she made when she climaxed.

He remembered the flickering oil lamp in the makeshift wooden hut. The coarse sheets and inadequate blanket on the small bed. The open trunk, half packed with her belongings. He could vividly recall his last glimpse of her sitting up in the bed, the sheet clutched around her, as he picked up his clothing from the floor in the grey light of dawn. And that last, lingering kiss goodbye.

All this flashed through his mind in those seconds as he stood rooted to the spot, both entranced and shocked.

He had never thought to see her again, though their passionate night still haunted his dreams, nine months later. What the hell was she doing here? He had barely formulated the question when she turned. Heart-shaped face. Huge brown eyes under fierce brows. Full mouth which formed into an 'oh' of shock when she saw him. She stood perfectly still, absurdly rooted to the spot just as he was, the colour draining from her cheeks, before returning, colouring them bright red, as she hurried towards him, pushing him out of the door and back into the entranceway.

'Hello, Isabella,' he said, as if there was any doubt.

Continue reading
THE LADY'S YULETIDE WISH
Marguerite Kaye

Available next month
www.millsandboon.co.uk

MILLS & BOON

THE HEART OF ROMANCE

A ROMANCE FOR EVERY READER

MODERN
Prepare to be swept off your feet by sophisticated, sexy and seductive heroes, in some of the world's most glamourous and rom locations, where power and passion collide.

HISTORICAL
Escape with historical heroes from time gone by. Whether your pass for wicked Regency Rakes, muscled Vikings or rugged Highlanders the romance of the past.

MEDICAL
Set your pulse racing with dedicated, delectable doctors in the high sure world of medicine, where emotions run high and passion, com love are the best medicine.

True Love
Celebrate true love with tender stories of heartfelt romance, from t rush of falling in love to the joy a new baby can bring, and a focus emotional heart of a relationship.

Desire
Indulge in secrets and scandal, intense drama and plenty of sizzling action with powerful and passionate heroes who have it all: wealth, good looks…everything but the right woman.

HEROES
Experience all the excitement of a gripping thriller, with an intense mance at its heart. Resourceful, true-to-life women and strong, fear face danger and desire - a killer combination!

To see which titles are coming soon, please visit

millsandboon.co.uk/nextmonth

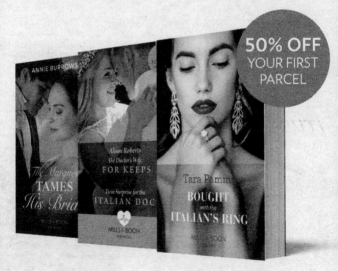

JOIN US ON SOCIAL MEDIA!

Stay up to date with our latest releases, author news and gossip, special offers and discounts, and all the behind-the-scenes action from Mills & Boon...

 @millsandboon

 @millsandboonuk

 facebook.com/millsandboon

 @millsandboonuk

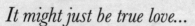

It might just be true love...